FROM THESE ASHES

FROM THESE ASHES

Tamela J. Ritter

Battered Suitcase Press

This is a work of fiction. Names, characters, places, and incidents are either the product of the author's imagination or are used fictitiously, and any resemblance to actual persons, living or dead, business establishments, events, or locales is entirely coincidental. All rights reserved. This book, and parts thereof, may not be reproduced, scanned, or distributed in any printed or electronic form without express written permission. For information, e-mail info@vagabondagepress.com.

FROM THESE ASHES

© 2013 by Tamela J. Ritter

ISBN-13: 978-0615777535
ISBN-10: 0615777538

Battered Suitcase Press

An imprint of Vagabondage Press LLC
PO Box 3563
Apollo Beach, Florida 33572
http://www.vagabondagepress.com

First edition printed in the United States of America and the United Kingdom, March 2013

10 9 8 7 6 5 4 3 2

Front cover art by Vasiliy Merkushev. Front cover designe by Maggie Ward.

Sales of this book without the front cover may be unauthorized. If this book is coverless, it may have been reported to the publisher as unsold or destroyed, and neither the author nor the publisher may have received payment for it.

Dedication

It feels hokey to dedicate this book to my ancestors, but it seems almost disrespectful not to, as I have used so many of their names and stories in this novel. So, this book is dedicated to my grandmothers Renna and Naomi, grandfather Amos, aunt Virginia, my father Charlie and especially to my brother Timothy Scott Ritter.

Your stories, lessons and love nurture me still...

Acknowledgement

So very many people I need to acknowledge with gratitude and devotion. This book wouldn't be written, completed or polished without the knowledge, constant encouragement and critique of a large group of people. Firstly to Chris Baty and his NaNoWriMo that pushed me to take this story to places that, given the whole of my life, I wouldn't have taken it; to the Fairfield County writing group Pencils! who helped me piece it together, with special mention of Cindi Siddiqui, Vance Fazzino, Kathryn Higgins and Kristi Peterson; to my Writers on the Rocks, Jill Bodach, Erika Zamek and A.J. O'Connell who provided inspiration, grammar checks and shared vast knowledge of incestual myths and legends of the ancients.

In the expertise of all things 18-wheelers, a special thanks to Travis Torman and to Bruce McPherson for teaching me all I needed to know (and more) about logging and the timber industry. There are way too many names, and too much time has passed, for me to remember all the many, many professors, guest speakers and storytellers from the University of Montana and the Flathead Indian Reservation that influenced, molded and shared their knowledge with me, either as a friend or a teacher. But thank you all, I hope you see the love and devotion I feel for your cause in my story.

Most importantly, to my editor, friend and benefactor of almost all of the good and writing-related things that have happened to me in the last eight years, N. Apythia Morges. The things we can do together will always astonish and amaze me.

FROM THESE ASHES

Prologue

The Phoenix Center for Cult Recovery
Phoenix, Arizona
August 1992

Dear Rose,

If it were up to me, I wouldn't be writing this. I don't want you to know anything about my life. You know I don't want to be here, that I had very few choices.

You want me to tell you all about me. Why? You don't care. If I've learned one thing in this life, it's that very few people really care. Not unless there's something in it for them. They might pretend, or they might even think they do, but I know better.

You want me to sit in your little circles and talk about my ordeal, but I will not talk to you. I will not give you that. If I have to write about who I am, then fine. I will tell you my histories, my ceremony.

In these pages are my formative years. The whens and whys of who I became. Some say I suffer in silence and count the minutes until I am free of this world; I am my grandfather's granddaughter. Some say I am defiant and disrespectful; I am my mother's daughter. Some say I am self-sacrificing and beyond human help; I am my brother's sister.

Is what I write here the way it happened? Probably not, but it is the way I remember it. The facts and fictions are irrelevant; it's what I do with it that matters. And you can do whatever the hell you want.

My brother has told me that you don't tell a story in the summer. That is a winter ritual and to do otherwise is a bad omen. You should know that. You should know the rules and regulations of being Indian. You can't tell me you know where I'm coming from if you don't know where *you* started.

Naomi West

Salish-Kootenai Reservation
Arlee, Montana
1980

The first memory I have is of my brother.

He was face down writhing and flailing on the dusty playground, a shoe on his cheek, holding him in place. There were other shoes assaulting his stomach, his back, and his legs.

I don't remember any of the faces attached to those tennis shoes. The only face I remember is Tim's.

His eyes flashed confusion and fear, but when they locked on me, they instantly turned to anger and, finally, shame. Then there was a shoe, and it seemed to be slow motion every time, dust flying as it swept the ground before making contact with Tim's nose, his mouth, his cheek.

After that, I don't remember seeing anything. My eyes shut tight, all I felt were arms holding me back, and all I heard were Tim's screams of pain and the boys' cursing: "Fuckin' half-breed. Learn your fuckin' place!"

It is a memory that repeated itself again and again.

Sometimes in the end, they threw me down beside my brother, where I wound up with his blood in the braids of my long, black hair, and my tears mingled with his sweat. For even then, I knew it was sweat and not tears all over his face. My brother did not cry. Ever.

Other times though, they brought me to the merry-go-round— my exposed legs stinging painfully from the sun-soaked metal—and spun me, hard. Thankfully, the contraption was so old and rusted that, even with two or three teenage boys' muscle behind it, it only went a few rotations before squealing to a stop.

I waited until they walked away, kicking up clumped dirt and gravel as they went, before I ran to Tim, cradling his busted head in my tiny lap. I started singing the soothing chant he had taught me. He called it our heart song. It was basically my name, every syllable stretched out.

"Na-ho-a-ah-me-i-ah
Na-ho-a-ah-eh-me-a-eh
Na-ho-a-ah-me-i-ah
Na-ho-a-ah-eh-me-a-eh
Na-ho-a-ah-me-i-ah"

I watched as his swollen eyes fluttered open, the shoe impression stark red against the dark skin of his jaw.

"Na-ho, you okay?" he whispered.

I fought the instinct to hug him tightly. Instead, I stopped crying, stopped chanting, and tried to sound confident and strong. "Just dizzy. You?"

He smiled and then moaned as if even that small gesture hurt. "I've been better."

Returning his smile, I wiped my eyes. "What do you need?"

He flexed his hands and feet, rotated his wrists and ankles, tested every muscle slowly and individually. I sat there holding his head on my lap, wincing every time he did. The only time Tim looked worried and his wince turned to a moan was when he got to his ribs.

"Should I get Mom?" I asked.

He shook his head but stopped almost immediately, as if he forgot and then painfully remembered that his head had only recently been pummeled. "No."

He started to slowly reach for his shirt to pull it over his head, and I scrambled to help him take it off. He clenched the end between his teeth and jerked it roughly so that it ripped before handing it to me.

"I need it in one, long strip, okay?"

I nodded nervously and finished what he had started. Meanwhile, he had gingerly stood up, holding his rib cage the whole time. Taking the strip of shirt, he started wrapping it tightly around his middle so that he wouldn't further distress any of the ribs. I would have been more scared if I hadn't seen this done before, too many times.

Still, Tim tried to make sure I wasn't too worried. He extended his hands out straight in front of him and began taking stiff-legged small steps while moaning, "I am not your brotherrrrrr. I am your mummy, rrrrrrrgh."

He wouldn't stop until I played along and began screaming and running away.

We slowly made our way home, not talking and not looking at any of the faces peering from windows or around corners. There were no taunts on these long walks home. Neither were there any offers of help or concern. Most people were just glad that he could walk so there would be no need for the tribal police to be called in. Police involvement was a hassle that was always to be avoided.

"Don't tell Mom anything," Tim said right before we turned the corner of our street.

I shrugged. "She's going to know. She always knows."

He groaned, but before he could agree with me, the screen door of our house opened and slammed shut as she ran down the sidewalk to meet us.

"What did those little fuckers do?" she demanded, looking from me to Tim and back.

Normally I thought of my mother, as an eagle: a solitary figure flying above us, hovering in the distance, barely recognizable, yet familiar. When it came to my brother though, especially when he was injured—whether it was physical pain or emotional bullying—my mother transformed into a Mama Bear ravenous for vengeance. Tim would attempt to soothe her, and I would focus on becoming invisible.

My mother had a routine she went through with each new scar of Tim's. It happened so frequently I thought of it as ritual. First was anger at those who had done this, then came concern for my brother. She would tend to him like she was Florence Nightingale and he was a soldier off the battlefield. Once the blood had been wiped away, the abrasions bandaged, and the bruises iced, her anger turned to my brother.

"How do you let them do this to you?"

"Mom, there were six of them."

She waved this fact away. "You always do that; you always doubt your own strength. You are bigger and stronger then all of them.

You just let them taunt you, then you just stand there and let them pound you."

This was partially true. At the age of 12, he was much larger than any other teenager on the rez, and he did stand there and allow them to taunt him. He had found that they would leave him alone if he didn't take the bait, so he never did. Or, almost never did.

I always hated the next part of her ritual the most. This is the part when my mother's anger would, rightfully so, turn to me.

"He was protecting you, wasn't he?"

I swallowed and tried harder to be invisible.

She didn't need confirmation anyway. "Of course he was. Always the hero."

She glared at me until my brother demanded she leave it alone. Only then did she finally drop it.

It was true though. We all knew it. The only reason he would fight them was because they started in on me. He could endure anything that they did to him: calling him names, questioning his right to live on the rez, or pushing him around; but if they said something even marginally threatening to me, and he would strike out. That was all they were waiting for: him taking the first punch.

All those times I remembered seeing my brother broken and bloodied, being ground into the dirt, I knew it was my fault. We all did.

The day after those incidents, my mother's ritual would be over, and my brother and I would just be starting ours. Ours mostly consisted of me hiding away in my guilt and vowing to never put my brother in that situation again. I would accomplish this by staying in the house, in my room for most of the day. This never worked, for my brother's part of the ritual was to determinedly prove to me that he didn't blame me and that he wouldn't allow me to take the responsibility all myself.

Even before the repetitive ritual of these memories, the thing I remember the most is Tim's voice. It was usually quiet and patient, a few times loud with worry or anger, but mostly there was a cadence I had always thought was a storyteller's voice. Every night, he would come into my room, and I would scoot over so he could lie beside me and take my hand in his.

"Let me tell you a story..." he would begin.

Tim loved being a storyteller. Sadly, I was the only one he got to tell them to; my mother didn't have the time, and no one else wanted to hear what he had to say. I loved all his stories though and would ask for more over and over. He would tell me about Coyote, Raven, and how joy was created; the stories he had heard from our tribe and stories he had read from books in the library.

My brother was everything to me: my babysitter, my bedtime story, my hero, and my best friend. He needed me because I was the only one who didn't see the white hope or the half-blood bastard but saw him for what he was: a boy who wanted to be accepted, who wanted to make everybody happy, one who would take what was given and wouldn't fight, no matter what they said against him.

Of course he wasn't the only half breed on the reservation. The truth was, he had way more Indian blood in him than the boys who tormented him, more than almost anyone on the rez. He looked like the rest of us; he acted like the rest of us. Actually, he acted more Indian than any of us. I thought it was one of the things that made him stand out and above everyone else.

For my mother, though, it was the other half that made him so special.

Everything I knew I was told by him. I believed every word of it. I believed it because I learned at an early age that my brother never lied. I didn't even know if he was capable of it. So, when I got older and heard all the stories of how the world had begun, how Turtle had swum to the bottom of the ocean and pulled up the earth, one piece of sand at a time, and how laughter came to be, I wanted to know the story of me. The story of him. He told me that to know that story, I had to know about my mother.

Virginia Lagueux-West, was raised by her mother's parents—respected council members who adored their granddaughter—and her father who would sometimes go on drunken travels, forgetting he had a baby at home.

The homes she lived in, values her grandparents and father instilled, and treatment of her might have been completely different, but one thing was the same: hatred for the white man. For her grandparents, the hatred was based on superiority and tradition. Her father's hatred was based on loss of human potential that he blamed on the whites.

As my mother grew up, she realized the hatred was widespread throughout the reservation, but she didn't understand it. She listened to her grandparents talk with pride about the tribe and their ancestors, but as she looked around, she didn't see what there was to celebrate.

The only time Virginia understood was when her grandparents would take her to the Powwows, and she would be mesmerized by the fancy dancers and tribal warriors. She would stand between her grandparents in their full regalia and war paint and the fire burning bright, illuminating the chanting dancers, and her heart would swell and flutter with what she imagined had to be pride. She wanted to grow up and be a dancer, like the girls there, like her mother had been in those pictures in her grandparents' house. They were all so beautiful; they seemed to belong in another world.

Later, when she could barely keep her eyes open, someone would take her to her father so her grandparents could stay for the council meetings. Her father threw parties every year during the Powwows, and she would try to hide in her room and keep this image of modern day Indian life separate from her beautiful Powwow images. She would tip-toe down the small hallway and open the door to her bedroom, only to find one of the drunken drifters who always found her father's house with one of the fancy dancers bent in half, her beautiful skirts over her head. Virginia would run out the back to escape into the woods and would bump into one of the warriors, still in his regalia and war paint, puking over the railing.

Soon my mother learned to hate being Indian. She didn't know what she wanted to be, but she knew it wasn't what she was, what her father was, not even what her grandparents were. The stories they told were fairy tales, wonderful bedtime stories that she soon outgrew.

She attended the Indian school at the edge of the reservation and met her first real-life, bona fide white man. He told her she could be anything, no matter what color her skin. He told her that they were a team, and he was on her side and that he was there for her. She fell in love.

The next year, he was gone, and there was another white man there telling her those things, and again, she was in love. In fact, in the six years of elementary school, she loved four different white men and loathed with a bitter jealousy, two white women. They were the only white people she had ever met, but she now knew what she wanted to be.

People who don't live in an extremely biased environment might not understand how Virginia saw everything: good versus bad, red versus white. Of course not all Indians on the rez were like her father, and not all whites were like her teachers, but that's all she saw, and that's what she believed, and that's why she hated herself.

I'd like to think that my mother was a rare case, but she was not. She wasn't alone when she started her daily pilgrimage to the edge of the reservation. By the time she was fourteen, she had a whole posse of girls stealing their parents' cars for weekend-long excursions to as far as they could get on a tank of gas. But she was a Lagueux whose blood could be traced to seers and chiefs and she was to be the example of how to live the good Indian life. Just because she had commoner West blood in her didn't mean she got to slut around in the white man's bowling alley, or whatever those devil children did.

It broke her grandparents' hearts that she spent so much time off the reservation. The rest of the tribe could have forgiven her if it weren't for two things: she was beautiful, and she was a great fancy dancer. She could have had her choice of husbands, her choice of futures, and she spit on them all and chose instead a race of people who had taken everything away from the Indians. Then she did the unforgivable.

After running away for a whole summer, she came home with a white man's child in her. When he was born, my mother took one look at my brother swaddled in her arms and found all she lacked and all she wanted to be. She named him Timothy after one of the white men who could very well have been his father.

That white men treated her no better and often times worse than her own tribe only caused her a small touch of sorrow. She knew she wasn't worthy of their devotion, so she had taken what she could get and had always gone back for more. But now, through my brother, she had all she needed and would no longer have to leave the reservation in search of the love of a white man. She would raise her very own, and he would be devoted to her.

No matter how much he looked just like everyone else in the tribe, they all knew he wasn't. Early on, they might've been able to accept him anyway if it hadn't been for my mother. Not only was she not ashamed of his heritage, she gloated about it and doted on him as if her child was better than all of them. He might have had more Indian blood then most of the tribe, but he was the only half breed in the Lagueux family. His great-grandmother would never let him forget it either.

When my brother was seven, two things happened that changed his life: his great-grandmother died, and exactly nine months later, I was born.

I am my great-grandmother's spirit. Everyone says they saw her in me from the very beginning. That explained why I was respected and embraced by the tribe despite the fact I had the mother I had, the brother I had, and one of many nameless, faceless Indian drifters for a father.

That was the story my brother told me. It was told in bits and pieces, and a lot of it was filled in by observation and pure speculation, but it all seemed to make sense to me, and my mother never contradicted it.

Later, when I asked him why my mother hated me so, he wrapped me in his arms, tucking my head under his chin, letting the slow, peaceful rise and fall of his chest relax me before he whispered in a soft, cadence: "For our mother I am the glass that she can look through and see all the things that are possible, all the things that she could be. You? You are the mirror. She looks at you and sees all that she is, all that she will ever be."

It was the first time I had wished he would have lied to me.

Continental Divide, Montana
Summer 1992

Tim woke to birds chirping in the distance and every bone in his body screaming. Opening his eyes made him wince with a searing pain behind his lids, so he closed them again. He had no idea what had happened, where he was, and, most terrifyingly, who he was. His mind raced, but that hurt too, so he took a breath to try and still his mind. A new pain exploded as the deep inhale re-opened a wound at his abdomen he hadn't known he had.

Mind and body fought for attention, and Tim forced himself to take the time to assess his injuries before anything else. Starting at his feet, he began testing his body. His feet were sore, but fine, his leg muscles ached but from strain, not trauma. His hands hurt, knuckles swollen, and his fingertips stung with burns. His face felt swollen and his lip was split.

Fight. Fire.

But who? Where? Why?

His mind was fighting for attention again, panic rising and almost making him reckless, until he tried to sit up. The screaming wound stopped him, and he clasped his hand to his stomach. The pain was excruciating. He swallowed the bile that rose in this throat and pulled his fingers away. They were sticky and smelled metallic: blood. Light-headed, he felt himself begin to lose consciousness.

When he awoke again, he tried to open his eyes and again they burned, tears blurring his vision, the salt adding its sting. Not allowing panic, he tried to search his mind for anything that would help him. He began to realize that in these moments when his thoughts were silent, he could hear everything. He didn't have to see to know he was lying on leaves under many trees. He could hear the wind blowing through them, could feel the nettles under him. There were small animals and rodents foraging in the distance and somewhere, not far off, was a creek.

He needed to get to that creek. Slowly, he pushed himself up to a sitting position. His head spun and pounded as a fresh wave of nausea washed over him. Stretching out his hand, he found the nearest tree and slid himself to it by pushing his feet into the earth. After a moment, he took another deep breath, shoving the irritation it caused to his wound out of his mind for the moment. Giving in to the pain and fear was pointless. There was nothing to do but survive it.

He pushed against the tree and stood up straight, keeping one hand on his side and one extended in front of him. He took a few steps before he tripped on a fallen branch. He caught himself before falling then wiped the sweat off his brow. It was then that he realized his eyebrows were charred. Raking his hand across his scalp, he sighed as he felt his hair in its ponytail. Tearing the ponytail holder out, letting his shoulder-length hair fall into his face, he ran his fingers through it and felt the crunchy tips break off. *Definitely fire.*

Again he tried to recall just what had happened. He searched his mind for any recollection. Nothing. In the void of memory, the desperation to get to the creek grew, as if it would answer all his questions.

Gingerly, he made his way to the sound of rushing water; squinting his eyes slightly open despite the burn, he could make out shadows and shapes between him and the water. As he walked, he began chanting under his breath. It was a nonsense song, and he didn't know what it meant or where it had come from, but it soothed him nonetheless.

"Na-ho-a-ah-me-i-ah
Na-ho-a-ah-eh-me-a-eh
Na-ho-a-ah-me-i-ah
Na-ho-a-ah-eh-me-a-eh
Na-ho-a-ah-me-i-ah"

Lowering to his knees with a whimper, he cupped his hands into the water and brought it to his eyes. He imagined he heard a hiss like a wet finger on a hot iron, but it felt like a fire had just been extinguished in his eyes. He held his wet fingers gently on his eyelids for a long time before he attempted to open them again. There was a definite burn, but it was no longer intolerable, as long as he didn't look directly into the sun. Next, he raised the water to his lips and gulped greedily. It was mossy and tasted a bit like run-off, but he disregarded that and instead marveled at how this bit of relief made him feel so much more secure.

He stood up, removed his jacket, and discovered the white T-shirt under it, along with the waist of his jeans, was crimson. He slowly stripped off his shirt, feeling a sharp sting when the sticky cotton disconnected from the gash in his belly and a sharper one when he lifted his arms over his head. Feeling as if he'd opened the wound again, he barked from the pain of it.

It was too bloody to investigate, so he dunked his shirt in the creek and used it to wash off the cut. After it was cleaned, he could tell it was a knife wound, caused by a swipe instead of a stab. It was about six inches long, starting at his hip and ending right below and to the left of his belly button. On closer inspection, he sighed; it wasn't that deep. He knew he should be stitched up, but looking around and listening hard, he also knew he was a long way from any hospital.

He began ripping his T-shirt into one long, thin strip and rinsed it off again. It wasn't something he wanted to do, but he had no choice. Biting down hard, he squeezed the two lips of the cut together and, tightly, very tightly, wrapped the material around his middle. It instantly turned crimson again.

He was going to have to continue to rinse and rewrap with the same strip of cotton until it stopped bleeding. If he found a way to boil the water, he'd have a better chance of avoiding infection, not to mention have safe water to drink.

Determined to clean up himself as much as possible, he pulled his jeans and underwear off, checking the pants' pockets first before submerging them. In the back pocket, he found a folded knife that didn't look like a knife that people carried for protection but for survival and some thin nylon twine. In the front, a book of matches from some place called Arlee Gas and Go. These discoveries asked more questions than they answered. Was this the knife that had cut him? If so, how did he have it, and if not, then whose blood was on it? Finding the matches was both good and bad news: Good because it was always a smart idea when stranded in the woods to have matches; bad because the last thing you want on your person when you wake up in the middle of the woods with no recollection of who you are, with no eyebrows and smelling of smoke is a book of matches.

Tim stood, completely naked except the torn up shirt wrapped around his waist. He looked down at his body, really looking at it for the first time. He was unusually tall, well over six feet, big, and broad. He looked as if he could have lived in these woods, survived on what he captured and killed. There was no visible ounce of fat on him, and he would have looked like a mountain rock except he also had no bulging muscle either. He was more like the creek: solid and liquid, smooth and rippled all at once. His skin was the color of a burnt sienna, brown and red swirled to make the perfect sunset, and his hair was so shiny black, it was almost purple.

As he waited for his pants to dry, he finally allowed the mounting questions and fears to take over his thoughts. At first, the sheer volume of questions and concerns almost made him hyperventilate. But then, like he had done with his injuries, he took a deep breath and forced himself to examine it one thought at a time.

Who are you? A list of names came to him: Amos, Marcus, Damien, Eli, Timothy, Andrew, Malachi, Larry…But none connected with him; no images surfaced to tell him who those names belonged to. *Okay, moving on…*

Where are you from? Again, his mind floated a list of locations but couldn't settle on one: Missoula, Phoenix, Arlee, Havre, Kalispell, Grand Canyon, Flagstaff, Portland… Arlee was the only one to which he had any evidence of a connection; he'd obviously been there at least once for long enough to procure matches. There was no association in his mind though, no image of where he had grown up and spent his time.

Family? Surely you have a family? Belong somewhere, to someone? Surely. Titles were easy, Mother, Father, Sister, Brother, Grandmother, Grandfather. Names though? Just like before: Virginia, Debra,

Naomi, Ruth, Thomas, Amos, Timothy, Malachi, Larry, Marcus, Damien and none of them meant anything to him.

If he had some sort of brain injury, he'd be able to understand this emptiness, give it a name—amnesia—but his head, aside from the ache all this struggle was causing him, was clear and uninjured. He just felt hollow and disconnected.

What do you remember? One thing... There had been a fire. Yes. That was obvious and wasn't really a memory; it was facts based on evidence. But earlier when assessing his injuries, he had deduced fire *and* fight. But why fight? Those injuries— swollen hands and face with a split lip—could have happened other ways besides a fight. Yet, that was the first place his mind went. Why? It could be he subconsciously remembered the fight, or he was familiar enough with the effects to assume. He didn't really like either choice.

He closed his eyes and tried to remember something, anything.

He lay on the ground, his body aching and sore. A girl leaned over him, stroking his forehead, chanting.

"Na-ho-a-ah-me-i-ah
Na-ho-a-ah-eh-me-a-eh"

Tim opened his eyes and touched his forehead where the hand had been. It had felt so real. A memory. But of what? Who? When? He closed his eyes again but nothing else came. Still, that feeling of someone taking care of him sometime in his past was a bit of comfort, and that was something. Not much, but still...

More would have to wait until he'd found some shelter and nourishment.

Before getting dressed, he unwrapped his bandage and cleaned the wound again with a tight-jawed grimace. After washing the blood from the cloth, he squeezed the skin that had turned clammy purple and rebound the bandage. He looked down and watched the blood swirl and skim along the soft current of the creek. As he did that, something caught his eye: a ripple in the water a bit downstream. A fish. Food.

Putting his pants back on, he pocketed the matches, knife and twine, pulled his boots on and headed downstream, hoping that this stream would flow into another; the larger the body of water, the larger the fish. He walked for hours, always staying close to the stream, before he found the first thing he needed: a six pack of Budweiser. They were still connected to each other by the plastic bindings; all but one had been emptied. He picked up the cans, brought them to his nose and took a deep sniff.

His knees buckled, and he staggered for a moment before he regained his footing. This time when he closed his eyes, the memory of the little girl came with no hesitation. Only now he was holding her, and they were crouching in a dark, small place, hiding. She was shaking with tears and her eye was swollen and there was that song again, him singing this time:

"Na-ho-a-ah-me-i-ah
Na-ho-a-ah-eh-me-a-eh
Na-ho-a-ah-me-i-ah"

When he opened his eyes again, he tossed the cans from him; they had something to do with that girl's suffering. By the queasiness in his stomach at the stench, he knew it caused the memory. After a moment, he shook his head and remembered the reason he had been relieved to find the cans and so he retrieved them. They could be sanitized and used to sterilize the water; the tab could be removed and fashioned into a hook for a fishing line. And that was two of the three things he would need to take care of before sunset. After he caught a fish or two, he'd look for something to make a shelter.

The fact that he knew what needed to be done and how to do it eased his mind considerably. It seemed much more important to have that information than the facts of who he was and how he had gotten there. For now.

Finally, he found a good spot where the water flowed wide and smooth. Finding a long stick that was strong, pliable and would make a good rod, he set about fashioning a hook and looking for bait. Worms would be ideal, but he'd take any bug he could get.

While he dug and overturned rocks, another memory came to him.

* * *

The boy walked through the forest holding the hand of a man much taller and much older. They both had poles over their shoulders; the older man also had an empty bucket.

"Grandfather, is this where our ancestors fished?" he asked.

The man said nothing.

They stopped at a plot of freshly turned earth. "Is this where our ancestors got their worms?" he asked.

The man said nothing.

"What kind of fish will we catch?"

Nothing.

"Am I doing it right, grandfather?" he asked, and supposed he was since he wasn't told different.

Later, when the sun was beginning its descent, they walked back out of the forest, still holding hands; the boy held both poles over his shoulder as the grandfather had the bucket half full of fish. The boy looked up at his grandfather from time to time but not saying anything, imitating the older man's peaceful silence.

"Grandfather," he said aloud, testing the word. It was the first thing he'd heard himself say since waking up. His own voice sounded strange to him, deep but delicate.

He fished for the rest of the afternoon and caught a few medium-sized trout that would do just fine. Now all he needed was shelter. Luckily, about half a mile farther downstream, he found the perfect spot. A bunch of trees had been knocked down in a storm and were lying on each other in an almost teepee shape. Layering them with more brush and crawling inside, he thought, *Yeah, this will do fine. This feels like home.*

As he watched the sun dance through the gapes in the shelter, heard the water in the creek glide over the rocks and pebbles, and smelled the trees and earth all around him, he felt warmth completely unrelated to the heat of the day.

"Maybe this is my home," he said aloud because he wanted to hear the sound of his voice, even though it almost hurt to use it.

An hour later, he was tearing off chunks of burning fish, scalding his fingers and mouth in his impatience. He ate half of his bounty and saved the rest, wrapped in wet leaves, for later.

He cut off the tops of the beer cans and filled each half full with water, setting them on the edge of the fire to cook out anything deadly. After they started boiling, he wrapped his jacket around the scorched metal and carried four of them to the creek to chill, surrounded them by rocks so they wouldn't be washed away.

Again he washed his wound, this time with clean, hot water. It felt much better, and for the first time, he was sure it would heal.

He watched the flames as they roared and then slowly burned out to dancing embers. It was unsettling how much he knew—how to fish, sanitize water and generally survive— and yet the why of how he knew was completely lost to him.

However, he had decided that the mystery of who he was would have to wait until he'd healed. He wasn't going to risk people looking for him until he was healthy enough to run from them if need be.

His eyes slowly began to droop. Before he fell asleep, he tried once again to answer questions:

Who am I?

Nothing.

Where am I?

Nothing.

Does anyone know I'm here?

Again nothing.

Does anyone miss me?

In the dimming light of the dying fire, he saw a woman, a very old, kindly woman and a teenage boy.

"From this day, and forevermore, in the tribe of Nopiinde, you will be Silent Stream. You are our family and we will always be a part of you."

The boy bit his lip, keeping his eyes on the ground to hide how hard he was struggling to not cry. "Thank you. I wish I could stay here forever but..."

"But you're needed."

The boy nodded; the woman remained silent until the boy looked at her again. "When you are ready, you will find us again. But until then," she reached into her bosom and pulled out a string necklace. On the end of it was a vibrant feather. It was so red that the boy didn't think it was from a real bird.

"Before I became what I am now, I was something else. Have you ever heard of a Phoenix?"

The boy shrugged. "Isn't it a mythical animal, like a unicorn?"

The woman laughed the sound of gold. "Yes and no. It is myth now, but at one time, the Phoenix was not only real, but their legend believed. Before I was the seer of this tribe, I was of another tribe. Our role in this universe was to protect and keep alive the magical bird."

She took the string off her neck and put it around his. "Now we will both be looking for something. I will, as I have for many moons, be looking for the Phoenix, and you will be looking for us. Take my advice; don't let the reward of the hunt take away from the beauty of the search."

He fingered the feather and nodded.

Even now, while he sat by a fire a million miles away for all he knew, he reached for the feather that he knew wouldn't be there. That did answer one question: someone did miss him. Now he'd just have to remember who she was to him.

Arizona
July 1982

The first time my mother tried to kill me, I was six.

We were in Arizona, at the Grand Canyon for a huge Powwow. We'd never been to one this big, and there were strange Indians we'd never met. My mother was showing off.

It was late. The council had already gone to bed and left the fire to the drunks. My mother was one of the drunkest. The alcohol, mixed with the natural high she got from being admired by so many men, made her reckless.

I was fighting hard to stay awake. I had this fear that if I closed my eyes, when I opened them again, everyone would be gone and I would be alone. The smoke burned my eyes, but I couldn't tell my mother. I had tried once, but she just sneered at me, "Smoke follows beauty." She had said it in that hateful sing-song way so many times I'd hear it in my head every time my eyes teared up at the fire. *Smoke follows beauty. Smoke follows beauty.*

I tried to go to her and tell her I was tired and wanted to go to the tent, but I couldn't see with all the smoke.

Then, suddenly, she was there, picking me up and spinning me around. For a minute, I was happy. Then she stumbled, and I screamed. She caught herself and held me tight. "Don't worry baby. Mommy won't lose you." She laughed hysterically, but before I could feel reassured, she threw me across the fire into the arms of a complete stranger. He danced while he held me over his head, one hand supporting the back of my neck, the other on my bottom like he was sacrificing me to the fire spirits. I was too terrified to move, but I screamed with all my might. He tossed me a little bit in the air and then caught me again down by his knees.

If he could see my tears falling like raindrops or hear my screams filling the air like thunderclaps, he didn't care, because he threw me to the next dancer to his right. This happened again and again until I was almost used to the blinding fear, which was being replaced with anger, a painful anger that demanded to be set free. Despite being restrained and the fire being so close, I raged with flailing arms and legs and a blood-curdling, vocal cord-straining shriek. The stranger tightened his grip on me, causing bruises that would stay for weeks, and I screamed even louder.

Suddenly a warrior jumped from the flames, red, yellow and orange feathers in his hair, a boned breastplate and tanned buffalo hide, fringed leggings and moccasins. He shoved the man holding me hard in the chest. The warrior's face was redder than usual, and his eyes, those eyes I'd been studying my whole life to gage my own mood, burned so brightly that it hurt to look in them.

The man dropped me, and the warrior hero, my brother, caught me effortlessly. His shouts at the crowd were so loud and shrill that I couldn't recognize them as words. Holding me tightly to him, he ran from the circle that had gone silent. We were out of sight before we heard the desperate calling of my mother that usually stopped him. This time, it made him run faster, but somehow he did it while still holding me tightly and making me feel so secure that my racing heartbeat slowed to normal before we'd even made it out of the campsite. And as he slowed to a walk without any sign of stopping or going back, the idea of running away calmed me further so that I began to doze in and out of consciousness.

I don't know how long we walked, but I woke up to him jiggling me in his arms. "We're here," he whispered.

I rubbed my eyes and looked around. In the dim light that the moon provided, I couldn't make out anything that would indicate a destination. "Where? I don't see anything."

"You will see something breathtaking as soon as the sun rises, believe me. This is the best way to see it for the first time."

"What?" I asked getting excited.

"The Grand Canyon."

I had begged my mother every day to go see the Canyon. Every day for a week, my mother had promised, "Tomorrow." That morning, she said if she won her dance competition, we would stay here another week and really explore: how would I like that?

She was in a good mood then; she always was the day of a competition. Besides, she had spent last night with a man who had promised us a ride home. Tonight though, she had come in second. Second place in a group of more than fifty, but still, second place. I had been worried that I'd never see the Canyon, but being thrown around a fire by drunks replaced that concern with something more important. Yet, here I was after all, and, in a few hours, the sun would rise, and I'd see the splendor for myself.

Tim carried me down a trail that, after a while, was no longer railed and put me down, right on the edge. I clung to him, both my arms around his leg. It was then that I noticed he was shaking more than me. I looked up to see if he was scared, too, and was surprised at the look on his face: cold rage.

"Tim, it's okay," I found myself saying, trying to comfort him.

He looked down at me, and his eyes softened for a moment before hardening again to match his stiffened stance. He knelt before me and stared intently at me. Looking away was impossible.

"No. *That* was definitely not okay. Something really terrible could have happened to you."

"But you saved me," I interrupted, placing my hand on his overly warm forehead.

He smiled as he stood up. "Yeah, I saved you." He put his hand on my head as I wrapped my arms around him again, and we stayed there like that until the sun was just beginning to rise. Tim put his hands up and pretended he was pulling a rope to raise the sun into the sky, like he would raise the blinds in my room every morning to wake me up.

I laughed, and it seemed to release something inside him, because he started to laugh too, then he raised his hands and faced the sky. The feathers in his hair moved with the warm wind. "Ah, Na-ho, this is where we belong. This is the place for us," he said, before releasing a long whoop of joy.

I looked at the wilderness around me—the big, beautiful rock formations coming into focus in front of me, revealing their many secrets to only us—and I had to agree; this was definitely the place for us.

We walked around the rim for about an hour before I said, "We're going to have to go back, aren't we?"

He sighed. "Yeah, but come with me; I want to show you something."

He started to walk through the woods on a narrow path that was obviously rarely travelled. After another hour, I got so tired that Tim picked me up and carried me.

We were still surrounded by trees when we started to hear chanting. As we got closer, the smell of meat cooking and sizzle of fry bread being dropped in an oil skillet carried on the air. Walking into a clearing, we saw a small tribe encircling a large fire. Children, wearing long shirts that looked to be made of some sort of tanned leather, were playing a game with sticks and giggling. About a dozen women were dancing around the fire with arms raised.

"What are they doing?" I asked. I'd never seen people dance and chant, except at ceremonies.

"They are praying to the Great Spirit. Thanking Him for the food they eat, the land around them, and the people who love them."

Tim put me down, and I walked fearlessly straight up to the circle. The woman who had been leading the prayer moments before was the first to notice me.

"Who is this beauty before us?" she asked.

I blushed. I had been called beautiful before, many times, but she seemed to be talking about something besides how I looked. I stood up tall, proud for the very first time. "My name is Naomi West, daughter of Virginia West, granddaughter of Naomi and Charles Lagueux, Chief of Salish-Kootenai Tribe of…"

I stopped as they started to chuckle.

"That's quite a mouthful. How old are you little girl?"

I couldn't tell if she was just teasing me so I didn't answer.

Another woman looked passed me and said, "Oh, Silent Stream, did you bring this little beauty?"

I turned to see who she was talking to. It was Tim. "You know my brother?" I asked, wondering why she called him Silent Stream.

"Oh, you're Silent Stream's sister," she said with a look like that explained everything.

Tim looked around but did not speak. I knew that he didn't talk to people he didn't know, and it surprised me that they knew him well enough to name him.

"Why do they call you Silent Stream?" I asked him.

He struggled to answer, the struggle I'd watched him fight all my life. Finally he just shrugged and looked from me to the woman. I turned back to her. "Why do you call him that?"

"We call him Silent Stream because he flows through us quietly and sometimes his current is slow, and he stays for hours, and sometimes it's fast and he's here and gone in a blink. Like the stream, no matter how silent, has many fish that swim in it, so does he; no matter how silent, he has many souls swimming through him."

I looked at the tribe members who all nodded in agreement and instantly respected them. They looked at my brother and saw what I saw: the grace that some saw as weakness, the heart that some didn't see at all.

"What tribe is this anyway?" I asked.

"We are the tribe Nopiinde," another of the women answered.

"I've never heard of you. Are you a member of the council?" They shook their heads. "Where are you from?"

"We're from here," she answered.

"Here the Grand Canyon?"

"Here America. Nopiinde means the Tribe of the People. We are nomads. Most of us were not born in this tribe but found it when we were looking for meaning and direction to our lives that our own tribes, in these modern times, have not provided for us. Do you understand?"

I nodded. I wasn't sure of the meaning of all her words but I understood enough. I found myself actually crying as I stood among this tight-knit community of strangers that talked to me like a person, not a child and who understood my brother without a word.

"Would you like to meet her?" the woman who spoke first asked.

"Who?"

"The Mother who names us all. Phoenix Daughter."

"Yes," I answered immediately.

She held her hand out to me. I looked back at my brother who nodded slightly, so I took her hand. I felt immediate warmth starting at my fingers and tingling throughout my tiny body. I wanted to wrap my arms around her and never let go.

She led me passed the row of tents that half circled the fire. Behind those were many more tents and teepees, a small village of people and activity, mostly women and children.

I was mesmerized. I had seen villages like this in books but never at any Powwow I'd ever been to before. Usually Powwows were full of old Indians getting together to reminisce, young Indians coming to dance and tell stories, drunk Indians coming to find new drinking buddies since they have alienated all their own tribe, and kids watching everyone, for these were the people they would become. Very rarely at these big Powwows are there more than a handful of people you know from your own tribe. The one thing these people had in common, besides being Natives, was their desire to show off when around each other. They all slept in teepees with elaborate designs and vivid paintings that probably only got used two weeks a year. The regalia they wore, especially the dancers, were reproductions that took all year to make and were reserved for these meetings only. You knew this because at night, the Powwow looked like a rodeo and a circus had blown up on the spot, but, during the day, those same people looked the same as any other tourists, with maybe a few more cowboy boots and longer hair.

These Indians in this tribe though, they were different. First of all, there were so many of them, and they seemed to all be up and going about everyday business in everyday clothes that looked homemade, from the teepees and tents, to the moccasins they had on their feet.

The first woman we passed looked up from breastfeeding her child to smile and exchange words. Two more women stood between tents beating sleeping bags and rugs that hung from thick hemp rope with heavy sticks. They, too, looked up and smiled their greetings. In fact, everyone we passed smiled at us and said hello as if I had walked into a reunion of long-lost family members.

We walked by another large teepee with the flap opened to reveal a wise woman sitting among dozens of children as she told a story, mostly with her hands. These were the only people too enrapt in what they were doing to notice us; I wanted to join them.

"Where are the men?" I asked, finally noticing their absence. "Are they sleeping it off?"

She laughed with sad eyes as she squeezed my hand. "No, the men are out gathering food."

I wanted to ask her why she referred to going to the store as "gathering food" but that was one of about a hundred questions I didn't get to voice.

She stopped in front of the only teepee that had any color. It was a vivid red with green, blue and orange shapes to represent the earth, sky and fire. She let go of my hand and stepped in front of me, motioning for me to wait.

She returned after only a minute and ushered me in. When I turned to thank her, she was gone. I turned back and, although I already knew it was rude to stare, I just couldn't stop. There was just so much to take in; I didn't have time to blink.

The floors had various animal hides of every shade of brown covered partially by rugs woven from vibrant blue, red and purple fabrics and ropes.

"You like my rugs?" a wise, old voice asked.

I tore my eyes away from all the colors and followed the voice.

"Step up child; let me see you."

I shuffled my feet a few slow steps. The voice told me there was nothing to fear, but I couldn't see her. Finally, curiosity won out, and I stepped closer.

I realized the reason I couldn't see her clearer was because she was standing in a fog of heavy smoke coming from the bundle of sage and juniper she waved all around her. She tore the bundle in two and put one half in a stand to her right and one on her left.

She was tall but didn't tower. She did not smile but seemed kind. She was old but still had a shine to her soulful eyes. Two long, grey braids hung over each shoulder and her skin looked as if cellophane had been placed on her face and hadn't been pulled tight, making her look wrinkled and slightly ashen. She was wearing a beautiful light purple dress and a white belt decorated with turquoise.

The room smelled strongly of sage, obviously, but I also smelled cinnamon for some reason, and I knew that, from then on, that would be the scent I would associate with Wise Women.

She put her hands palms up, and I instinctually put my hands in them. "You are very small to have the wisdom you have," she said.

I didn't know if that was a good or bad thing, so I tried to explain: "They tell me I have my grandmother's spirit. Maybe I received her wisdom as well."

Her eyes twinkled. "Perhaps. Tell me though; haven't you ever wondered what it's like to be a six-year-old?"

I thought about all the other kids I knew and the ones I'd seen in books and on TV, being held and snuggled, read to and sung to, having a mother and father who made their babies their world. "Yes, all the time," I shrugged, knowing I would never be like them.

"Come here." Before I knew what was happening, she had pulled me to her bosom with both her arms around me tightly. After my heartbeat slowed to match her measured rhythm, I realized I was being rocked back and forth. She was chanting a soft, mournful song. Without knowing the words, I found myself overcome with an odd sort of peacefulness, yet was shocked to realize that I was simultaneously shaking with painful sobs. She held me for what seemed like days while I wept for things I couldn't even name.

"You and your brother have the biggest hearts I've ever felt from outsiders. You both are very special," she whispered in my ear.

I pulled away, feeling warmed from the inside out, and wiped at tears I was surprised to discover weren't there. "My brother talked to you, didn't he?"

She sighed. "Yes, although I had to hold him to me much longer than you. The hurts run deep in him, but you know that, don't you?"

I nodded. "He feels the pains of both of us, and sometimes I think, for our whole tribe."

"Yes, I feel that in him as well. I fear there is nothing we can do to ease the pains, but it's up to the ones who love him to make sure he also feels the joys and pride of his tribe. Can you do that?"

I nodded again and vowed in my heart to do all I could.

She cleared her throat. "Let's talk about you now. Some things I will say, you will understand, and some will make little sense now, but long after you forget me and this place, you will find understanding." She paused as if she were listening to a voice I couldn't hear. "Many tribes believe that inside of us are many spirits and that these spirits take on certain animal characteristics, we call them totems. In our actions and beliefs, the animal is revealed to true seers. I have been honored, along with all my ancestors, to be a seer and I see that in you too."

I shook my head to argue, but she raised her hand dismissively and continued, "You are young, but I see it in your eyes. The eyes tell the story of your life. The wise owl sees many things with its powerful vision but does not seek counsel nor desire fortunes in this life or the next. The owl uses her wisdom to help and never to harm. She has no enemies in nature and only hunts for food and not sport.

"These are the good things that Owl People have to their credit, but as with any animal, there are disadvantages as well. Your strength of wisdom comes with a desire to show off; your strength in compassion can lead you to disregard your own needs. Being able to see others' weaknesses might leave you blind to your own. Most importantly, the independent spirit of the wise owl might forget that the most important thing in life is to need others and to be there when they are in need." She paused and studied me. "Does any of this make sense to you?"

I shrugged. I wasn't really sure what the Owl had to do with me or how she knew who I would be by looking into my eyes, but she had already told me that I probably wouldn't understand.

I tried to look in her eyes to see her story, but all I saw was a lone Indian, tall and strong, standing on a precipice. He chanted as he wept and took handfuls of ashes and released them into the wind and watched them spread among the trees below. I didn't understand that at the time either, but it made me go to her arms again, and this time the tears flowed.

After a long silence where she simply let me cry, she asked, "Will you join me in the ceremony of name?"

I nodded then answered, "Yes please."

She turned us around. "We face the East and acknowledge that today is a new day where we can be born again, erasing past hurts and pains." We turned again. "We face the South as we ask the Great Spirit for what we want to be and need to accomplish." Again we turned. "We face the West and ask the winds of the great waters to blow away the spirits that work against us." Finally we came full circle. "Now we thank the Great Spirit for this new life and promise to honor the gift we have received."

She faced me, dipped her fingers into the ashes of the burning herbs, and wiped my tears that refused to stop flowing. "No need for more tears. In the tribe of the Nopiinde, you will be known today and evermore as Soaring Fire."

I smiled and felt the love flow through me. She put her hands on my shoulders, and I felt the connection between me and her, me and the earth, me and my people—all my people.

"Will I ever see you again?" I asked, clinging to her.

She rocked me back and forth, chanting something soothing. Finally, she pulled me away. "We will meet again; if not in this life, then in the next."

When I got up to leave, it felt like I had been in there all day long and was shocked to realize the sun was still in the sky. I was almost outside, having already said my goodbyes before I thought to ask, "Hey, what animal is Silent Stream?"

She smiled with laughter in her eye. "Ah, I never tell. That is between him and the spirits, just like yours."

I shrugged, again not really understanding, but liking that I had a secret of my very own.

When I got out to the sunlight, Tim was waiting for me. Without a word, I took his hand, and he led me out of the village of tents the opposite way we came in. We walked in silence; the only sounds our footsteps and the wind singing through the tops of the trees. "So, did you like her?" he asked.

I squeezed his hand. "No, I loved her. I think she is my second favorite person in the whole world."

He squeezed my hand back. "Mine too. Don't tell Mom though."

"I'm not telling her about any of this. This is ours. Do you think when we're old enough to find our own tribe, we'll find them again?"

He nodded, and we walked in silence.

We got back to our campsite as the sun was setting. My mother, who was talking to a few men, looked up to acknowledging our presences for only a split second, her expression revealing nothing. She said nothing. The next day, we left, without her ever taking me to the canyon. I was not surprised, nor did I care. I'd already experienced it, and it was all the better for her not being there. She thought she would punish us the whole ride home, all four and a half days of it, by not speaking to us. She never understood; that was her greatest gift. We were so wrapped up in our own American thoughts and our Indian dreams that we barely even spoke to each other.

Years after that, every Powwow in every state we went to, we would search for our lost tribe. They became our three ring circus; when we dreamed of running away, we dreamed of them.

Highway 280, Montana
Fall 1992

Tim walked out of the trees and stepped on the concrete of the one-lane highway. His knees buckled at the difference of the hard surface of the road compared to the soft earth his feet were accustomed to. He didn't know the last time he'd walked on a road, but he knew he didn't like it much. He didn't like the way it felt; he didn't like being in the open, but mostly he didn't like the way the buzzing of the telephone wires muted the symphony of the forest. This new silence was eerie, and it made him want to run back to the cool shelter of the trees.

He had come out in the open because he knew that he would need to find a place with walls and a roof and warmer clothes soon. Though he had found a great many things abandoned by campers and hunters, none would keep him from freezing to death, and none would help him remember the answers to the growing number of questions that had been haunting him.

He had found another white T-shirt like the one he had been forced to use as a bandage. Unfortunately, this one was about two sizes smaller and, oddly enough, had a blood stain on the shoulder. He had washed it as best he could against rocks by the river.

He had lived on fish and huckleberries for so long he was starting to crave things he didn't think he'd ever tasted. He had started to imagine that he'd never see another soul, and there were times when he was fine with that, forgetting he'd ever known anything else.

He hadn't even thought of what he must look like anymore, his only indication was his own reflection in the smooth surface of the water he fished in. His hair was a mess that he tied back to keep it out of his face. His wounds had healed, but the scars remained. He tried to keep clean, but there was only so much he could do with the frigid stream and plants rubbed into his skin to remove the loosest of the debris.

"Hey Chief," a voice beside him suddenly called out. He jumped slightly, not realizing a car had driven up to him.

It was a small, beat up, multi-colored Mazda pickup. A guy in his early fifties with a deep tan and a John Deere hat was driving. He took the toothpick out of his mouth before he spoke again. "Ya need work?" he asked.

Tim shrugged. "What do you need done?"

"Just need some lumber chopped. I'll feed ya lunch and dinner and pay ya twenty dollars when you're done. Whatdya say?"

"Sure, thank you," Tim answered, walking around and opening the door. He didn't know which part he looked forward to most, getting further down the road, having a meal, which hopefully didn't include fish, or earning some money.

The minute the car started moving, the man started talking. Thankfully for Tim, he didn't require many answers.

"The name's Steve. What's yours?"

"Johnny," Tim answered, studying the Johnny Cash cassette tape case sliding back and forth along the dashboard.

"Well, Johnny, it looks to me that you've had a rough night."

Tim shrugged.

"Yeah, I guess we've all had nights like that; no shame in it. But I'll tell ya, some of my best drinkin' buddies are Indians. I don't know how you guys do it. I'll get myself away from the missus and rug rats once a week or so, if I'm lucky, and get down to the taverns to have a few, but every night? I'd die within a month."

There was a long pause as he waited for Tim to say something, but Tim had no idea how "us guys did it"; he didn't even know what "it" was.

"I'll tell ya what, it's a shame how the drink has torn apart the reservations. I agree with those people who say alcoholism is a disease, don't you?" Steve asked.

"Yes, sir, I do."

"Yes, sir? Well I'll tell ya, that's a word I haven't heard in a while. How old are you? Seventeen? Eighteen? That's how old my youngest is. I don't think he's ever said that. Hell, his high school lets him call his teacher by their Christian names. Hell in a hand basket if ya ask me."

"Yes, sir."

Steve laughed. "'Yes, sir,' I like that. Someone obviously raised you right."

They drove another forty-five minutes until they came to I-90 and went west on that until they got to a small town called Superior.

Tim looked from the gas station-slash-casino on one side of the highway to the vast emptiness on the other and wondered what had prompted the name. As they proceeded south and crossed the Clark Fork River, he started to see what those first frontiersmen might have seen. In the distance were mountain ranges that rose and receded, met and mingled, filling the world with never ending and majestic trees with only a few small trails encircling them, crossed and followed by streams and small rivers.

There were a lot of rafts on the Clark Fork, getting the last of the summer sun. Tim wondered what it was like to be that happy and carefree. He wondered if he had *ever* been like that. He was pretty sure, deep down, that he never had.

"Well, here we are," Steve said.

They had just turned onto a long, winding dirt road that cut through a small apple orchard. "This is beautiful," he said.

"Why thank you. I know, apples in Montana don't really make sense, but it gets us by, and it has for generations."

The house was about a mile from the road and looked like a one-story doll house surrounded by tall trees.

"I'll take ya 'round back where the wood has been gathered. I just need ya to cut it into firewood," Steve said and veered right in a fork in the driveway that went around the house.

The chopping block had just come into view about a hundred yards from the house when Steve started cursing, "Goddamn-Good for Nothing! Jesus, have mercy, I'm gonna kill that boy!"

Tim looked at the empty space surrounding the block on all sides.

Steve slammed on the brakes, and Tim slid to the edge of his seat, throwing his hands straight out instinctually. Steve got out of the truck and stomped around, looking like he hoped the wood would appear somewhere in the near distance. He swore louder and louder and kicked at the ground angrily.

Tim studied Steve's face intently, as a boy who has been raised around volatile men might. Even though he didn't know this man, he knew he was struggling hard to control an explosive, unexpected rage. Tim comprehended that he had gotten into a vehicle and been driven to the hole of nowhere by a man who might be unstable. It wasn't fear he felt at this realization; it was weariness. He sighed and got out of the truck.

After a few moments, Steve came back to where Tim was leaning against the truck. He seemed to have gotten his emotions under control and only appeared to be slightly out of breath as he spoke, "Hey Johnny, I'm awfully sorry. It seems my son, Matthew, in his mad dash to get to Seattle, has once again neglected his chores. I'm afraid the wood hasn't been gathered."

Tim saw the tractor, with an empty flatbed attached, at the edge of the clearing. "That's okay. I can gather it if you need. I see the tractor is right over there. Where's the wood?"

"Ever driven one before?" he asked.

"Sure," Tim answered, pretty sure he was lying.

"Well, that'd be great. There are downed trees out past the clearing. Ya shouldn't have to go too deep; we only need one load."

"Okay, sounds good."

"Keys are in it," Steve said. "Make sure not to get yourself somewhere you can't get out of."

"Yes, sir."

Steve smiled warmly. "Yeah, I knew I liked you. Now, if you'll excuse me, I need to have a few words with the lady of the house."

Tim headed for the tractor but not fast enough to avoid hearing the nasty words being exchanged on the porch.

"Ella, Goddamn it, get out here!" Steve shouted. He repeated himself two more times before a slender woman in a floral sundress two sizes too big adorned with a pink apron opened the door, looking both timid and fierce.

"Jesus! It's good we ain't got neighbors. What's it now?"

"What is it now? Two guesses. I know you were kind enough to let Matthew take the Dodge to Seattle, even though you knew I had a market run to Butte, but did you also give him permission to shirk all his chores?"

She put her hands on her hips. "You know I didn't. I told him he needed to help out before he went, and the reason I told him to take the new truck is because that piece of shit you're driving wouldn't even get him out of the godforsaken state! Now, if you'll excuse me, I have a pie to finish."

She had almost gotten all the way around before she caught sight of Tim getting onto the tractor. She swung back and shouted, "Who the hell is that?" She pointed her finger at Tim, who was trying to start the machine as fast as possible.

Steve barked with a laugh. "That? That's the son I bought to replace the Good-for-Nothings you bore me."

"Steven James, I won't have it! You get that Goddamn Injun off my..."

BROOOOM. Tim sighed, put the tractor in gear and slammed his foot on the accelerator.

He drove the tractor as far as he could into the clearing, turned around, and parked it, all the time wondering how people could talk to each other that way.

He jumped down and scanned his surroundings. There were trees downed throughout the tall pines. He grabbed an ax from the cab and walked to the furthest tree. Raising the ax over his head and with confident, swift slices, Tim took off branch after branch and continued from that tree to the next and to the next. He was chopping them into thirds so he could easily load them when Steve showed up.

"Hey, I have a couple sandwiches and Cokes." He stopped and looked around him. "Well, will you look at this? You are on fire."

Tim stood up straight and beamed, wiping the sweat dripping from his face. "Thank you, sir. It feels good to be working."

"I can't imagine you have problems finding work."

Tim picked up one of the Cokes with a shrug.

"Well, if you want, we could always use help around here. Picking season is about to start, and we could sure use you."

Tim took a swig of pop and looked into the distance where Ella was hanging the wash and stealing glances at him. He couldn't see what her eyes might be saying, but he still heard her voice as she said, "Goddamn Injun," and knew he couldn't stay. "Nah, thanks for the offer, but I gotta be movin' on."

Steve followed his gaze. "She's really not as bigoted as she sounds, but I am sorry you had to hear that." Tim shrugged in reply, so Steve continued, "No, that ain't right. She's just mad at the world sometimes and decides to blame it on people she don't know rather than examine her own heart."

Tim didn't think that excused anything, but it was none of his business, so he just shrugged again and begun to unwrap his sandwich. It had an unfamiliar smell, but his salivary glands instantly informed him it was a good one. Steve caught him examining it. "Meatloaf. I hope that's okay."

Tim took a bite and closed his eyes with an audible moan. Steve laughed. "I guess that means it's acceptable."

Tim nodded sheepishly. "It's amazing."

Steve laughed again. "You're an easy person to please. Wait until dinner, though. Ella might have her faults but not in the kitchen."

At the mention of Ella's name, the food caught in Tim's throat. He took a swig of the Coke and contemplated if the food was worth sticking around. He took another bite, and the ground meat, tomato and Wonder bread once again exploded and opened every taste bud. *Definitely,* he thought.

Steve stayed and helped load some wood before he excused himself to "get back to the business of business." Steve promised to call Tim when dinner was ready. He showed him a water pump on the side of the house if he got thirsty.

Before he drove off, Steve said, "Good job, son. Keep it up."

Something about that phrase *Good job,* or perhaps the *son* warmed him and kept him going through the heat of the day, urged him on as the trees he loaded got heavier and heavier. It was those words feeling like a pat on the back, a scratch behind the ears for a pet who wanted nothing more than to please that got him through the increasing blatant, hostile glares coming from the woman who spent entirely too much time hanging wash, sweeping the back porch, and picking beans in the garden.

By the time he was called to dinner, he had finished gathering the downed trees and was just finishing chopping them. Steve was standing on the back porch holding out a fifty dollar bill.

"What's this for?" Tim asked.

"Whatdya think? I pay well for a job well done, plus I'm trying to convince you to stay on."

"Thank you, sir," Tim said, taking the money, "and I'll think about the job."

"Great," Steve said, holding the door to the kitchen open. Tim followed him. "We could really use the help. Matthew is a senior this fall, and he's working towards a football scholarship."

Steve almost sounded proud of his son, but as his wife entered the kitchen, his tone changed. "Of course, he was practically useless before he wanted to be the next Joe Montana."

Ella glared at him as she went to a drawer and rustled around for silverware. In these close quarters, she didn't even peek at Tim. He didn't think he'd ever felt this uncomfortable. "Would it be alright if I wash up before dinner?"

Steve stopped staring down his wife, who was now setting the kitchen table, and turned to Tim with a grin. "Of course you can. Let me show you to the *guest* bathroom."

He walked Tim down the hall to the bathroom and then went back to the kitchen. Tim was just about to close the door when he heard the shouting.

"Goddamn it, Ella! Knock this shit off. What have I told you about having guests for dinner? We're not sitting in the Goddamn kitchen, like Goddamn field hands. Where's your—"

Tim quickly shut the door and turned on the faucet to drown the noise. He looked around the bathroom. It was too pretty, all pink and roses. All the towels matched, and the flower-shaped soap looked untouched. He looked at himself in the mirror but couldn't see how he really looked; he could only see that he was contaminating her beautiful room with his Injun presence and manly odor.

He searched all the drawers and shelves for the ugly towels, for the hidden, stained ones that the regulars of the house used; there weren't any. The closest he came was a rag that he found in a bucket of cleaning supplies. He took it and ran it through the water, which had become so hot the room was steaming and sweating.

The smell of bleach wafted from the rag and burnt his nostrils. He delicately looked through the soap dish and found a petal that had broken from a rose of soap and scrubbed that into the rag until the bleach smell lessened. He put it to his forehead and cheeks and in hard, circular motions, released the dirt, sweat and tension he had felt since he had heard *Injun* in that hateful tone.

He felt so much better as he turned off the water that he had resolved to take his money and sneak out the front door while they continued to bicker in the kitchen.

He opened the door to total silence and without the noise to guide where they were, he stood, thinking hard which way to go to avoid them.

"Hey, there you are. I thought maybe you fell in. Come on, dinner's ready." Steve said from behind him. Tim sighed and walked back to the kitchen. "No Johnny, in here."

Steve motioned him into another room that was too pretty. The long mahogany table that looked like it could sit eight comfortably was set for three. The plates were barely used china with gold lining that matched the gold plated silverware and had roses around the border, to match the table runner that matched the napkins that matched the wallpaper.

He was told to sit down as Ella entered from the kitchen with a heaping bowl of mashed potatoes.

"Hey, Johnny, can I get you a beer?" Steve asked.

Ella snorted as she dropped the potatoes with such force, it rattled the silverware.

Tim ignored this. "No, sir, I don't drink beer. I'd love another Coke though."

Ella snorted again as she went back into the kitchen, returning this time with a platter of fried chicken and a bowl of green beans.

"Everything looks so delicious," Tim said, to show her how civil he could be. She glared at him again; this time he could read her eyes. She seemed to be blaming him for something. He looked away, feeling guilty despite himself.

Steve came back with two glasses of pop and one mug of beer. As soon as Tim saw the golden yellow with the tiny bubbles, dancing to the top, his nostrils flared, and the smell overwhelmed all other senses. He closed his eyes and willed himself to survive this dinner.

Steve placed the Cokes in front of Ella and Tim and sat down at the head of the table. He took a swig from the mug and moaned. "Ah, that hits the spot."

This caused Ella to snort again. Steve shot her a warning glance and said, "Ella, do you have something caught in your throat?"

She forced a condescending smile. "No dear. Would you care for some potatoes?"

Steve matched her tone. "Yes, darling, I would love some taters."

Ella and Tim both grabbed for the bowl to hand to Steve. Tim noticed a mark around her wrist that made him recoil and rub at his own wrist. He knew what caused that mark, knew it was called an "Indian Burn," and he knew exactly how it felt to have your skin twisted and pulled like that.

She noticed his revulsion and put her hands on her lap. Then with an evil smile, telling him that she had thought of a way of getting back at him for pitying her, she asked, "So Johnny, are you one of my husband's drinking buddies?"

"Sorry ma'am?" Tim asked, not understanding the question.

Ella rolled her eyes and spoke loud and slow. "I was just wondering if you were one of the drunks my husband hangs out with."

Steve slammed his fist on the table, and Tim looked from him to Ella. "I don't drink at all, ma'am, and I just met your husband this morning."

She turned her glare to Steve, who smiled at her. The silence that followed was terrifying.

* * *

They had almost finished the meal when Ella said, "So I talked to Matthew today. He really loves the school and says the coach is impressed with him. So, now it looks like a decision between UDub and Michigan."

Steve scowled. "Good riddance."

Tim looked down and tried to ignore them so he could enjoy the best meal he'd ever tasted, at least that he remembered. He knew what they were doing to each other. He was just glad they weren't using him to do it anymore.

"You're just jealous that he's going to be getting out of this hell hole, just like the rest of them, and you never could."

"Some of us are perfectly happy staying where we are and working the land that God has blessed us with."

"While the rest of us, who think there's more than the Goddamn apples and the Superior Church of Goddamn Christ are sinners. Right, Steven?"

"Woman, that's enough. You're embarrassing our guest," Steve said through clenched teeth.

She got up, marched into the kitchen and began throwing around utensils and silverware. She came back in with a pan of pie that smelled like apples, cinnamon and sweetness. She walked slowly with a smile on her face to the head of the table and slammed the pie down in front of her husband. Pieces of apple and crust flew everywhere. That was the only bit of the pie any of them tasted.

Ella started screaming, "Our *guest? You're worried about embarrassing* our *guest?* You bring a *drifter* into *my house* and you're worried about embarrassing *him?*"

Tim was on his feet apologizing and trying to get out. "I'm sorry; I'm just going to…"

At the same time, Steve had flown out of his chair and had his open hand raised and across Ella's face before Tim knew what to do. "Shut up! Shut up you stupid, stupid woman. All I asked is for one night. One night with a little bit of hospitality, a little bit civility and…"

"…go now." Tim finished.

Steve had her hair in his fist. "Are you happy now?"

He spun her around the table by her hair and thrust her in front of Tim who staggered backward, still trying to escape. "Now I want you to apologize." Steve said.

"Are you crazy?" Ella screamed, trying to get free. "Get your hands off me!"

He pushed her forward so that Tim had to decide to catch her or get out of the way. His inability to run forced his decision, and he caught her, hoping that would be the end of it.

Words spluttered out of her, too wet to be understood as she flew back at Steve, arms flailing. Steve looked at her, amused, and Tim looked amazed, until Steve swung back. It only took one, solid connection to land her on the ground where she crumpled like a wet towel.

"Hey, hey, hey," Tim said, still believing he could stop it with words.

Steve and Ella didn't even realize he was still in the room, and it certainly wasn't Tim that Steve was referring to when he began chanting, "Apologize, apologize, apologize," as he straddled her and pounded his fists into her face and chest.

Tim was screaming inside. He didn't want to be there; he didn't want to see this—this was none of his concern, none of his business, but he knew it was wrong, and he knew he had to do something.

Before he even knew what he was doing, before he'd even fully convinced himself to do anything, he had Steve by the back of the neck and was lifting him up like a baby cub. Steve yelped and flailed his arms and legs as Tim held him above the ground, his hands so large and his arms so strong that with one hand, he securely held him, and then, with both arms, tossed Steve away from himself and Ella, who lay on the ground watching this overhead with fear and astonished wide eyes.

Steve sailed across the room and slammed into an antique glass door of the china cabinet. The force of the throw caused him to bounce off the cabinet and slump to the ground, shards of broken glass raining down upon him.

No one said anything for a long, painful minute.

"Are you okay?" Tim finally asked Ella without looking at her. He was gasping in deep breaths as he watched the heap of Steve with amazement. *I did that. I did that,* kept running through his mind, then was replaced with, *What have I done?*

She answered by getting up to her hands and knees and crawling to Steve, ignoring the glass digging into her flesh.

"Is he...?" he couldn't ask the question.

She felt his pulse. "He's okay, just knocked out." She turned and studied Tim. This time the hatred was replaced with bewilderment. "Why did you do that?"

"I didn't mean...I only wanted..."

She stood up and came to him, eyes puffed and her face a bloody mess. "You're shaking," she said, surprised.

He swallowed. "I'm sorry, I should..."

"No, don't be sorry. He was hurting me. He could have...but...why?"

"I don't...I don't understand."

She continued staring at him, ignoring the blood falling into her eyes from her temples and her bloody nose dripping onto her rug. "The way...my behavior...well...you should have been the one...you should have been helping *him*...not me."

Tim looked horrified. "No. I could never...a man...a man wouldn't..."

He still wanted to run away but he couldn't, not yet. "Sit down," he said, guiding her to a chair and helping her into it. He went to the kitchen, and, this time, he found the old towels in a bottom drawer. He got one, soaked it with warm water, and went back to her. He sat down, cupped her face in his hand, and gently dabbed at the blood dripping from her nose.

She looked puzzled again. "Why are you helping me?"

"You're bleeding."

"No, I mean, why?"

He shrugged. "Do you have a first aid kit?"

She told him where it was. He left the towel with her and went to get it. When he returned, she had cleaned up her face and was digging glass out of the palm of her hands. "You have to get out of here," she said.

"Let me help you first."

"No, don't worry about me. Take the truck. After you're gone, I'll call the neighbors for help. You can't be here when Steve wakes up."

"You shouldn't be here either," he said.

"No, I'll be okay. He won't hurt me anymore. Just leave the truck somewhere the police can find it and don't worry about us. You've done enough; I don't want you to get in any trouble."

Tim still didn't feel right about it, but with the mention of the police and trouble, he broke out in a cold sweat, and he knew he had to get away, fast.

She handed him the keys, walked him to the door, and with a fat-lipped smile said, "Thank you."

Tim followed the roads Steve had taken to get to the house, but instead of getting on the eastbound highway back toward Missoula, he went west to the sign reading Coeur d'Alene.

He checked the gas meter, a little less than half a tank. He hoped that would get him out of Montana. West, that was the direction he longed for; a fresh start, a new day.

He rolled the window down and tried to clear his mind of the horror he'd just left. The air blew his hair, and the breeze smelled like wheat, cattle, and new highway.

Suddenly the scene changed, and he was no longer driving down the highway; the windshield that had shown the night stars and empty stretch of road was now flashing a scene of a burning inferno. The wind that had been blowing in his hair had become hot, blazing hot and not moving at all but suffocating still. The smell was no longer sweet and familiar but of burning metal, brick and wood.

Sweat poured from his temples, and the roar of the flames was deafening. He wanted to cup his hands over his ears but they were inexplicable glued to a steering wheel.

The image of a chaos of people appeared before him screaming:
"Fire! Fire!"
"The house is on fire!"
"Where is Naomi?"
"Where is Virginia?"

"*Did they…?*"
"*Are they…?*"
Then his own voice strained above the others. "*Na-ho! Na-ho!*"
The house exploded.

And then, just as suddenly, there was a crash that was much closer.

What amazed him as the truck slammed into the billboard is that he heard the crash before he had felt it—heard the bending metal before he felt the lurch of the sudden stop throw him against the steering wheel until the seatbelt slammed him back again.

In the stunned silence that followed, his mind raced with the only emotion he was painfully familiar with: fear. Smelling gas and seeing smoke escaping the bent-in front of the truck, Tim fought against the wave of nausea, pain and the light-headed need to lose consciousness, and opened the door. After struggling with the seat belt, he finally freed himself and made it a safe distance before his legs gave out. As he glanced up at the stars and the billboard advertising someplace called the "10,000 Silver Dollar Bar" through his blood-soaked vision, he thought to himself, *Yes, this is my spot. This is where the journey ends. I'm glad to go. Glad the mysteries will finally be solved, or become unimportant,* before he succumbed to the dizzying urge to pass out.

Kootenai Salish Indian Reservation
1983

The first time I lost my brother, I was seven. He had just turned fifteen, and some of the slightly older boys had offered to take him on a vision quest. He walked around feeling truly accepted for weeks beforehand, and my mother beamed at him. I was the only one who wasn't buying it. First of all, I didn't think any of them knew what a vision quest was; it sounded like one of those things that might have once had a meaning but had long-since lost its relevance.

Besides, none of the boys taking him on this great quest had been friends of Tim's before. I thought they were using the fact that he would do almost *anything* to be a real Indian and to be included in tribal matters as a new form of torture. He was gone for two weeks. The boys he left with returned after only one.

It was the first time that I spent Saturday night in the closet by myself.

Every Saturday, my mother threw a party. Sometimes it was an all-day barbeque to actually celebrate something, and sometimes it didn't start until after two in the morning when the bars would close, but it was always at our house until the sun rose the next day.

Every week, my mother would find it hilarious to play the "humiliate the offspring" game; she was a master of it. She would spend all day cooing over me and making me feel special, doing my hair and putting makeup on me, like a big girl, for the party, only to smudge the makeup all over my face or cut off one of my ponytails right before people came. Then she would parade me around, telling people how naughty I was. *How was she supposed to deal with a child filled with the Devil?*

She continued to tell these stories as she drank, so by the time everyone had heard about what a horrible, disappointing, stupid child I was, she would be so drunk she forgot that I hadn't actually done any of those things. Then she would drag me into the bathroom and whoop me until I went limp or she grew bored. The whole time, Tim was on the outside, pounding on the door. She'd yell back that she had to teach me a lesson, that she couldn't take my disobedience, or my smart mouth, or the look of me anymore.

This was an every week thing for a long time until Tim came up with a plan. Saturday mornings, he made breakfast in bed for our mother, packed her a lunch, and then took me out of the house. We'd walk around town, spending long, cold afternoons at the library, hitching rides to the lake to go fishing in the warmer weather, or to his favorite place, the junkyard.

Tim loved the junkyard. Sometimes I think he would live there if he could. Most of the times that I couldn't find him, he'd be there. When he took me the first time, I felt he was taking me to his sanctuary, and he was. He loved it for many reasons; it was quiet and never demanded anything from him. What he liked most, though, was that it never really changed, and when it did, the only differences were positive. Unlike real life, it was never one thing on Monday and something completely different on Tuesday. His treasures were well protected in other people's garbage, and there was nothing he wanted that he couldn't find there.

He would try to keep my mind off home on those Saturday adventures, but there was always a time when I would want to go back. No matter how she treated me Saturday nights or how much she loathed the sight of me the other days, there were always those rare moments: the times where she'd snuggle with me after the aspirin kicked in. I would rub her temples, she'd smile at me, and all was forgiven. There were days when she would really do my hair, and she'd let me play dress up in her Friday night fancy clothes. There were even those small glimpses of times when she had the patience to show me how to do beadwork or let me help her in the kitchen. It didn't matter to me that I knew she did these things when she was bored and had nothing better to do. I lived for the days when my mother needed a playmate. *Those* were the moments that kept me coming back home.

Tim knew this about me. Knew I would trade the abusive Saturdays for the snuggles of Sunday morning. So when I cried for home, he took me back and created a safe, comfy place for us.

In our house, two bedrooms—my mother's and mine—shared a large closet that had hung clothes on both sides, and in the middle had spare blankets, pillows and miscellaneous shoes. It was large enough to hide us and comfortable enough for us to camp out all night.

There were bad things about this hiding place, very bad things. Since no one knew we were there, and we were situated between bedrooms, we heard a lot of things that no child or teenage boy should hear. He tried to drown out the noises with chanting, stories, even jokes, but since we didn't want to be heard, and they couldn't care less, we heard it all.

That's why I was so angry with Tim that second Saturday without him. Without his chanting beside me, all I could do was shove my fingers in my ears and pretend that wasn't my mother screaming, "Fuck me! Oh God, Fuck me!" and it wasn't someone I was told just that morning to call "Uncle Danny" moaning, "You dirty whore, you dirty, dirty whore!"

The next morning, I woke in my bed, but I wasn't alone. "Uncle Danny" was curled up next to me, his arm around my shoulder, breathing stale beer into my face. My first thought was of fear, but he wasn't hurting me, wasn't yelling at me, wasn't undressed, so I relaxed and quietly scooted away from him.

I decided I would never talk to my brother ever again. *How dare he leave me alone!* But to give him the silent treatment, first I'd have to find him.

"Tim! Tim! I know you're here," I shouted then listened. There was a loud pounding coming from somewhere in the middle of the junkyard. I knew that Walter, the guy that ran the place, never walked that far in, so I was pretty sure it was Tim. I didn't know what he was doing, but it sounded like he was destroying something.

I walked past the abandoned furniture, ripped-apart couches, highchairs with bent legs, past the pieces and bits of demolished or burnt out doors, windows, shingles and bricks, past the cars, most of them stripped of everything of value.

The noise was becoming louder, but I still couldn't see him. Someone had taken about a dozen hoods and stood them in a circle. The commotion seemed to be coming from there.

"Tim!" I shouted.

"Na-ho, is that you?" he finally asked.

"Yes. Let me in."

There was a silence, and then the hood in front of me slid away. The sudden sunshine off the hot metal sent Tim into shadow, but I knew instantly something was different.

"What are you doing here?" he barked.

I froze, terrified by his tone. I'd never heard him talk with such dislike, not to me. I realized that I'd never be able to give him the silent treatment. How could you not talk to the only person who really cared if you lived or died?

"Here," he said, throwing me a pair of goggles. "Take cover."

I hid behind a back seat that had been removed from its car and was off to the side of the windshield of a Volkswagen Beetle he was destroying. One...two...three times he lifted the sledgehammer over his head and slammed it down on the already crushed-in front window.

"What are you doing?"

He shrugged.

"Where have you been?"

He shrugged.

"Did you have a good time at your *vision quest*?"

He turned away from me and started pounding on the windshield, harder and harder.

My worst fear had been realized. "So now that you're a man, you don't talk to your little baby sister anymore?" I asked in between swings.

His hammer slipped out of his hand mid-swing, and he looked at me with tears in his eyes. I had never seen tears in my brother's eyes—never. I'd seen him scared, I'd seen him angry, and I'd seen him sad, but this was all three at once, each fighting for control. Part of me wanted to run from whatever had done this to him, but the other part wanted to make him better, like he'd always done for me.

As he swiped at his tears, unsuccessfully trying to make them stop, I realized for probably the first time how young he was. Then as if to prove this point, he stammered, "I am *not* a man. They did *not* make me a man."

He put thick gloves on and began tearing the sheet of shattered glass out of its frame.

"What did they do to you?" I asked in a whisper, pretty sure I didn't want to know.

He didn't answer, didn't even look at me. He just continued his demolition. A long time later, so long I wasn't sure if he even remembered I was there, he spat into the dirt. "God, I hate this place!"

"The junkyard?" I asked, confused.

"No. Not the junkyard, every inch of the rez that's not the junkyard; every person who owned any of these things; any Indian who ever drove by this place." He laughed bitterly. "I can't believe I ever wanted to be one. Ever wanted anything they've got." He spat again, as if trying to get the taste out of his mouth.

"Why don't we go?" I asked, hoping I wasn't included in his hatred; for the first time in my life, I wasn't sure.

He sighed. "Oh, Na-ho, I wish we could. Where could a seven and fifteen-year-old go?"

"We could go find the Nopiinde. They'll take us." I answered, the hair rising on my arms just thinking about it.

He sighed again, bringing me back down. "She'll never let us go."

Now it was my turn to be bitter. "She'll never let *you* go."

He smiled at me. We both knew the irony of our lives. Aside from ourselves, Tim had one person love him, but yearned for the love, or, the very least, acceptance of the rest of the tribe. I was accepted by the whole tribe, but yearned for that same one person's love.

"Nah, I don't want to give those bastards the satisfaction of running. Besides, I don't think the fates are quite done with us here. We're still being tested," he said.

I hated tests. I had always hated them, since the first one in kindergarten. They wanted to flunk me because I wouldn't recite the ABCs backward. I didn't see the point. Once they explained why it was necessary, so they could tell I knew the letters and not just memorized the song, I of course, had no problem. They told my mother that I had the markings of a genius. Not because I could say my ZYXs, any idiot can do that, but that I asked the question and understood the answer. My mother told me I'd do better to keep my mouth shut and do whatever they asked.

I sat in the junkyard all day trying to lose the frightening feeling I had when I first saw Tim and sensed he was no longer the boy I knew. He stood with an unusual slouch, and he appeared to be holding an inner debate with himself, sometimes seeming angry, sometimes sad. He was usually slow and precise, but that day, he was full of energy, constantly moving from project to project, never stopping, and never sitting down.

As the sun began to set, I asked, "So are you coming home?"

He shook his head as he failed to look me in the eye. "I can't, not yet."

"When?" I pleaded.

He went back to working. "Soon. As soon as I can walk tall again. I won't let them see me hurt and cowering. I won't give them the…" He stopped talking when he saw the fear in me. "Don't worry."

"You won't leave without me, will you?"

He finally looked me in the eye and smiled his old, sad smile. "Never." He picked something up and brought it to me. "Here, these are for you."

They were small baby food jars with the labels ripped off and filled with sparkling blue water. He rotated them up and down and held them to the light of the low horizon. There were tiny pieces of glass inside that shimmered as they danced in the beautiful water.

"I love them," I said, taking the two jars from him and turning them in the light myself.

"Good. I knew you would. But if anything happens and they break, you *have* to throw them away. It's beautiful but dangerous and highly flammable: glass and Montana windshield wiper fluid, pure methanol. I know you're a smart girl and will know what to do with them."

I nodded my head solemnly and carefully put them in my jacket pocket before hugging him tightly. I wanted to give him my little bit of strength to see him through this. I remembered what Phoenix Daughter had told me at the Grand Canyon about taking care of my brother, and I felt that I wasn't just letting him down, but her as well.

He finally pulled away and changed the subject. "So, everything's okay at home?"

"Oh, yeah. Everything is exactly the same at home. We have a new uncle."

He laughed. "Of course we do. Who is it?"

I shrugged. "Some guy named Danny. I only met him yesterday, but he may be around for a while."

"Yeah, we'll see. He wasn't mean to you, right?"

I shook my head. He hadn't been mean to me, but I knew I should tell Tim about this morning. I knew that he would be irate though, and I wasn't sure how I felt about it, so I didn't. Truth was, most of mother's boyfriends left because of Tim. They didn't like my mother's devotion to him or the way he watched them closely to make sure mother and I were treated right or the way that my mother wouldn't let them slap him around.

Tim helped me off the hood of the Chevy S-10 I had been sitting on. "Don't tell anyone where I am, okay?" he asked.

"Of course not. You'll be here if I need you though?"

"Right."

I left and tried not to think about what they could have done to him to have finally convinced him that they were nothing special.

Life in my house without Tim sort of sucked. My mother had "Uncle Danny" to occupy her interest, and I discovered my grandfather, but it still was no fun without Tim.

My grandfather was a statue in our house. He'd always been there, but since I'd never seen him move from the bench by the fireplace, and he never exerted any more energy than it took to light his non-filter Camels in between the yellowed pointer and middle finger of his right hand, I never thought about him.

Our entire relationship consisted of this: Every morning, I'd pat him on the head on the way to wherever I was going and say, "Morning, Gramps." Then he'd pat the front pocket of his faded Western shirt. I'd reach in and pull out a stick of Wrigley's Big Red. I'd put the gum in my mouth and pocket the wrapper, adding it to my collection later.

It wasn't until Tim was gone that my boredom sparked my curiosity. I decided I would spend a day investigating him. He couldn't possibly live on that bench all day and all night. He and Tim shared a bedroom that was originally an enclosed back porch, but I didn't think he actually slept there.

I woke up, wiggled quietly out of bed, so as not to disturb "Uncle Danny." I had woken up with him curled up next to me, his face in the space between my shoulder and neck, for about five days.

It no longer shocked me, and I stopped wondering why. I actually kind of liked it. Tim had told me about the Bad Feelings so many times, I knew how to detect them before I was out of diapers. Uncle Danny never made me feel bad though. I thought maybe he liked me like a daughter, and I'd never had anyone besides Tim in my everyday life care about me as a person.

This made sense every morning, but the rest of the day, he treated me no differently than any of my other "uncles," who all seemed to understand the relationship between my mother and me better than I did. They understood that unlike other single mothers, she wasn't actually looking for a daddy substitute, so it was not required that they be involved in her children's lives. The more time they spent being nice to me or trying to get to know Tim, the less time Mother would keep them around as a sleeping partner, so they left us alone.

I went into the closet, got out of my princess PJs and into my summer uniform of Daisy Dukes and a tank top.

"Hi, Gramps," I said, patting his head and taking my gum from his pocket. I bent down and stared into his eyes, looking for any sign he knew I was there. Nothing. I sat down beside him and tried to see what he saw, what he watched all day.

After thirty minutes, I'd seen enough of his view to last a lifetime. These are the things I wrote down in my notepad:

ded flys in window—12.
Socks under cowch—3.
Stains in carpet—4
Stains that look like 3 leged dog—1.

Feeling pleased with myself, I tucked the notepad into my back pocket and stopped for breakfast. I brought my Pop-Tarts back to the fireplace, offering Gramps one. He didn't want it. I sat down beside him and noticed his breathing seemed a lot slower than mine. I got closer and decided to count how many breaths he took in a minute.

Gramps breath—10.

Then I counted mine.

Me—25.

I wondered which one of us was not right. Probably him. I also wondered if I could get mine as slow as his. I tried. By the time I'd actually gotten there, I was exhausted. I wanted to take a nap, but what if he did something interesting while I slept? I got an idea.

I went to the bathroom and found some dental floss. I came back to him and began tying the end of the floss around his cowboy belt buckle. No response.

"What are you doing?" my mother asked. She was standing at the kitchen door with a beer in her hand.

"Playing with Gramps."

"That's nice," she said, no longer listening. "Dad, I have to go pick up Danny. Can you stay here with Naomi?"

I watched his face. She must have seen something I didn't. "Thanks. We'll be home soon."

She left without a goodbye. I waited for her truck to pull out of the dirt driveway, and then I continued my work. I stretched out the dental floss until it was long enough. I tied the other end to my belt loop and went to the couch to take a nap and watch my stories. *The Electric Company* was still my favorite, but my brother loved *ZOOM* so I liked that one too.

I slept on and off all morning. I never felt a tug on my string, but, on closer inspection, I did discover something odd: crumbs on my grandfather's shirt. I picked one off his shirt to look at it closer. I studied him and the crumb, both revealing nothing. I put the piece to my nose, was that sugar I smelled? It dawned on me what it was: my discarded second Pop-Tart from that morning. He had waited until I had gone to sleep to eat it.

I wrote this in my notepad and gave him a sly smile. "I'm on to you, Gramps."

His lip twitched, but he put his cigarette in his mouth to disguise it. I sat next to him again, determined not to miss a thing. I only left his side twice: once at lunch time to make a PB&J sandwich; the second time, when I realized mother and Danny were not returning, I made another sandwich for dinner. Both times I made one for Grandpa too. Both sat uneaten.

As the sun was setting, I realized what a quiet, peaceful day we had just shared. Yes, most of it was incredibly boring, but it was nice nonetheless. I had no proof, but I was pretty sure he knew I was there, knew what I was doing, and was enjoying it too.

I went back to the couch and turned on the TV, shouting out letter suggestions at *Wheel of Fortune*. I had fallen into a light sleep when I felt a slight tug. It wasn't enough to signify him standing up and walking away, but enough to awaken me. I kept my eyes closed all but a squint to mark his movements. He was standing up!

I almost jumped with excitement and a little bit of fear, but I controlled the urge as he approached. He bent down so that his horrid, smoky breath tickled my nose and almost made me gag. He kissed my forehead and slowly headed for the front door.

I waited until he was gone to get up. The floss was still tied to my belt, but he had cut off his end. That must have been the tug I felt.

I grabbed my notepad, a camera that I wasn't really sure even worked, and my flashlight, and I followed him. I hoped he was going to stay on foot and wasn't going too far. We walked past our street, past the grocery, crossed the highway, and finally came to the only place he really could be going, *The Broken Arrow*.

I watched him walk in, heard a chorus of "Amos!" and sighed, *Him too. Of course he was one too.* Of course he spent all day smoking cigarettes, not eating anything, breathing extremely slowly, counting the minutes, seconds until he can get his next drink. *Of course.*

I sat on a parking block to think. I couldn't go in there; that was for sure. I would definitely blow my cover. That only left sitting out here all night, and was it worth it?

I didn't get too far in my ponderings when I heard a familiar engine pull up. I knew it was my mother's truck before I heard her voice, along with five or six others coming out of the cab and truck bed, laughing. I hid behind a dusty Cherokee with Bureau of Indian Affairs plates.

"What do you mean you're not allowed? You work here," someone said, and everyone laughed.

"I know, but they said my paychecks never cover my tab, and they don't want me drinking here no more."

"That's retarded," I heard my mother's voice reply. "They'd rather you took your business, and all ours with it, somewhere else?"

I couldn't hear the answer to this over the twang of the guitar from the jukebox, meaning that they had gone inside. I stood up straight and went to the truck, jumping into the back.

There was no way I was going home now. I just realized that my house was completely deserted. All my parental guidance was in the saloon, so I figured I'd better stay too.

I lay down and got comfortable; *this was going to be a long night.* The stars were out bright, and I tried to find the constellations that I knew. Tim had been teaching me, but I only knew the Big and Little Dipper so far. After that, I tried to count the stars. Every hundred or so, a shooting star would race across the sky and make me lose count. They were pretty to watch, but they started to irritate me. My friend Donna told me every time I saw a shooting star, I was to close my eyes and make a wish, but I didn't believe in making wishes.

I watched the stars so long that when I closed my eyes, they were still there. I didn't know I had fallen asleep until I was jerked awake by nearby shouts. The angry voices didn't alarm me at first since I recognized one as my mother's, and I'd heard that sound too many times for it to worry me. It wasn't until my sleeping mind registered where I was that I woke up fully.

I rolled over on my stomach and crouched low on my hands and knees, for a quick, quiet retreat if she was carpooling again.

"You really need help; it's not natural," she was saying, calmer now.

"Shut up! Please!" Danny spat. "It's not like that, not about *that*."

"Then what the hell is it? What turns you on? I thought I used to know, but now…What? What?"

Danny was quieter now, like he had been wounded. I knew the abuse was only beginning. "It's about purity. It's not about sex. It's… innocent and…clean."

"You're disgusting," she spat.

"Shut up!" he shouted this time.

I peeked over the side of the truck in time to see my mother attempt a drunken swing at him that missed and would have knocked her on her ass, if Danny hadn't caught her from behind.

He held both of her arms around her chest tight. She tried to buck away. "Get off me! Get off me you, motherfucker!" she screamed. Then she started laughing. "Wait, you're not a motherfucker; you've stopped being a motherfucker. Now you're a babyfucker."

He threw her to the ground, hard. She began chanting, "Babyfucker! Babyfucker!"

He opened the passenger side door, picked her up by her hair, and threw her in the truck. She howled as he slammed the door shut.

He cursed all the way around the front of the truck, "Stupid slut. Dirty whore." But he didn't have much conviction, and he stopped as he opened the door. I saw in his eyes that she was worth it to him.

We drove away, and through the red of the taillights, I saw my grandpa standing in the parking lot. He looked so sad as our eyes locked. Then the truck turned the corner, and he was gone.

There was no talking from the front cab, but by the way Danny was all over the road, I knew they weren't finished. He pounded on the brakes in our driveway so hard that I slammed into the cab. This time the stars were inside my head, and then I saw nothing.

Next thing I knew, I was being lifted by someone who reeked of beer, cigarettes and dirt. I had spent all day with that smell; I knew who it was. I put my arms around his neck and held on tight as he carried me to my room. He laid me down on my bed and put the thin sheet over me. He stroked my face and forehead; I felt a bump forming there. He left and came back moments later with a cold, damp cloth. Throughout this, I kept my eyes closed, trying to pretend I was asleep.

I heard the sounds in the room next to me and wondered how long I had been out. I knew by the screaming of the bed springs that the fighting was over, knew by Danny's joyful moans that he had forgiven her calling him a babyfucker, knew from my mother's complete silence that her love affair was over, and knew that tomorrow, "Uncle Danny" would be gone.

My grandpa sat next to me and, as if trying to drown out the sounds next door, did the most amazing thing. He reached into his pocket, pulled out a handmade flute and began to play a slow, mournful melody.

The rest of the world stilled, and I felt drops on my face that I didn't recognize as tears until I tasted the salt in my mouth. When he was finished, he tucked the flute between my arm and body and leaned over to brush his lips against my forehead.

When I woke up the next morning, the familiar-by-now breath on my neck told me last night's fight had been a bad dream. I was more than relieved, because it had dawned on me what Danny and my mother had been fighting about in the dream, what she had meant by "babyfucker." It hurt me in ways I couldn't even understand at the time.

If she really thought he had done only half the things she accused him of, then shouldn't some of her outrage been on my behalf? Did she *really* not care about me at all? Even a little? But it had been a dream, so I didn't need the answer to that question.

I sighed with relief and had just started to shimmy away when my bedroom door was thrown open. Three men in cowboy hats, ponytails, badges and shotguns stormed in.

There was a lot of shouting, and I was yanked into one of the men's arms. I looked around me, trying to make sense of all the noise and people. That's when I saw "Uncle Danny." He didn't have any clothes on and was trying to cover up while they forcefully pulled him out of the bed. He was yelling, "No! No! This isn't right! It's not right!"

I had never seen a naked man's bit before. The way it was bouncing around like a dead fish, and the clumpy hair with bits of grey surrounding it made me feel dirty.

The man holding me must have noticed where I was staring, because he shoved my face into his chest and ordered the other men to put some clothes on Danny, before he turned me around and walked me out the bedroom door. My mother was in the hallway wailing, "What has he done to my baby? What has he done?"

I glared at her over the policeman's shoulder. I knew she had done this, and I would never forgive her. I wanted her to know, and I wanted her to always wonder if this little revenge of hers was worth it.

I saw in her eyes fear and a bit of understanding. Then the tears in my eyes blurred everything and made her look far away. By the time I had wiped my eyes, she had turned back into her pretend face and started to perform for the strangers.

"Where are you taking my baby? Naomi, come back to me!" She fell to her knees. "My baby, give me back my baby!"

They dragged Danny down the hall behind me. He was wearing a pair of sweats and handcuffs. Now he was shouting at my mother who was still on her knees flailing her arms in the air.

"You bitch! What have you done?" he screamed over and over.

Everyone was shouting at everyone else. I was the only one who hadn't opened my mouth. But as I looked around one last time, I saw that wasn't true; Gramps was in his usual position by the fireplace as if he was blind and deaf.

That's when I lost it. I thought I had gotten through, had touched him somehow. Now, my being forcefully pulled from my home couldn't even wake him. I put my arms out to him and called his name between sobs that strained my throat, but through the smoke of his cigarette, I couldn't even tell if he knew I was there. And then I wasn't.

I was put into the back of one of the men's car. The man who carried me put on my seatbelt with delicate care, the way people who don't have children and don't know how very much it takes to break them would.

I swiped at my eyes angrily.

"Don't worry, sweetie. We'll get this all sorted out. You did nothing wrong," he said, ruffling my hair and then removing his hand as if I stung him.

We had to wait for the car that Danny had been forced into to move before we could pull out. I watched the whole scene from the backseat window: Danny and my mother screaming at each other, the neighbors standing at the end of their drives, and a teenage boy riding a bike fast down the street. This vantage point made it all seem far away and unrelated to me, as if I could reach over, turn the knob, and catch the end of *Donahue* instead of this show.

I closed my eyes and turned away, resting my cheek on the cool, blue vinyl. I knew this wasn't a nightmare I would wake from, but I still wanted it all to go away, but where? And what would be next?

As we pulled out of the driveway, I turned for one more look at my mother. I wanted to see if there was anything about her that I could ever remember loving. She was on her knees, her hands in the air, screaming. My brother, the boy on the bike, was now the man running across the yard to her. By the time she was in his embrace, we had turned the corner, and he didn't even know why I was being taken away.

I was met at the Bureau of Indian Affairs office by two men and a woman who was wearing too much turquoise and patchouli to be a real Indian. They spent more than two hours trying to get me to talk. First they asked me a million questions—everything but what they really wanted to know—trying to gain my trust. How old was I? What was my favorite color? Food? TV show? Did I like to jump rope? Play on the Monkey Bars? Color with markers?

Apparently they took from my total silence that, yes, I did like to color. I was given markers and a big roll of paper and instructed to draw how I was feeling.

I didn't see the point; these people didn't care. I remembered my mother's words though: *You'd do better to shut your mouth and do what you're told.* So I tried to draw.

I didn't want to draw what I felt now; I didn't want to think about any of it. I tried to think of something that made me happy.

I thought of the river where Tim took me sometimes to fish. It was a long hike, and I always felt exhausted and sore by the time I got there, but I would never complain. It was worth every sore muscle, every mosquito bite, every scratch and stumble. It was a place in the river that no one else had ever been before, and it was the perfect spot. The river was wide; its two shores shallow and calm, but the center roared, pumped, and screamed life, drowning out all other noises and all worries.

After the hours it took to get there, the rocks that I kicked down the highway, the warnings about hitch-hiking the tourists who picked us up would give, after the taunts from the boys at the Arlee Gas and Go, where Tim would pick up bait, and then into the fields, where the only noise was the buzzing of the biting horseflies and the grasshoppers that bounced off my legs, we would be in the woods. It would be another hour of me chasing after Tim, trying to catch up, before we would even hear the river. After that, it was about fifty yards of climbing under, over and around fallen trees until we would finally get to the swamp where we'd have to remove our socks and shoes or lose them in the mud, and then run to avoid the mosquitoes on the way to the river.

Tim would climb onto a rocky ledge that hung over the raging, swelling, beating heart of the river. He would sit on this rock, bare feet dangling, fearless and happy. I found a large branch that hung just above the smoother part of the river and would straddle and shimmy myself to right where it started to sag from my weight. Though I had no fear for my safety, Tim would always position himself in a way that he'd be able to jump in if a rescue were necessary.

By the time I got to that log, I would be so exhausted that my favorite thing in the world was to go to the end, lie on my back, and lean my head over the edge into the water. The first thing that I would feel was biting cold that seemed to penetrate every hair on my head and move along each strand to my scalp.

After I became accustomed to the cold, I'd place my arms in the water and let them float wherever they desired. I would put the rest of my head under the water, so that all that was visible was nose and mouth. I would listen to the water, quiet and inviting, feel my long hair, removed from its ponytail, dancing around me. My brother would smile down and I'd laugh as he tried to splash me with pebbles he'd toss, never hitting me.

After that, before it got too late, Tim would go off and find a long, thin branch and pull the twine he always carried from his pocket and somehow—he explained many times but I never got just how—made a fishing pole. I would watch him concentrate on his task, his tongue between his teeth, his gaze steady along the line of the pole.

When Tim stood on the boulder above me with the sun behind him, I could see his silhouette long on the water. When he wasn't blocking the light, the sun would burn my eyes so I would close them. All I could see behind my eyelids was the color red seemingly pulsing.

So when I drew how I was feeling, I drew that moment: me with my head under water, my arms floating akimbo along with my hair, Tim standing over me with his fishing pole in his hands and a big, relaxed smile on his face, and all around us, the red I saw behind my eyelids.

When I was done, I handed it over to the three of them. They studied it, studied me, looked at each other, conferring without words, then back to me. They each had different expressions on their face, but they all conveyed the same meaning: They hadn't understood the picture at all. If they had, the woman wouldn't be looking so sad, her eyes looking like they were swimming in her sockets. The policeman wouldn't be looking so angry, his face red. The other man's eyes wouldn't have been looking everywhere but in mine.

The woman cleared her throat and began questioning me again, this time about the picture. Why was that one's hair doing that? What was the other one holding in his hands? Why was one person standing over the other? Why the color red? What did that mean?

All day I'd been there listening to them, one at a time or all together, questioning me, wanting to *help* me, to be *there* for me, and I hadn't opened my mouth. There was no way I was going to say anything now. Besides, my art teacher said you should never have to explain your artwork, and I knew they wouldn't believe me anyway.

They were starting to look exasperated when the door opened and another man in a tribal police uniform leaned in. "There's a visitor here to see her."

No one had to guess who the visitor was. We all heard Tim shouting what sounded like a foreign language at someone. The other person didn't seem to be saying much, but by the sounds of scuffling feet, he must have been using all his capabilities trying to restrain Tim instead. The two men in the room went to help. Before the door closed, I heard the big policeman telling Tim everything would be all right, just like he told me when he had taken me in his car.

"Timothy, relax. You will get to see your sister, I promise. But first you need to come with us. We need to ask…"

The door shut, and my last captor and I stared at each other. She smiled; I didn't. She looked away; I didn't. I counted 256 seconds before my continuous silent gaze finally raised her to her feet. "I'll be right back. There are toys over there if you feel like playing."

After the door clicked shut, I sighed and finally looked at the room I was caged in.

There were windows on every wall, but only one looked outside. It was the smallest window, and the only one without blinds. Two of the windows had their blinds open, but one showed the hall, and the other just a darkened room. The room across from me though, that was where the party was. The blinds were shut, but there were a few fingers pulling the slates apart, and I saw at least two sets of eyes on me. I locked on them until they pulled away. I was starting to enjoy this new power I had somehow received to make people squirm with my eyes.

I contemplated the toys, but they all looked in even worse shape than the ones at school. I never understood why anyone would treat toys that way. I was very careful with the few I had, so much so that some of them were still in the boxes they came in. The ones here looked like they had been playthings for gorillas before they had been donated.

Finally the door opened, and Tim walked in. I was off my chair and in his arms before the door closed behind him. The moment I realized he was alone, I started crying and begging, "Tim, you have to get me out of here. You got to tell them she did this to me!"

He didn't say anything, just wrapped his arms around me, rocking back and forth, letting me sob on his shoulder while he tried to calm me. He held me a long time before my breathing became normal. He sat down, took a tissue from a box on a corner table, and began wiping my tears and snot away.

"Na-ho, you have done nothing wrong," he whispered.

A rock dropped in my stomach. "I know. She did this to me."

He looked shocked and doubtful. "You have to tell me exactly what happened. What's been happening: the truth."

I shook my head; the tears welling up again. "You have to believe me. Please, please, please."

Tim sat me down in a chair next to him, took my chin in his palm, and squeezed my jaw, not painfully but sternly. "Na-ho, have I ever lied to you?" I shook my head. "Have you ever lied to me?" I shook my head harder. "So if you tell me the truth now, I'll believe you."

I nodded my head, took a deep breath and began. I told him about waking up with Danny in my bed, that I didn't think it was a big deal. Then I told him about the fight I heard the night before and watched as his face slowly changed from calm, to doubt, then to anger.

"He'd never been in your bed with no clothes on before?"

The rock floated away. "No. Never. She did that; she did it all to get back at him."

He stood up and began pacing with a heavy step.

"You believe me, don't you?" I pleaded.

He came back to me and kneeled down to look me in the eye. "I believe that you're telling the truth, but I also know that some things are so bad and so scary that we don't want anyone to know—ever. You have to tell me those things too."

I wanted to scream, but then I saw in his eyes, the bad things were his, not mine. He knew more about the evil of the world, and he didn't trust that everyone wasn't out to get him, to get us.

I sighed and placed my hand on his forehead. "Tim, listen to me. I would tell you everything, but there is nothing."

He looked me hard in the eye, read my determination, and nodded slowly. "Okay, but one more question. In the picture you just drew, what is it the bigger person is holding?"

That was the last question I expected. "What?"

He asked again, and I laughed. "It's a fishing pole. What does it look like?"

He laughed with a blush. "Nothing else."

After a few hours, we were allowed to leave. I was surprised that it was my grandfather who had come to sign all the paperwork and bring us home. Tim explained that our mother had been forced into rehab for a month.

"How was she forced?" I asked.

"They threatened to put you in foster care," Tim answered matter-of-factly, without looking at me.

I knew there was more to the story, but I didn't ask. I needed to believe, if only for a minute, that she was that concerned about *my* welfare.

I-90 12 miles east of Idaho/Montana border
Fall 1992

When Tim regained consciousness, his first thought was, *God, not again.*

He recognized the feeling of lying in dirt with aching muscles and loss of blood. He tried to open his eyes to discern exactly where he was and how bad it was, but this time, the burn was caused by the sting of blood in his eyes. He heard voices close by and instantly froze and tried to appear as close to dead as he could.

Tim heard one of them approach. "So how ya think he survived this?"

There was a hock-spit from farther away. "Dunno, he's probably drunk. Crashed his truck and passed out trying to get away from the scene. Serves him right."

The man bent over him. "I don't smell booze, but that don't mean nothing, right?"

"Nah. Could be intoxicated with something besides liquor. You'd be surprised the ways these fellas find to fuck themselves up. You ever heard of Robo'n?"

"Huh?"

"Robotussin. I guess ya drink enough of it, you'll get hallucinations and shit. They call it the 'over the counter peyote.' Then there's the sniffin' of household products, the snorting of twigs and such. It's amazing what they find to dull the senses."

Tim heard a lighter and smelled burning tobacco. "So what should we do?"

The man standing next to Tim moved away. "I dunno. Maybe we should get to a phone and call the po-lease. They'll know what to do."

Tim waited for the men to drive away before he started to slowly test his aches and pains. He wiped at his eyes so that he could see. He was still looking at the billboard, and the truck was still wrapped around it.

The space under his temples pounded so strongly that he turned his head and vomited. His neck creaked painfully and his shoulder throbbed where the seatbelt had tugged and then snapped out of its joint in the collision. He used his right hand to massage his neck and shoulder, before taking a deep breath to brace himself and rotating his shoulder back in its joint. The pain washed over him, and he vomited again. After a long moment, he tested his head from side to side this time. It still hurt, but it was lessening.

A few other cars slowed down and then drove by. So he used his elbows to slither out of eyesight from the road and then hobbled to his feet, leaning against a tree that seemed to sway with him. After a moment, he continued into the security of the trees, ignoring the pain in his body and the blood blurring his sight until he no longer heard the sound of the highway.

Leaning against a boulder, he sighed, resigned to once again survive. He took off his shirt and wiped his face with it. There was a cut over his right eyebrow that had a knot forming around it. As he shimmed up the few steps to sit on the flat top of the boulder, he tried to clear his mind. It hurt to think.

He was tired of all of it: not knowing who he was, why he was there, or if he would ever know. He was incredibly tired of being in constant pain.

He laid down on the cold rock and studied the stars above him. Somehow, they calmed him.

"Ursa Major, also known as the Big Dipper, the Great Bear, right there…and there is Cygnus, the Swan also known as the Northern Cross and next to it, Aquila, the Eagle." He recited aloud just to hear knowledge coming up from the lungs to the vocal chords and dispelling out into the wilderness. He thought of the Eagle, the Great Spirit, the sun and the sky as he drifted off to sleep.

The eagle not only controlled fire but also the soothing rain.

* * *

When he awoke, the sun was peaking over the eastern horizon, and the air was visible as it exited his nostrils. He stretched and got to his feet. He had, sometime in the night, covered himself with his jean jacket, but it hadn't been nearly enough warmth. He blew in his hands then rubbed them together briskly to gather some warmth. He knew he needed to keep walking. There would be snow on those mountain tops soon; he could almost smell it in the chilled air.

He walked a few more miles west, on and off a deserted, barely paved road and then headed back south.

It was on the other side of a mountain range that he came across the first valley town. It looked like a ghost town, but he thought that might be because of the hour. It couldn't be much earlier than seven. He found a truck stop with about two dozen rigs in the huge parking lot, but the restaurant and gift shop seemed empty. He walked in the convenience store door and was met by a glaring clerk.

After a moment the man asked, "What'd you need, boy?"

Tim advanced toward him. "May I use your bathroom?"

The clerk gestured to the back of the store, between the gift shop and the restaurant, then turned away mumbling to himself.

"...Goddamn Indians..." Tim heard as he walked by.

"Excuse me?" Tim asked.

The man's demeanor completely changed as he perceived he was being challenged. "Look, I don't want no trouble. Just do your business and then go along your way, alright Chief?"

Tim hung his head and followed the restroom signs. It all became clearer as he got his first look of himself. He really looked like a man who could start some trouble. Actually, he looked like a man who had been in some trouble.

Along with the open wound on the top of his head and a few cuts along his cheekbone, he had a scar on his upper lip, one at his hairline, both looking like cheap stitch jobs, small but inaccurate. That was just on his face. As he took off his shirt in the deserted bathroom, he got a look at his other scars. The most recent addition, the one along his gut, that one was never going to heal right. But it wasn't until he turned around and saw his back for the first time that he got the worst of it.

From his shoulder blades to his waist, there were about a dozen burn marks. They were nearly the size of half dollars and as he stared at them, trying to remember. He was shocked to realize that he was looking at Ursa Major; he had his very own Big Dipper. He slumped down under the sink as a vision came to him. He closed his eyes tightly and tried to get it out of his head.

He was standing in a cave surrounded by a half dozen other Indian young men looking at him; the fire before them the only light. There was a low hum reverberating through the walls like a chant.

"From the old times, sacrifice has been a rite, an absolute requirement of manhood. For our ancestors, it has always been human sacrifice. Sometimes it was scalping of the devil white man, but most of the time, it was self-sacrifice. Since you have the white blood of the devil in you, if you want to be a warrior, the sacrifice must be double. We have to purge the devil. The spirits will require much from you. Are you prepared young scout?"

"I will do what is required."

He already had his shirt off and was told to turn around. There was an uneasiness that he swallowed down when he turned his back on them. Nothing good had ever come from having his back to these men, these boys. However, they were including him for the first time; this would be the price he paid for being accepted as a member of a tribe. He continued to tell himself that as hands grabbed his wrists, his forearms and his shoulders.

"I will do what is required," he repeated. This time his voice was shallow and he wasn't sure if he was reassuring them or reminding himself. It calmed him though.

For a minute.

He sensed the heat approaching for a split second before he felt the flaming ember being pressed into the small of his back. Writhing away from the sizzling burn, he screamed but he couldn't hear it; all he heard was the blood pumping in his veins.

After a moment, he stilled. The hands grasping and tugging against his resistance lessened but did not let go. He knew they were not done and barely had time to comprehend this when the sting was there again, this time higher on his back but just as monstrous. He fought against the searing pain, his scream guttural and echoed along the cave. He bit down hard on his lower lip though when the scream verged on the edge of a plea. He would ask nothing of these people.

"That's right, brother. Call out the devil. Expel his vile blood."

The voice was right behind him so he knew it came from the man administering the burning punishments, but it was inconceivable that a man could talk so peacefully and reassuring while essentially branding the flesh of another.

Again the ember touched to his skin, higher still, and again he raged against it, tugging and writhing, cursing and spitting. The more he struggled, the more hands he felt on him, until the pain on his back was matched with the strain of his body being tugged in opposing directions, his skin being twisted and rubbed raw. Sweat flew from his temples and rolled down his back, the salted moisture burning the flesh all over again.

They got him down to the ground. Lying on his belly, he heard a chorus of pants around him that matched his own. The satisfaction of knowing it had taken all their strength to get him down was soon replaced when the calmed voice once again spoke:

"The devil is strong in him. The strongest I have ever seen."

Again and again they held him and burned him and again and again he raged against it. Lifetimes passed it seemed, until, at last, the world went black.

Taking a deep breath under the sink, he stood up and splashed water on his face. He put his shirt back on and studied himself in the mirror. He recognized the feeling of blacking out when the pain got too much, when the rage was inescapable.

He stayed in the bathroom until he pulled himself together. He was walking back to the front of the store when he saw that, in the far corner, they sold pants, shirts, socks and underwear. Behind the clothing was another hall that led to showers. Grabbing a pair of everything, along with a first aid kit, he went back to the counter. He paid silently, daring the man to open his mouth again. He didn't.

In the showers, Tim found the cleanest stall, took off his clothes, put his quarters in the machine, and was sprayed with tepid water that got warmer and warmer until it was like liquid sunshine. He put his head underneath the spray, closed his eyes, and smiled.

Forgetting about anything else, he put another quarter in the shampoo machine, and gingerly massaged his scalp until the bubbles were so mountainous, they fell from his head and ran around his toes before drowning the drain. He did the same with the soap, scrubbing until the water ran clean off his body. He rubbed so vigorously he wondered if it was possible to take off a layer or two of pigment, and if doing so would really change anything.

He got out of the shower and shook himself dry like he'd seen a bear do once. That was another thing he had forgotten—how good it felt to be clean. He put on his new pair of sweats and another white T-shirt. This one had no blood stains, and he vowed to keep it that way. He put on his new socks and regretted that he had to put back on the work boots that he came in with. It took away from that brand new him he was feeling. They were good boots though, and chances are he'd owned them for a long time; they'd traveled many hundreds of miles together.

Finally he dressed the wound on his head with a cotton swab and tape. He wasn't looking forward to the day where he'd have to rip it off, but he needed to protect it from dirt and bacteria somehow. Covering it with a green and yellow John Deere baseball cap, he walked out of the dressing room with his head held high and contemplated food. The rest of the looming deliberations would have to wait until after he had some coffee and breakfast.

As he was deciding between buying a to-go coffee and a bag of donuts or splurging at the restaurant, he walked by the phone stations and caught a bit of conversation between a man and someone Tim supposed was his wife. "...no, it's fine really. It feels like I've never stopped...yeah... Tacoma tomorrow, head back home the next...I will...I'll call if something comes up...no, you were right...I did need to...I'm just going to grab breakfast here in Mullan and then back on the road...I love you too."

Tim decided on the restaurant. He sat at the counter and ordered a coffee before even considering other choices. He counted his money while he waited for the waitress to return. She placed the mug in front of him and looked at him and his pile of singles scornfully. She must have seen the corner of the twenty peeking out from the bottom, because her mood picked up. "What can I get you, honey?"

"Hmmm. I'll have"—he wanted it all, everything—"pancakes, eggs, bacon, um, no, sausage, no wait, ham…uh."

"Why don't you get this one down here? It has it all." She pointed to a selection called Trucker's Special, and it was perfect.

"Yeah, that's it. Thank you."

"How do you want your eggs?"

"My eggs?" Tim asked.

She rolled her eyes and spoke slower. "How would you like your eggs prepared?"

Tim blushed and shrugged. "Fried, a little runny?"

"Sure. Now toast: white or whole wheat?"

He looked at her and saw she was smiling now. "Why don't surprise me? Anything else?"

"Yeah, you want cream in that coffee?"

He chuckled. "No thanks, just more sugar, lots more sugar."

He put about six heaping spoonfuls of sugar in his coffee, took a sip and watched as the man from the phone walked into the restaurant. Tim was hoping he would sit at the counter, too, and was relieved that he did. Tim nodded his hello; the man returned it and ordered his coffee from the waitress.

Tim got his breakfast and was so overjoyed he almost laughed out loud. It smelled incredible, and as he took his knife and slowly spread the half-melted butter all around the top pancake and then the one below it, he thought of ritual. He put the eggs between them, poked holes in the pancake until he saw the yoke of the eggs bleed through, drowned it with syrup and took knife and fork and crisscrossed them along the breakfast, making dozens of gory, gooey, bite-size pieces. He put the silverware down, closed his eyes for a moment of thankful silence before slowly taking his first bite.

He moaned and then blushed as he heard the man beside him chuckle.

The man took a sip of his coffee and then asked, "So which one of those rigs is yours?"

Tim smiled, this was exactly what he was hoping would happen. "Oh none, I'm on foot."

"What do you mean 'on foot'?"

"I have to get back to school. My ride fell through, so I had to resort to hitchin'."

"Which school?" the man asked, almost too eagerly.

"UDub," Tim answered.

"Seattle? Wanna lift?"

"Definitely, thanks. The name's Matthew," Tim said, extending his hand.

"Charlie, pleased to meet you."

They exchanged small talk through their breakfast. Charlie was from Utah, had been driving truck since his early twenties, had taken some time off, and hadn't been on the road for a while. He told Tim that was why he was so willing to give a stranger a ride; he had forgotten how lonely it got.

In addition to lying about his name, Tim told him that he was from Superior, Montana, his parents owned an apple orchard, and he was going to UDub on a football scholarship. They each paid for their breakfast and made their way outside. The clerk gave them a wary look that said he'd be watching the news looking for one of their mangled bodies in some rest stop. Tim ignored it; he was getting away.

"Wow, nice rig," Tim said, loving the sound of lingo on his tongue, feeling again that he was becoming a different person.

"Thanks. It belongs to the company. Had one of my own once but I sold it..."

It sounded like he had more to say, but he didn't. Tim climbed into the cab, sat down on the roomy passenger's seat that felt like it was made of air and looked around. From the large windows in front and to the side of him, he could see the whole world beneath him as they slowly pulled out of the truck stop and patiently made their way through the narrow town streets onto the highway. The cab definitely had a lived in look and smell, with an unmade bed in the back and an empty gas station coffee cup in every holder.

"You drink a lot of coffee?" Tim asked, smiling.

"Yeah, you have to. It's the trucker's water. Wouldn't survive without it."

They traveled up and down mountain ranges, past closed weigh stations and small town after small town, Charlie telling stories the whole time. They passed a town called Wallace; Charlie told him it used to be a mining town that had more prostitutes per capita than any other town in the Northwest. They passed a town called Kellogg, and Charlie asked him if he skied. He told Tim a story about the first time he'd done it and how he'd hit every tree coming down the mountain. They passed Coeur d'Alene Lake, and Charlie told him of this time when he'd almost crashed his truck on the 4th of July Pass because he saw the biggest full moon he'd ever seen, and it looked to be setting right into the lake. He still dreamed about it and hoped to see it again, but never had.

They got off I-90 in Coeur d'Alene and headed north toward someplace called Sandpoint. Charlie stopped telling stories. Tim didn't notice at first, but he started to get a deep-in-thought feeling from Charlie and figured the man would talk if he wanted to. They were about five miles from a place called Newport when Charlie said, "I have to make a stop, you mind?"

"No, not at all," Tim answered, but he felt a bit uneasy when Charlie pulled into a cemetery. They followed the thin, dirt road up to where the military tombstones were, and Tim thought maybe he was visiting an old war buddy, but Charlie passed those and stopped on the other side.

Charlie turned off the engine, and Tim asked, "You want me to stay here?"

"Nah, you don't have to. You should walk around, get some air. It's going be a long drive."

Tim nodded and opened his door, found the ladder, and climbed down. He waited until Charlie walked away, and then went in the opposite direction.

He was surprised by how different each tombstone looked. A few had messages on them that told a bit about the person, who they were, who had loved them, where they were going now. He liked to add up the ages from birth to death in his head and imagine the life that was lived in between. Until he got to some that had only a few years difference, and then the game wasn't fun anymore.

He found one that was truly unique; it was the exact size and shape of a Harley Davidson motorcycle handlebar, and it had an American flag hanging from the clutch and a POW flag from the brake. In the middle was a Semper Fi bumper sticker, and the ground around it was littered, not with dead or dying flowers but with Jack Daniels and beer bottles, some empty but most with at least one shot left in them.

He gave Charlie his space, but after an hour, he started to get curious. He slowly ambled his way in and out of markers until Charlie was a few graves away from him. He was holding a bunch of flowers that Tim hadn't noticed before and was reading something from a piece of paper that he finished as Tim watched, unnoticed. He put the paper in an envelope, put it with the flowers and placed them both on the ground beside the tombstone.

Tim turned around just in time to avoid Charlie's eyes that were bloodshot with the effort to not cry. He walked away, and Tim followed him, stealing a peek at the headstone. "Scott Ashdown: Loving Son, Gentle Brother and Kind Friend: November 26, 1966-September 24, 1980."

Tim did the math, almost fourteen years old and had been gone for twelve years. Charlie didn't look old enough to have a son that would be twenty-six now as he, himself, looked like he was in his late thirties. Tim decided it didn't matter. Charlie would tell him if he wanted to, and if he didn't, that was okay too.

They got back in the cab and onto the highway right before it started pouring. Tim had forgotten about rain and thanked the heavens that it had held off while he had been shelterless, lonely and scared. Now the splunk of it on the metal roof, the swish of the wipers and the silence of the cab was lulling him to a deep sleep.

He opened his eyes and was blinded by the heat around him. He felt as if he were in the fire but realized that he was lying beside it. His back was turned away, but he felt the fire burning there, where the scars of his sacrifice had seared.

He had made a terrible mistake; he knew that now. He had assumed that people who had what he wanted, knew what he did not, had seen that part of him that was the same and were bringing him to their mystery.

"Here," someone behind him said, nudging his shoulder.

Tim sat up, readying himself for fresh assault. He would not let that happen again. He also had secret, dark places that he could send them; just let them come at him again.

"Here." A pipe and a lighter were handed to him. "This will ease your mind a bit."

Tim took them and looked in the direction of the voice, the darkness of the cave around them and the shadows of the fire dancing along his face made him impossible to recognize. "Why are you doing this to me?" Tim asked.

The fake voice of the shaman they had all been teasing him with was gone. "Cuz, you had it comin'," he answered.

Tim thought about this as he put the pipe to his lips and allowed the man to show him the way to light it. Had it Comin'. Had it Comin'. He would never understand.

He drew a deep breath of the smoke that tasted like musk and wondered, as he coughed with his mouth closed, what to do with it. He swallowed, coughed again, this time opening his mouth and expelling the fog from his lungs.

The man laughed and smacked Tim on the back. Tim cringed away from the hand, feeling the burn all over again and stopped coughing.

"Jesus, sorry man. I forgot."

He forgot. For some reason, Tim found that funny. He took another hit, and somehow it became even funnier. He tried not to laugh, not wanting to give them that, but he couldn't stop himself. It wasn't until he had the third hit that he stopped laughing. His head became incredibly clear, and the flesh on his back stung all over as if he had just realized that it should.

"Where is everyone?" he asked. It just dawned on him that this all could be a trick to lower his defenses for a fresh attack. He rubbed at his eyes, but the fog that hovered in front of them would not go away.

"They went for provisions."

"Provisions?" Tim asked, growing cold.

"Beer."

Tim relaxed, but only slightly. Drunkenness he could deal with, but a drunken mob was different.

His mind raced and he prepared himself for anything...almost anything.

There was a jolt, and suddenly Tim awoke with a lurch and a tug against his seatbelt. He noticed that it was barely raining now, and they were no longer on a highway but instead on a city street. When he looked over to Charlie, he sat up straight. "What's wrong?" he asked.

"I'm sorry...I can't...hold on." Charlie pulled the truck into an empty Albertson's parking lot. He was shaking so badly the steering wheel looked like it was going to disconnect from the base. The sweat of his brow was pouring down his face and around his collar.

"What happened?" Tim asked trying to understand.

Charlie opened his door and stepped out without a word. Tim looked around for some clue to explain. He didn't know what he should do, but he had to do something. He climbed down from the truck and found Charlie was pacing back and forth, tears mixing with the sweat, mumbling to himself.

"Did something happen?"

Charlie shook his head and turned away, taking a deep breath. "I'm sorry, man. Just give me a minute, please. I just got...got...oh God, I can't do this!"

Tim came to him, not knowing how close was too close. "Hey, it's going to be okay. I can help you; I can. You just have to tell me what it is I can do."

He waited as Charlie pulled himself together enough to talk. "I can't drive *this* truck through *that* intersection," he said, first pointing to the truck and then to the cross walk they were about a hundred yards from.

Tim followed his finger. It didn't look out of the ordinary. There was a Denny's Restaurant on one corner, a Taco Time on another, across from a small strip mall and on the fourth corner a Safeway grocery store.

Tim considered what was needed before he said, "Okay, alright. Well I see two ways around this: We can turn this rig around and go the other way, or I can drive it through this corner."

"Have you ever driven a truck before?" Charlie asked.

Tim thought about it. He had bluffed his way through many things but he didn't think he could pull this one off. "No, but how hard could it be?" he said, chuckling.

Charlie turned around and tried to smile. "You must think I'm some sort of freak, huh?"

"No, not at all. We all got our things, right?"

"Sorry, just give me one minute, and then I'll tell you what to do."

Charlie walked around the truck a few times holding a heated debate with himself before he seemed to come back to his senses. He stood before Tim. "I'm sure you're going to want to know what this is all about. You have every right to wonder, and I swear to God, get me out of this, and I'll tell you. Okay?"

They got back in the truck; this time Tim was in the driver's seat, and it had a whole different view. He hadn't noticed how many buttons and knobs there were from the other seat. That was frightening enough, but when he looked out the window and saw those huge mirrors, all three of them, he forgot where exactly he was. He closed his eyes and forced himself to focus. "Okay, give it to me."

"Alright, first thing you do is put your foot on the brake. Now you see those buttons there, one yellow, one red? Yeah, push those in, that releases the parking brakes. Now, you know how to double clutch?"

"Clutch twice?" Tim said, feeling stupid.

"Right. Once to get it out of one gear, and then once to put it in the next. In town here, we'll only need the first five gears, so we'll worry about the rest as we go. Feeling okay?"

"How many gears does this thing have?" he asked, trying unsuccessfully to sound calm.

"This one? Eighteen, but it's simpler than it looks. So, let's put it in gear and see what you can do."

"Just like that?"

"You want me to give a written test?"

Tim took a deep breath, put it in gear, pushed on the gas as slowly as he took his other foot off the clutch, and before he had time for terror, they were across the parking lot. He eased out into the road, and it was like he had been doing it his whole life, until he steered the trailer over a parking barrier and almost took out a hydrant. "Oops," he said.

He sighed and looked over to Charlie, who was breathing hard, his head between his legs. Tim needed to get them back on the freeway; he wasn't sure why they had gotten off it. He was pretty sure it had to do with that grave and this intersection, Pines and Sprague, he read as he drove through.

Tim didn't bother Charlie until he'd gotten over twenty miles per hour and needed to go past fifth gear. After Charlie showed him how to flip the switches to get to the higher gears, the man leaned his head back and wept silently. Tim didn't know if he'd ever heard a man cry before, and he wondered if he had, did it always make him feel that useless. Luckily, though, he had the road to concentrate on.

They had driven out of Spokane and were heading to Medical Lake when Charlie finally started talking again. "Well, I guess you've figured out that you picked the absolute worst day to hitch a ride with me."

Tim smiled but remained silent, letting Charlie tell the story he needed to tell.

"I used to be a really good truck driver. I loved the open road, where it took me and what I got to leave behind. I met a woman who liked the road as much as me and we shared this. Then she got pregnant, and we settled down in Utah. I still drove truck, and I still loved the road, but there had become something to come back to, somewhere else where I belonged and my mind sometimes took me there.

"Twelve years ago, Jesus almost to the day, I didn't realize… anyway, twelve years ago, I was on my way home, had just been to Nevada, Oregon, and Washington. My wife was close to poppin' and I was stopping every hundred miles or so for updates. I got to Spokane, that town we just left, and it was around two in the afternoon. I called her. She said she was checking into the hospital; she was having contractions. I told her I could almost see home from where I was and I would get there as soon as I could. She said not to rush: Seeing my son's first breath wasn't worth risking my last."

Tim could tell by the way Charlie was breathing that he was getting to the hard part. "In my hurry, I must have made a few wrong turns because I found myself lost in a part of town I'd never been before. I passed a junior high where school was just getting out. My mind wandered to my son; any minute, I'd have a son. I wondered about him. I came to an intersection, that intersection. There was a kid on a bike...he was wearing a football jersey and his hair was blowing in the wind and you could tell by the way he was swinging his head to get it out of his eyes, that it irritated him...I remember wondering if his parents had been threatening to cut his hair, if he was wearing it long just to drive them crazy...I wondered if my son would play football, would we fight about the length of his hair, his friends, his homework...

"I realized that I needed to make a right turn to get back on the freeway, and it would be a close turn since I hadn't gotten into the left lane...the truck bumped and swung back and forth from the curb...I was a half block away before the cars around me finally got my attention to stop..."

He rolled the window down and started wailing into the misty rain. Tim found a safe spot with a large shoulder and pulled over, setting the brakes. Charlie was out of the cab retching against the tires before Tim could get to him. He grabbed Charlie before he collapsed there, right into his own sick. Tim wrapped Charlie in his arms and supported him as Charlie screamed and heaved with painful sobs until he was weak from it. Tim only thought vaguely what it must look like: two men standing in the pouring rain as the sky became dark around them.

"Oh God! I killed him! I hit him without even realizing...I dragged his bike half a block...oh God! Oh Jesus! He was someone's son, someone's brother...and I...I...he's dead and I killed him...I look at my son and I think...I killed..."

Without realizing it, Tim had begun quietly chanting into Charlie's hair.

"ah chi et da, woe ah chi et da
bay ya chi et da, woe ah chi et da
ah chi et da, woa ah chi et da
bay ya chi et day, woe ah chi et da"

"Oh God…oh…huh…ho," Charlie moaned, pulling away. He walked around the truck a few times before he stopped again in front of Tim.

"Feel better?" Tim asked awkwardly.

Charlie shook his head but answered, "Yeah, a bit. But I really shouldn't. I shouldn't be allowed. Every time I think I'm going to be okay, something happens that should make me happy, it reminds me of what has happened. I was sitting in a police station when my son was born. The day he came home from the hospital, I was hiding behind a tree watching a burial I most definitely wasn't invited to. For years, I would make an excuse and go to that cemetery and share in the grief of the family that would visit their lost son, their lost brother.

"The investigation proved it was an accident. The police told me it wasn't my fault. I had the right of way. I wasn't to blame. Everyone told me that. I tried to believe them all. I really did.

"My wife threatened to leave me, and I tried to put it behind me; got a different job, and focused all my energies on my family. We had a daughter three years later. It all came back. I had this perfect family and, out there somewhere, there was a little girl whose brother I had killed. My son takes his little sister's hand when they cross the street, and I fall apart."

Tim put his hand on Charlie's shoulder for a moment to lend his support and force eye contact. "Man, you have got to let yourself off the hook. I know it was awful, I can't even imagine just how much, but it has to be alright to live now. You're a good person, I know it, and I've known you for about eight hours. Your wife knows it; I bet your children know it. Give this up and let them in. They deserve to have their father. Don't you think? You can't stop living because this boy did. Your life has to go on."

Charlie nodded halfheartedly but looked away.

"This little girl, the one you see in your dreams every night, the one without a brother, she's not a little girl anymore," Tim continued. "I can bet you money, she's gotten on with her life, and though it will always be sad that she lost him, don't you think you've punished yourself enough?"

They stood there in the soaking rain in silence for a long time before Tim said, "Come on. Let's go."

"Do you want me to drive, or do you think you'll be okay?"

"I'll be okay." Charlie said.

They climbed back in, Tim in the much more relaxing passenger's seat. Charlie went back into the sleeper, closed the curtain and changed out of his wet clothes. After he came back out, he looked over to Tim.

"Don't you have a change of clothes?"

Tim raised his empty hands. "Nah. I should be home soon but until then," he shrugged.

"Go back, in the wall cabinet, there is a change of clothes, take whatever you need."

"You sure?"

"Am I sure? Yeah, of course I'm sure. It is quite possibly the very least I can do to repay you."

Tim smiled. "Okay."

He changed his clothes and peeked out through the curtain. "Mind if I take a nap back here? It's been a long couple of days."

"Sure thing. I bet you're probably regretting ever getting into this rig, but, man, I sure am glad that you did."

Tim laughed. "You want to hear something tragic? You're the best ride I've ever had."

They both laughed, and Tim laid down for sleep. He thought back on what he had told Charlie out there in the rain to reassure him. He was pretty sure all but one part was completely true: that the girl had probably forgotten her brother. Tim had forgotten his whole life, had forgotten where he was from and who he was, but he remembered one little girl and the only word he had for her was *sister*.

With sleep, came the continuation of the nightmare he'd been having every time his mind wandered or he closed his eyes.

"Bind his hands and legs." A new voice demanded sternly.

"No, we've done enough," said the voice Tim recognized as the one who had smoked with him earlier.

"I say when we've done enough. We don't need any pussies here, so if you got a problem, leave now."

There were no more complaints, and Tim heard them approach. He was naked, and his whole body ached. He didn't know how either of those things had happened, but when they approached, and he got a look at them, he realized he must have put up a good fight. Each of them bore the mark of his wrath, but there were six of them and only one him.

He struggled against them again as they sat on him; one holding his hands behind his back, one sitting on his thighs so yet another could tie down his legs. He got a nice chunk off of one's shoulder with his teeth as he was raised up before he was punched in the stomach so hard he couldn't breathe. They gagged him and dragged him to the back of the cave.

"What are you going to do?" the voice asked.

"Justice, my friend, justice and payback. We have been fucked in the ass by the white man since the beginning of time. Now, we're going to show them what it really means to be fucked."

There was a moment were the only sound was Tim's fight against the ropes that bound him. He flailed and squirmed violently, but he would not beg and he would not cry. He swallowed blood and vomit and glared at his captures.

"Rob, we can't. It's fuckin' sick, man."

"We're not going to fuck him, stupid. We're just going to teach him a lesson. Now go find a stick."

Tim rocked back and forth trying to find some way out. He began slamming his head into the rock wall. If he couldn't get away, he could at least be unconscious when it happened.

Tim could tell that a few of the men had left in some sort of silent protest but that didn't stop the rest from approaching him, breathing hot, foul-smelling curses in his ear. Tim couldn't see what they were going to use or if they even had anything. It didn't matter as they grabbed him and spun him around, forcing him to bend over, spreading his butt cheeks and…

"Jesus Friggin' Christ, what's going on?" Charlie called out from the driver's seat.

Tim opened his eyes before he stopped screaming, before he stopped thrashing around in the bed. It took him a full minute before he realized he was no longer in that cave. He sat up and looked around, waiting for an attack. His breathing was raspy and his heart was beating so fast, trying to get out, it hurt his chest.

Charlie had pulled over, but Tim wasn't sure if that was just recently or if they'd been stopped for a while. "What's wrong?" Charlie asked. He sounded a lot like Tim had only four hours before.

"I...I don't...I...must have been a bad dream. I'm...fine now."

That of course was not true. He was not fine, had never been fine, and didn't know if he ever would be fine. He just wouldn't even know where to start on this one.

"You sure?" Charlie asked.

"Yeah. I can't even really remember what it was about," Tim lied again.

"Okay," Charlie said sounding a bit unsure. "Well, we're about twenty miles from Seattle, and I'm stopped here in this truck stop for some coffee. You hungry?"

Tim's stomach roiled and his head pounded, but he looked at Charlie's expectant face and lied, "Famished."

"Great, let me buy you dinner, and then I will deposit you on the University's doorstep."

"Thank you. Just give me a minute, and I'll be right in."

After Charlie left, Tim put a hand to his forehead to gauge his temperature. He was still warm but the sweating had stopped, and it had become, in the last few seconds, possible to close his eyes without images of unimaginable pain flashing behind them. The borrowed clothes he was wearing were actually wetter with sweat than the ones he had hung over the passenger's seat to dry. He changed his clothes again and tried to recapture that feeling of putting on new skin.

In the restaurant, he joined Charlie, who was hunched over the table writing something. He had already ordered two mugs of coffee and had the sugar bowl right in front of Tim's seat, as if remembering Tim's affinity for sweetness. That alone made Tim wish he didn't have to get out in Seattle. He knew that, technically, there was no reason for him to be there, but he also knew that things would get weird if he asked to continue on Charlie's journey. They had been through a lot in their day together.

When Tim sat down, Charlie swept the paper off the table, and they ordered their food, both getting T-bones and French fries. "So, you're an American Indian?" Charlie asked.

"That obvious, huh?" Tim answered, smiling. Nothing good had ever come from that question.

"A bit, but no, it's just back there, on the side of the road, you, well, you were singing another language. What was that?"

Tim shrugged. "You know, I really don't know. Must be something from my childhood; maybe my mother sang it to me when I was having a bad day." He gave an honest answer for once.

"Well, it was nice." Charlie said, sipping his coffee and looking away. Then he smiled. "But if I might suggest, if you don't want people to know you're Indian, you might want to think about cutting your hair."

Tim smiled as he wiped his mouth.

After dinner, they sat and drank more coffee; neither in that big of a hurry to get where they were going. "Can I ask you a question?" Tim asked.

"You just did."

"What made you come back to drivin'?"

It took him a minute to answer. "I have been dead inside for so long. My wife thought if I battled these demons, maybe I could come back to the family and be the man I was supposed to be. I guess it was that 'get back in the saddle' thing. Do you think it worked?" He laughed to let Tim know it was supposed to be funny.

When they got to Seattle, Tim was overwhelmed with its size and bustle. The traffic alone terrified him; it was chaotic in flow, and its speed was flinchingly fast. He was regretting ever telling that lie. It was too late now. They were there, right in front of the school. It was packed solid as well, full of happy, laughing or handsomely brooding young people. Who was he fooling?

"Ready?" Charlie asked.

Tim shrugged. "I guess."

Charlie reached behind his seat, grabbed a backpack that was there and handed it to him. "I know you have things in your dorm room, but here, just in case."

The jig is up, Tim thought. He took the bag and just smiled his thank you and goodbye.

He waited until Charlie drove away before he looked around and wondered, *What next?*

Walking around the campus area, looking for anything that would get him back out of town, he found the bus station. However, since he only had about twelve dollars in his pocket, he didn't think he could go very far. It was a warm building, and there were lots of chairs for loitering and a lot of people already occupied in this way, so he joined them.

He opened the backpack and smiled. There were, in addition to the clothes he had been wearing earlier, two more pairs of jeans, two T-shirts, a package of new underwear, socks, toothpaste, and a toothbrush. But it was the side pocket that had the real gift. An envelope. Inside was a letter and wrapped in that were ten 20-dollar bills. He looked around to make sure no one had seen the money and then shoved it back into the envelope. He read the letter.

Matthew,

I don't know what it is, but something tells me you are going through something similar to me. I only wish I could return the favor you have done for me. All I really can do is help you with these few things and say one thing. Follow your own advice. Let yourself off the hook and allow yourself to live. You are a good person.

I really appreciate that you were there when I broke down. You have no idea what it means to me. If I can ever return the favor, my address and telephone number are enclosed. Don't hesitate to use them.

Charlie

The Way Compound
May 1986

For the next three years, my mother had been in and out of tribal-mandated rehab, and I had been in and out of foster care. It had been an almost tedious routine. For my mother, it had been a long cycle of fighting addictions, trying to be a good person, good parent before the inevitable backsliding and then repeating it all over...and over.

For me, it had been a sequence of almost giddy good times with my mother, moments that I had always wished for. They had been followed by physical and mental abuse, all the more cruel because she had successfully convinced me over and over that she was not like that anymore. Then I would be removed to foster care again where my confusion, anger and finally hatred would fester until the cycle restarted. Each time she had to work harder to convince me, but in the end, I fell for it, was still desperate to believe.

Through it all, Tim had tried his best to protect me from the upheavals but he had his own problems, and since he didn't share them with me, I couldn't help him. He had been spending more and more time away from home, sometimes gone for weeks.

He had still seemed to want to be an Indian more than anything, but he hadn't seemed to want to be from our tribe anymore. He had started avoided all his peers, even more so since his "vision quest." Their taunts had caused him to flinch and occasionally break out in a cold sweat. He'd started carrying a knife, and I would find him with bumps and bruises. When I had asked about them, he had told me to mind my own business.

When I had been in foster care, I had missed Tim so much that I had tried to run away at least once from each home. It didn't matter if it was another reservation in another state.

I had gone to four different schools on three different reservations in three years. He had found ways to keep me company though. If I was on our reservation, he'd meet me every day after school and either walk me to my foster home, or, if they'd allow it, he'd take me with him until sundown. If I had been on another reservation, he'd either come to visit or call, or at the very least, send a letter every day.

Tribal Social Services had never removed him; they'd trusted him to be fine with just my grandfather as his guardian, but they hadn't trusted the two of them to take care of me. It had made no sense to me. Tim had told me that once he turned 18, he'd make sure he got to keep me, even if he had to fight for custody.

The last time my mother entered rehab, she was kicking, screaming, cursing and spitting all the way to the trooper's car. Telling me all the ways she would kill me when she saw me again. I was ten.

I picked up the almost empty jug of Mad Dog and chucked it at the car's rear window before another trooper grabbed me and brought me to the other car. The last thing I saw was a wild-haired woman so drunk that she didn't even notice she'd knocked her head to a bloody pulp against the window.

Six months later, she came home a shiny, beautiful, soulful person full of the love of a Higher Power...and Larry Harrison.

Tim and I were out in the yard. He was just getting ready to drive me over to my foster home when a shiny, new, black Dodge Ram pulled in. The first thing we registered, after we got over the truck, was that our mother was laughing, really laughing. When she saw us, instead of instantly stopping, she beamed, waving hysterically. She almost jumped out of the truck before it had completely stopped.

"My babies! My babies!" she screamed, running across the yard. We stood there, dazed. She took us in her arms and held us tight. "Oh God, I missed you."

I glared at her, squirming to get out of her grasp; I wasn't falling for that crap. "Both of you," she said, holding us at arm's length and looking at me in particular.

Before she got even weirder, the driver of the truck emerged, and all the world froze. He was the very whitest man we had ever seen.

Not only was he white, he was a cowboy. He was wearing a beat-up, once-white cowboy hat, a Western-style shirt, a bolo tie, Wrangler jeans and boots with pointy, steel tips. I rolled my eyes as I wiggled out of her arms.

"Darlings, I want you to meet Larry, Larry Harrison, your new father."

"Our what?" Tim asked, beating me to it.

"Larry and I just got married. Kids, I know it's fast, but it's right, for all of us. Larry's going to help me be a better person. He's already started."

He was standing right in front of us, smiling in a way that I thought was just a little off; not exactly the creepy I was used to but not right. We chose to talk about him instead of to him. "Where did you meet him?" Tim asked.

"We met in rehab."

"Rehab?" I finally got out. "You married someone you were in rehab with? Isn't that against the rules?"

She smiled, and a chill ran through me. There was none of her usual disdain in that smile. The *wait until I get you home* smile. No, this one I'd never seen before, and it scared the shit out of me.

"Sweetie, he wasn't *in* rehab. He runs rehab. He is the director of The Way."

"That definitely has to be against the rules," I replied.

He finally addressed us, bending down to look me in the eyes. "A rule follower. I like that."

I smirked. If he thought I was a rule follower, he was going to be in for a surprise. I waited for my mother to say something to dissuade him from talking to me, but she didn't. She just beamed at us, like she couldn't be happier that we might get along.

He stood up to address both of us. "I know this is sudden, and it will seem scary, but, believe me, we are going to do everything possible to heal the wounds that life had inflicted upon you up to this point. I'm not like any other of your mama's friends…"

I snorted at that euphemism; they just continued to smile creepily.

"She knows she deserves that. We've discussed her failings as a mother up to this point, and we're going to ask you both to take a huge leap of faith that things are going to be better."

Now it was Tim's turn to be speechless, so I answered for both of us, "Larry, no offense, but we've heard this before."

I braced myself for the slap, but, instead, I got to witness Larry bend over with laughter, mother smiling at him. "Uh-huh, your mama told me you were a pistol."

I rolled my eyes, wishing I *had* a pistol.

We went into the house, and they poured out their love story and their plans for the future, our future. We were going to leave the reservation and move to The Way. We were going to be one of those happy families that I had only heard about, and we were going to teach The Way to nonbelievers.

We were what?

"Tim, what the hell? I don't want to go with these people. What are we going to do?" I asked when we were finally alone. Mom and Larry had gone to talk to the family that I was supposed to be staying with. Then they had to do paperwork, talk to official people, all the things needed done to sever all ties to everything we were.

"What are we going to do?" Tim repeated my question as if he were in a daze. "We're going to move. We're getting out of the rez. We'll give it a try, okay?"

I looked at him doubtfully. "But our home? Our friends... hmmm? Grandpa? What about Grandpa? Why do you want to do this?" I started pacing.

"Relax, you're getting hysterical. Listen to me." He put a hand on each of my shoulders, forcing me to stop. "It doesn't matter where we go as long as we're together right?" I nodded. "And we don't have to trust her or this new crackpot she's found. We have to go; don't you want to escape this place, these people?" He looked hurt by my unwillingness to see this as a good thing. "But we can go along, and if it's weird, or not for us, then we can go."

"Go where? And how? We'll just pack up and hit the road if we don't like it?"

Now he started pacing. I couldn't believe how excited he was by this new development. "Yeah, yeah, yeah, listen...just listen. Let's make a pact, a deal between the two of us. We'll give her one more chance…no listen, one more chance to prove she deserves us. Then when…*if* she hurts us again, we will go and find our own way. We can even go find the Nopiinde." He stopped in front of me and got down on his knees to look me in the eye. "I promise."

"Pinky swears?" I asked, offering him my pinky, like we had done when I was small.

He took it in his and shook it.

Within a week, it was all figured out and we were packing our house. The speed in which everything was happening was unsettling, but it was nothing compared to the transformation of our mother. It was as though I had never met her.

I wasn't buying it. I had, after all, seen this before, about a hundred times. They all said this time was different, but I'd heard that, too, so I would just wait to see how long it lasted, or if it was some elaborate plan for new tortures. I didn't care how her smile reached all the way to her eyes now or that she was always touching us softly, tossing our hair, patting us on the back; I wasn't falling for it, not again.

"Baby, can you bring me that box? The rest of this stuff can go in the garbage. We aren't going to need it."

I brought the box to her, dropped it at her feet, and waited for the explosion when she heard breaking glass. There was none, so I tried again. "Don't call me Baby; I haven't been a baby for a long time… not that *you'd* know."

No explosion. She swallowed, smiled. "I love you."

I snorted and turned away. I went back to my bedroom and found the box I had hidden under my bed. They had told me that we'd only bring what we needed, that where we were going, there would be no need for material entertainments or attachment to possessions. None of that made me feel any better about this move, so I had started collecting all the things that I would not part with, no matter how much I didn't "absolutely, positively *need* them."

In this box was who I was; I didn't want to leave that behind. I had the bottles of sparkling water Tim had given me all those years ago, a Raggedy Ann doll that my mother didn't realize I had stolen from her—her grandmother had made it for her when she was a child. It was the closest thing I had to an heirloom. I had the flute that my grandfather had whittled and used to play me asleep every night when my brother took his journeys away from us. I had every letter my brother ever wrote me, and I had a picture of my father that my mother had thrown at me one night. "I'd rather be with a man I'd never meet than with you!" I had shouted. She had flung the picture at me and said, "That's the only bit of him you'll ever get, and it's better than the bit I got."

"So Larry, what is this place we're moving to like?" Tim asked, as we drove away from our home.

Larry, for some reason, got a whole new tone to his voice that made Tim and I steal glances at each other and forced ourselves not to laugh. He was so excited. You could tell that if he weren't behind a wheel, he'd be jumping around. "Sweet Lord, you're going to love it! You know how you been living your life in this little piece of earth? Someone telling you where to live, who to live with, where you can go, where you can't?"

Tim nodded his head vigorously; I snorted and looked out the window.

"Well, that's no way to live. What we've done is take all that negative stuff and turned into positive. We took the community and sense of family from the America Indian and took out all the hopelessness, the cycles of self-destruction and the...well the ugliness that has taken over on the reservation.

"We love and take care of each other; we love and take care of our community, and we don't need anything else. We are God's children. We pray at the altar of the Great Spirit and dance in the glory of Malachi's teachings."

"Who's what?" I asked, my deaf pretense failing.

"Malachi, he is our spiritual leader. One day, God spoke to him in the form of an Eagle on the mountain. God told Malachi that He was God and God was the Great Spirit and He was Jesus, Buddha, Allah, the beginning and the end. He was the truth, the light, love and Life, He was Malachi and He was you and me."

"What does that mean?" I asked.

Larry laughed and looked at me through the rearview mirror. "Your mama sure was right about you, little lady. You are truly full of spunk! I don't blame you, no, not at all. You are exactly how we white men made you. We put you in a corner and told you that all you could possibly achieve would never get you out of it. We taught you that everything you learned would be a lie, and that the things your soul sought would be lost to you always. All of this was because the color of your skin in relation to the color of mine."

I wanted to ask my mom if she was actually falling for this horseshit, but I caught a look at my brother and stopped myself. He had an insanely dreamy expression I've never seen before. Was I missing something here? I shrugged and assumed it was over my head. I tried to stay awake while Larry droned on.

We drove for hours until I wasn't even sure if we were in the same country anymore. Finally, we arrived in the middle of nowhere; by that time, I was numb from the constant yammering and didn't care where we were, as long as I could get out and find a bathroom.

We saw a sign above the driveway saying "The Way: Where the path to redemption starts." We turned down that road. It was newly paved and looked like it was not supposed to be there. The trees that lined it bumped and nudged the shoulders, trying to destroy them. These trees, in turn, looked like they were being shoved by the millions of trees behind them. I looked out the window and could not see sky and wondered that if I were a bird in the sky, would I even be able to see this place.

After a few minutes, the trees gave way to a large, wooden lodge with a wooden gate that had the slogan posted again. I was beginning to get worried that my brother and I were going to have to live in a nuthouse I mean, really, *where redemption starts?* It sounded so hokey.

But then we drove past that and came to another gate. This one had no slogan and was barbed wire and had no trespassing signs on many surrounding trees. Suddenly, hokey was the last thing I was thinking. Sinister was a much more apt descriptor.

Larry stopped in front of the gate, pushed a few buttons, and it swung open. I suddenly felt more like a millionaire than a prisoner.

The only time I'd seen gates open like that was on *Hart to Hart* reruns. We drove along this road, which was no longer paved but bumpy and dusty, for a few more minutes, still unable to see anything through the crowd of trees.

As we drove to a clearing, I felt my breath being taken away and heard the intake of breath that should have been mine from the seat next to me. I looked at Tim, and I saw in his eyes the feeling I was struggling not to think: HOME.

All the doors to the cabins along the road started opening, and people started emerging, like a village coming to welcome its heroic warriors back.

Before the truck had completely stopped, there were women and children surrounding us, laughing and waving. As we got out, they were upon us like locusts, shaking our hands, hugging us, telling us who they were and how happy they were that we had joined them. In between awkward hugs and back pats, I watched them with my brother. I might have been welcomed like a lost member of a tribe, but Tim was their bronze statue, the God in the desert.

While I looked around, I noticed that these people were all shades of red and white, mixed and mingled. They looked more like Tim than I did. I squirmed out of their arms and took my brother's hand tightly. He looked down at me and smiled, jingling my hand, telling me everything would be alright.

Suddenly, the sea of people parted, and I felt like I was in one of those Sunday school picture books where the sky opened up and shone down on us alone. The door of the largest of the many multi-level cabins opened, and the Messiah emerged, long hair, flowing robes, and everything. Even before I was ready to admit he was real, there he was.

The smallest of the children left our side and ran to him. He took the littlest, a girl of about three, in his arms and walked toward us, the children following him as though he were Jesus. All he needed was a lamb and maybe a lion to make the picture complete. He wasn't as tall as Tim, but standing next to a gaggle of children, he looked ten feet tall.

He gave the little girl to one of the women, came to me and without any warning, took me in his arms and spun me around. His laugh was musical until I started screaming and flailing my arms and legs. Then he brought me to his body and forcefully, but not harshly, held me there until I stopped screaming and let my legs and arms hang.

"Sh, sh, shhhhh, it's okay; it's okay. No one is ever going to hurt you again," he said.

I looked at him like, *who are you kidding?* But then I looked into his eyes, and I began to wonder instead of doubt.

I had never been held by a man like that who wasn't my family or didn't want something from me, so I stiffened to indicate that I wanted to be put down, and I wasn't talking to anyone. He smiled at me and set me back on my feet.

He turned to my brother who stood on guard. The man put out his hand and with a laugh said, "No, you are too much of a man to take in my arms and spin around. I wish I could though, so that I could tell you as well: Everything will be okay. No one is ever going to hurt you again." Then, without any warning, like he had done to me, he embraced my brother, who was less used to physical affection from people than I was. He flinched at first and then stood there silently once he realized the man was not going to attack.

The man stepped back, still smiling sweetly, looking from one to the other of us. "Timothy, Naomi, my name is Malachi. Welcome home. We've missed you."

Our mother came and stood next to him. He put his arm around her lightly and whispered in her ear. "Why don't you take them to their cabins, show them around, and then bring them to dinner where they can meet everyone formally."

My mother nodded and kissed him on the lips. I looked at Larry for some reaction, but there was none. He still had that stupid grin and the "gee shucks" eyes. My mother took both of our hands. Too stunned by the events to pull away, we allowed her to lead us to one of the cabins closest to the main one. A few others followed her, and I got the distinct feeling that no one did anything alone here.

The first floor of the cabin had one large room with a wall of windows framing the forest beyond. There were doors to bedrooms on each side. This floor was for parents. She took us up a narrow, circular staircase to the top floor which was laid out exactly like the floor below. This one was for the children. The big room had tables, chairs and bookcases in one corner where mother told me I'd be taking classes. Another corner had couches and beanbags where the young people "hung out" and another corner had mats and pads for individual prayer or yoga.

I rolled my eyes and asked where the hell the TV was. They laughed and told me that with all the great things for us to do, we wouldn't need TV. I tried to stay calm, but then they dropped the next bomb. They showed me my room, which, it turned out, I would be sharing with two other "happy, delightful" girls. One was six and the other was twelve; they were siblings and anxious to meet their new "sister." That was bad enough, but then they informed me that Tim's room was in the cabin across from us.

"The young men have a home of their own. They need more space, more privacy and different training."

"But I don't...I don't know anyone...I..." I was losing it.

My mother put her hand on my shoulder. "Baby, you will know everyone soon enough and until—"

I swung around. "Stop calling me baby, you stupid whore! I hate you! I hate this place, and I'm not staying!" I put my backpack over my shoulders and stormed down the stairs.

I heard my brother call after me, but my mother said, "It's okay; just let her cool off."

I slammed the front door and looked around. It was a beautiful place where everyone seemed happy. *Yeah right.* I walked back down the dirt road, kicking rocks along the way, trying to keep my mind off of everything else.

I got to the gate but couldn't find any way to open it. The barbed wire fence had a low hum that I knew meant it was electric. I wondered vaguely what they were keeping out, or if it was there for the sole purpose of keeping us in.

I found a large, thick stick and brought it back to the fence. Placing it on the middle wire and pulling up, I shoved the other end of the stick into the ground, making a hole large enough to shimmy through. The hardest part was not to get nervous and shaky. Once, I had saw a kid freak out so much doing this, he accidentally kicked the stick, had seizures, and stopped breathing right there in front of me. Luckily for us, it was by his house and his uncle came out and revived him.

I had passed the rehab center and was on the highway, kicking my rock and wondering where I was going to go, before my mother caught up with me in the truck. I refused to get in, so she pulled over, got out, and started walking beside me.

She didn't say anything for at least a mile, and I wasn't going to speak to her, obviously. I'd said everything I wanted to say; now I just wanted to get away.

Finally, she said, "You know, that wasn't very nice what you called me."

I didn't respond. Truth was, I didn't know really what that meant; I've just heard my mother called that many times, and it was never said out of love.

She didn't say anything else, and after a half hour, I answered, "Well, it wasn't nice what you called me either."

She stopped. "Baby? You really hate being called that, don't you?"

I stopped too, not believing we were talking about this, about anything, I couldn't remember any conversations with my mom that she'd ever started. "Mother, no one's here so you don't need to be all honey-sweetie with me, okay? You've never called me *baby* before in my life and meant it, never said it when you weren't teasing me or throwing me around a fire or using me in a game. So all of a sudden, I'm *baby* and you're hugging and patting and wanting to be around me. Why?"

She looked down and studied her feet for a long time. "Come with me," she finally said. She almost took my hand but stopped herself. "Let's get off this road and really talk because I need to tell you something I should have been telling you your whole life."

I followed her, wanting to know, despite myself, what she had to tell me. I knew she was going to say she wasn't really my mother, that my brother and I had been dropped on her doorstep and she couldn't very well throw us away. That would explain why she never liked me, what I had done to make her hate me.

We walked through the woods for about fifteen minutes until we came to a brook. I wondered if she had been here before. She was one of the only Indians I knew who really didn't "do" the outdoors. We waded across the water—it only came to my knees—and went around a bend where there was a log hanging over a few rippling rapids. We shimmied onto the middle of the log, facing each other. She glowed, and I stared, amazed. This was not my mother.

"Alright, so I promise I won't call you Baby again, okay? What would you like me to call you? Naomi, or can I call you Na-ho like Tim does?"

I shook my head. "That's *ours*. Not yours."

She nodded and again hid her face. "I understand. I haven't earned it. I will call you Naomi and hope for a day when we have created a name of our own."

I rolled my eyes. "Is that what you wanted to tell me? Why you brought me here?"

She sighed, pulled off a branch and started to tear off the leaves and drop them into the water. I'd never seen my mother this fidgety; I finally understood where I got it from. "I want to tell you I'm sorry. I know that doesn't mean anything, but please give me a chance to show you I've changed."

I crossed my arms over my chest. This wasn't why I came out here. I wanted to hear that she was returning me and my brother to our true family, the normal family that has been looking for us all this time.

She went on. "You are too young to be this angry. I know it's all my fault, and I wish there was some way I could instantly make it better, but there isn't. All I can do is show you that I'm not the same person, and I'll do that every day through my actions. You're going to see soon. Everyone who comes to The Way is changed forever." She started to get really excited. "You're going to see just how good life can be once you're in a family that's not screwed up and you're surrounded by a tribe that truly loves you and is full of the same sort of people, people who are trying to find what has been lost or taken so many years ago."

It took me a good minute or two to weigh my options. I didn't believe her, of course, but I really had no choice but to give her a chance. Putting up one finger, I said, "One chance. You hurt me one more time, and I'm leaving, and I'm taking Tim with me when I go. Okay?"

She nodded, and we climbed off the log. As we walked the long way back to the truck, she asked if she could hold my hand. I let her.

"I can't wait to get to know my daughter," she said as we finally were back in the truck. I didn't respond. I didn't want to fall for this, not again, but like I said, it was a cycle that repeated throughout my life, and it repeated mostly, because I *allowed* it to happen. Instead, I turned the radio on; "Delta Dawn" was playing, and I started to sing along. She joined me, whether to get a reaction or not, I didn't know, or care. I didn't give her one.

We had only been at the commune a week before Malachi started pulling Tim away for private conversations. The first time, we were sitting by the fire where Larry was teaching me a hand jive, and Tim was staring silently into the flames. A couple of people were checking him out, not quite sure what to make of him yet, when Malachi came up to him. He whispered something to Tim, who rose and, without a backward glance, followed Malachi to the main house.

I didn't think anything of it, but when Tim didn't return to say good night to me, which he'd done every night we had been there, I went looking for him. I saw that the lights on the third floor were on, and I knew that that was Malachi's floor.

The first floor of the main house was devoted to kitchens, large dining tables, bathrooms and group meditation nooks. The second floor was for the men. The third floor was Malachi's. It had a sparse bedroom with a pad on the floor, candles for light, a few shelves filled with the books he was reading at the time and his guitar. Next to that was his office, which looked like anything but. It did have a table with a typewriter and a lamp, but looked hardly used. The rest of the room though, was where all the living took place. There were two velvet, plush beanbags, more bookshelves, a large oriental rug with deep, hypnotic colors and designs, incense burning constantly;

it was very lived in but very dusty. Obviously this room didn't get cleaned like the rest of the housing did. In fact, I don't think that he let many people in this room.

I snuck up the stairs and followed the voices to the open door of his study. I didn't know what I should do, but I didn't have to worry.

"There's a little one outside the door. I think she wants to say good night," Malachi said quietly, but loud enough for me to hear him and wonder how he knew. "Come on in, Naomi."

I came in slowly, waiting to get reprimanded for being where I shouldn't. Instead, he smiled and reached his hand out for me; I relaxed. I went in and sat with Tim as they continued their conversation. I tried to follow it, but it wasn't for me, so I only got bits and pieces.

"Do you know what Columbus and his people thought they had found when they landed here? They thought it was Atlantis and Avalon, The Fountain of Youth and the Garden of Eden. Do you know what the first Pilgrims were looking for when they came here—exposing themselves to months, even years of hardships and the possibilities of death on the journey alone? They were looking for Nirvana, for Utopia. They wanted to create a heaven on earth where they could live and believe as they chose.

"They wanted this. They wanted what we've created. Do you know why it's taken over 300 years to create what they strove for?"

Tim and I shook our heads.

Malachi continued, "Because they weren't willing to create the changes they longed for. They simultaneously craved and feared this new life they were to create. So they became everything that they left behind. Only it's actually worse than that. Not only did they create another hell, but they enforced it upon the people who were already living here, already living that life they yearned for."

When I woke the next morning, those words swam in my brain, so that the next night, I couldn't wait to sneak back up there. Malachi talked about God and His many names and how all wars were fought in His name and all science was created to find a way to live in a world without God.

"It's not God, it's man's perception of him. Just like the Europeans tried to decimate and destroy what they didn't understand, Christians and other people of religion try to mold and reshape a God that they don't understand. If they only knew how easy it was to worship, how little God required of us to lead a holy and worthy life. Do I look like I'm suffering from my relationship with God?"

We both shook our heads.

He continued, "Absolutely not. The moment that I realized what exactly was required of me, my life only got better and better. I tried to convince the world, but then I realized that was making me unhappy and God is something that can't be taught."

Every night, after dinner was eaten and cleared away, after the fire was built and the children had grown tired of dancing and playing, the mothers and fathers would put their children to bed, and Tim and Malachi would go to the main house. I was never invited, but neither was I ever sent away when I joined them.

I learned more in that room, listening to lectures I only half understood, than I did in school.

There were a lot of new things to get used to. First of all, I was shocked to discover my mom and her new husband didn't even sleep in the same room. She shared her room with two other women, and it turned out that Larry wasn't her "actual" husband but something like her "spiritual mate," whatever that meant. The other women in her room were also his "spiritual mates." It all sounded sort of weird to me. I just knew my mother had never even let a man get close to Tim and I, let alone two other women. When I saw her around Malachi, I thought, maybe Larry wasn't the only one sharing, but then, all of these people seemed to be more affectionate than any I'd ever been around before.

Breakfast, lunch, and dinner were prepared and eaten in the main house with everyone: eighteen children, twelve women, six teenage boys, six teenage girls, four men and Malachi. It was hard to figure out who belonged to whom; everyone was mingled. All the mothers slept in one house with the children, all the fathers slept in the main house with Malachi, and all the teenagers had their own rooms in a house by themselves.

There was no separation of women's work and men's work. The adults took turns working in the rehab clinic, teaching us, helping us prepare meals, and generally playing with us. The teenagers did as well. If you had a problem, any adult around would do; if you did something wrong, anyone could punish you.

But it was punishment like I'd never experienced. If you threw a tantrum, they'd hold you tightly and whisper in your ear that you were loved and special. If you got in a fight with another kid, which happened less and less frequently as you got used to your surroundings, they'd take both children and talk to them, sometimes for hours. They would tell parables, some from the Bible and some from Indian folklore, on the virtues of peace and understanding. They wouldn't tell you to resolve your conflicts, but it was impossible not to after hours of instruction.

The thing was, after a while there, you really did want to be a good person. You really did want everyone to get along. All the people there had similar backgrounds. As much as I'd always wanted a normal family, on the reservation in these times, truth was, my family *was* pretty normal. Now, Malachi was giving us a chance to create a new reality, create a new family out of love, shared experiences, and community. How could you not want to be a part of that?

It wasn't easy though. It took at least a year to stop trying to run away any time someone said something I didn't believe. In those early days, there were a lot of things that I didn't believe. I didn't believe I was special, that I was worthy of love, but, most importantly, I didn't believe that when an adult made a promise, it would not be broken. The treaties I'd made with adults up to this point had never been honored, either due to backsliding alcoholism, short-term memory loss, or just plain vindictive meanness.

Tim tried to make it easier for me, but he didn't know how to deal with someone who didn't instantly love it here. Tim treated The Way as if it were an answer to a prayer he'd been making his whole life. Not only was he included, he was singled out as being extra special. His talents were honored; he taught the Salish language to us children. We learned how to make our own clothes, pottery and beads. We learned how to survive in the wild on the plants and herbs all around us. The teens learned to hunt with only what they found in the wild and a few essential tools that you should never be without: a knife, book of matches, and twine.

Tim spent more time with Malachi than any of the rest of us. If Malachi was God to us all, Tim was his Jesus. We were all disciples.

Finally, after over a year or so, I learned how to trust, how to love, and how to be part of a true tribe. My mom was another person, and she proved that to me every day just like she promised. We became something more than mother and daughter; we were friends. I also had friends who were like sisters and brothers to me. The adults were like aunts and uncles, mothers and fathers who loved me like their own, and God was everywhere, and He was in me.

Seattle, Washington
Winter 1992

"Hey Chief, you lookin' to score?" he heard a voice ask.

Tim had been in Seattle for three weeks and had really been careful with his money, finding a temporary residence in a flop house and eating barely a meal a day. Six days ago, he was down to twenty dollars and had decided instead of using it on lodging, he'd hit the road and save the money.

He was having a tough time getting out of town, though. He didn't know where to go or what to do when he got there. He needed to find money—that much was obvious—but without knowing who he was and without any documents to prove it even if he did, he was stuck. A man had asked him if he was interested in making a buck, but he didn't like the look of him and he had a strange smile, which told Tim that whatever he wanted done wasn't worth the money.

He'd been on the street for six days now, and the only places that didn't shoo him away for loitering or threaten to call the police for shivering too loud were those where everyone wanted to score. As soon as Tim had found out what "score" meant, he'd wanted to get out of town.

"Hey Chief, you lookin' to score?" the voice asked again.

"No thanks. I'm clean," Tim answered.

A new voice came out of the shadows. It belonged to either a very tall, muscular woman or a man in a light pink, spaghetti-strapped, sequined, thigh length dress, walking slowly around him before bending low to Tim's neck for a sniff. "Yeah, you is mighty clean."

Tim leaned back to avoid contact. "Can I help you with something?"

The man reared and laughed, giving the sex away. "No, the question is, can I help *you* with something?"

Tim swallowed and squirmed away. "No thanks, I'm good."

He walked down the sidewalk with hookers and dealers heckling him. He had gotten used to it, actually. He wondered how someone got street smart. Was it something you were born with or was it something you learned after enough time living on them? He didn't want to know. He liked that he wasn't street smart. At least that was one thing he knew: he'd never been homeless in a city before.

The police lights at the end of the road forced him to turn down an alley. From bad experience, he had learned alleys were the very last places you wanted to be. Well, second to last, the very last was anywhere the police were.

He had realized that during the day, everyone loved the homeless. They came out with coffee and soup, blankets and Bibles so they could tell all their friends how conscientious they were and how they had looked upon the face of despair that day and were better people for it. At night though? At night they stayed in their warm houses, snuggled under their even warmer blankets and sent the police out to take care of the *problem*.

"Ya here to fuck with me motherfucker?" a voice inside the dumpsters shouted out as Tim's footsteps reached it.

"I don't want to mess with anyone. I'll leave you alone; you leave me alone, alright?" Tim answered.

There was a grunt and half a face emerged. "You ain't one a Sisco's cronies?"

"No, I don't know any Sisco. I just came in here to avoid the cops hassling people down the road. I'll be out of your way as soon as they leave."

The kid heaved himself out of the dumpster and into the light. Tim saw that he was a boy, maybe thirteen or fourteen. "You okay?" Tim asked.

The kid snarled, "Whassit to you?"

Tim raised his hands. "Hey, it's nothing to me. I was just wondering if there was anything I could do for you."

"Oh Christ, tell me you're not one them do-gooders? I don't need to be saved; I don't need no place to stay that includes sharing my story or singing no Goddamn hymns, alright?" he said as he went to the next dumpster, jumped up to balance on the rim, and looked down. "Damn, Mondays never have leftovers."

"Look I'm no do-gooder; I'm a guy, just like you."

The kid lifted his head to look Tim up and down. "Nah, you ain't like me. You're new at this, ain't you?"

"How can you tell?"

The kid jumped back down and moved to the next one. "First, your clothes are too clean. Second, you're talking to me. If you wasn't new, you'd be pushing me outta the way and taking it all for yourself."

"You're right; I am new at this. How long you been on the streets?"

"I'm not on the streets; I'm at home. Been my home my whole life," he answered, not too concerned.

"Your whole life?" Tim asked, mortified.

The kid shrugged and picked out a pizza box and opened it, exclaiming, "Bingo." He took out a slice and handed the box to Tim. "Want some?"

Tim thought about it for only a second. He didn't want to be rude—this kid was the only person who actually talked to him on the street—and more importantly, he was hungry. "Thanks," he said, taking the smaller of the two pieces left.

The kid looked in the trash again, found an empty bread bag, flipped it inside out, put the last piece of pizza in it and put it in his coat pocket. He looked Tim up and down again and whistled. "You are some tough lookin' sommabitch. Ya ever thought about body guard work?"

"What do you mean?" Tim asked.

"Ya know, protection? Body work?"

"What would I protect?"

The kid shrugged. "I dunno, stuff like...well, like me for instance."

Tim laughed. "What would I protect you from?"

"Man, you are new to this. Protect me from what? From people, jackass. You could protect me from people bigger than me, smaller than you." He bounced on the balls of his feet. "Yeah, yeah. We could help each other. I could show you around, and you could keep Sisco and his gang off me."

Tim pretended to think about it. There might have been a time when he liked the solitary life, but it wasn't now, and it wasn't in this city. "Okay, but first I have to ask, who is this Sisco, and how big is he?"

"He's like I said, bigger than me, smaller than you."

"How many buddies does he have?" Tim asked, sensing there was something not being said.

The kid shrugged and kept moving. He slithered through, in and out of the crowds and around all obstacles. Tim lost him three times before he started to catch the kid's pattern and learn his system. After about an hour of snaking through the city, he discovered the advantages of the kid's technique: You avoided trouble by not being in one place too long. Also, the maneuvering required so much concentration not to get lost, that was all your mind could focus on.

"Hey, what's your name kid? Mine's Char—" Tim started to say. The boy stopped and spun around mid-stride, putting up his hands.

"No, no, no, never give your real name. Never. They call me Mutt and that's all ya need to know." Tim laughed and Mutt scowled. "What's so funny?"

Tim couldn't stop laughing. He laughed so hard his sides hurt, but it was a good hurt. He laughed so long he had forgotten why he was laughing in the first place, and when he remembered, he realized it wasn't that funny, but he still couldn't stop. Mutt looked at him with mild concern.

"You're crazy man. No, that's a good thing out here. Crazies get left alone. No one hassles them."

Tim finally stopped, holding on to his sides and massaging the rarely used muscles there. "I don't think I'm crazy. It's just been a while. Sorry I startled you."

Mutt looked like he wasn't convinced and then asked, "So what was so funny anyway?"

Tim shrugged. "I don't really know. I was just laughing because you thought I was giving you my real name, and the truth is…" He stopped. He was about to tell this kid that he didn't even know his real name. Why would he tell someone that? *Maybe I'm just tired of carrying this world of mystery on my shoulders alone.* "Well, the truth is, that's one thing you don't need to teach me."

"Oh," Mutt replied. "Well, I don't get the joke, but hey, that's nothin' new for me."

"Never mind. It's really not that funny. So where is it we're going?" Tim asked, changing the subject. Mutt was giving him that crazy look again.

"Home."

Mutt started his mad weave again so Tim couldn't ask questions: Where was home? What was home? And what was going to happen to them when they got there?

They navigated the maze of the city for a long while until they were off the avenue, had long left the pushers and hustlers, and had come to the center of a salvage lot for abandoned cars. Tim was overcome with an unexplainable sense of joy and peace. For the first time since he'd arrived in town, probably since he had awoke smelling of fire, he felt like he was protected, that nothing bad could happen now. He touched the windshield of a Chrysler LeBaron in front of him; the warmth of the glass that had been exposed to the weak sun magnified that heat on one side of his hand as the biting cold breeze brushed against the other. Again he felt he was *home*, that this was where he belonged.

"It's the coziest thing I could find without having to worry about police and poachers," Mutt said.

"Poachers?" Tim asked, letting his stupidity show again.

"Ya know, other dumb punks looking for shelter from the cold. They come in and push you out or start a war for territory. This place is big enough that no one bothers you."

"It's great," Tim said awestruck.

That night, they started a fire in a metal barrel and shared the last slice of pizza and a bag of vegetables Mutt had found earlier in the day. He told Tim that vegetables weren't that hard to find in the garbage of nicer restaurants. It was amazing how many people in those places didn't eat their veggies, assuming they were a garnish to add color but not to be eaten.

Later when they had settled in, Mutt in the front and Tim in the back of a two-tone Lincoln Town Car without its wheels, Mutt asked, "So what did you say they called you?"

He was going to tell him Charlie, but that didn't seem right. He was tired of being someone else. So until he knew who he was, he would be what everyone had been calling him. "Chief."

"Chief," Mutt echoed and then repeated again, trying it on. "Chief. Yeah, that sounds right. Chief and Mutt; that's the making of a great story is what that is. They call ya that 'cause you're Injun?"

"Yeah, I guess. Why do they call you Mutt?"

"Hmmm. Probably the same reason. I got everything runnin' around inside me. Mom's Puerto Rican and Spanish, Spic and Span, and my dad's from all over the world, German, Polish with a bit of British for fun. How they ever hooked up…" He shrugged.

Tim wanted to know more about Mutt's family, but he didn't want to be questioned about his, so instead he asked, "Why don't you give your real name to people?"

Mutt was silent for a while and then explained, "It's yours, the only thing that belongs to you. You don't just give it away. Plus, if you go away tomorrow, I can say to myself, oh well, I didn't really even know him anyway. If you watch me get knifed to death, you can say, 'There went Mutt.' That's a hell of a lot better than sayin', 'There goes Sam Smith from Tacoma' or whatever. It don't mean as much; I don't mean as much."

Tim pondered that for a long time, finally deciding it was another bit of street smarts that he wished he didn't know. "So, you're not Sam Smith from Tacoma?"

Mutt groaned. "You're kinda an idiot, aren't you?"

Tim sighed, sleepily. "Yeah, I guess I am."

They spent weeks together like that, digging through garbage for food and cans for recycling. Mutt showed him how to pan-handle, but Tim never made as much as Mutt did. It must have been the kid thing. But it was probably the Indian thing. There were so many Indians in Seattle, and most of the homeless reeked of alcohol. People took one look at Tim and didn't stick around to smell him or give him anything.

Sometimes Mutt would disappear for a couple of hours. When he returned, he would have money and cigarettes and wouldn't talk for the rest of the day. Tim didn't want to think about what Mutt might have done to get the money, so every time that would happen, Tim would find more ways to make money: he would spend more time digging for cans, try squeegeeing windshields at red lights, anything to make that scared little boy look go away from Mutt's face.

More and more kids showed up at the lot daily. At first, Tim thought it was only because he was some sort of novelty, a great big tourist trap that baffled the locals. Then he figured Mutt had rented him out as protection. But it seemed to be more than that. They hung on his every word and followed him around like puppies that were starving for a pat on the head and a game of fetch.

At first, they would come only in the mornings, bringing him coffee and talking about their lives, what parts of it they were willing to share. They would then scatter and work the streets. Some would come back later that night; some wouldn't until the next day. Eventually they started to show him around the city, and often, they would come back to the lot with coverless books that the boys had rummaged from the bookstore's dumpsters and Tim would read to them.

Tim wondered where the band of boys had come from and where the people who should be missing them were. Were there people out looking for them? He wanted to know, but he didn't question. His role was just to be there the only way he could.

"Hey Jose, what did you bring today?" Tim asked.

Mutt had been right when he said that no one gave their real names; everyone had a nickname. Jose was called that because he always said, "No Way," and everyone else always finished it with, "Jose." Domino was a black kid who had extreme dry skin that gave him small patches. Cobra was just a "slithery mofu."

Parkay was a kid about twelve or thirteen who had an amazing ability to swipe anything he needed, which was surprisingly little. His thing, though, was he didn't want anything used or discarded if he could have it shiny and new instead. So Parkay would come in with books that not only hadn't been mutilated but looked as if they'd never even been opened. Every time he brought them a new book, the first thing they'd do was pass it around for that new book smell. For some of the boys, that was the best part of the story.

"I got *The Great Gatsby* and *Oliver Twist*. Ya read either?" he asked, sounding like he hoped the answer was no.

"No," Tim lied, because he knew Parkay liked when he could bring something to him that he'd never read.

Of course, he read *Oliver Twist* first, knowing they'd relate more to that one. But it turned out that they loved *The Great Gatsby*; it was like a fairy tale to them, all about a magical kingdom that they would never get to called Long Island. They had him read the parts that described Gatsby, his house, his clothes, his car, over and over. When the story was over, Jose stood on the hood of a pickup and proclaimed that from now on, he would be known as Gatsby. Then they spent the rest of the day playing pretend that they were in the Hamptons, at parties that lasted days. They played this game like the boys in the suburbs played games of war.

As the months wore on, Tim started telling stories he had never read but couldn't remember where he had heard them. He told them about how Raven had created the world, why bears hibernate in the winter, and how joy was created. "Imagine a world without joy," Tim began.

"Gee, I wonder what a world like that would look like," Mutt said as he scanned his surroundings. The other boys snorted their agreement.

Tim smiled and continued, "I know you think you're pretty familiar with that world, but imagine not even knowing what joy is, not even having a word for it. Not knowing how to sing, to dance, to smile. Imagine, if you've never laughed at something that's funny to you and no one else, imagine that."

They all managed to look horrified.

"There was a time when joy didn't exist, where every day was working, eating and sleeping and nothing else. There was a hunter and his wife and they had three sons. The sons grew up to be hunters as well, and two of the sons went out and never came back. This made the parents very worried about their last son. If something were to happen to him, what would become of them in their old age? But a hunter's got to hunt, and one day while looking for caribou, the last son saw a great eagle circling overhead. He pulled back on his bow, but as the eagle came down to him, he lowered his weapon and watched as it landed and became a man."

There were a lot of oohs and ahhs from the crowd, and Tim looked at these children and thought, *This is what I can do; this is what I can give them. Their childhoods back.* He continued, "The eagle man told this hunter that he wanted him to throw a festival and sing. 'What is festival? What is sing?' the hunter asked, scared of words he didn't understand. 'I will take you to my mother and she will show you,' the eagle man said. When the hunter told him he was too frightened to go, the eagle man said, 'You must. Your brothers died because they refused to accept this gift I offer. There is no reason to refuse; fun should not kill you.' The hunter didn't know what fun meant, but he didn't want to die, so he went with the eagle man to the eagle mother.

"She was old and withered, and the hunter was astonished that someone could be that old and still live. She told him how to throw a festival. She told him to build a lodge because you needed a large space for dancing, to make a lot of food because all the people would be hungry. He told her he would build the lodge and would make the food but that he didn't know any people besides his own family. She laughed and said that once he built the lodge and made the food, people would come and, as for the rest, she would teach him.

"He went home and told his parents, who were as frightened of joy as he was, but they were even more unwilling to lose their son. So they built the lodge; they prepared the meats and breads for the feast. He went back to the mountain top to the eagle mother and learned to dance. He came back to the village and was surprised to find the lodge full of people. People he'd never met from all different tribes, wearing different furs, and as he showed them the dance, something amazing happened. Can you guess what it was?"

The boys sat mesmerized; they didn't say anything, couldn't say anything.

"The people laughed, they sang, creating the songs right there. They danced and they became great friends. They said from now on, the world should have joy, and we should have feasts every year to share the joy.

"When the hunter went back to thank the eagle mother for the gift of joy, he couldn't believe his eyes. She had transformed into a beautiful, vibrant eagle, and she laughed at his surprise and told him, 'An Eagle cannot live in a world without joy.'"

There was a moment of silence before everyone started whooping and cheering.

"That is the coolest story I've ever heard!" Gatsby proclaimed, as the rest agreed.

Two days later, Tim came back to the lot after pan-handling the entire day, collecting all of seven dollars and feeling pretty low about the whole situation. There was a particularly large crowd of kids bustling around with activity. "What's going on?" he asked.

They jumped at the sound of his voice. "Jesus man, wear a bell or sumthin'. Ya scared the crap outta us," Gatsby said.

"Sorry, you all were so busy in whatever you're doing. What are you doing?"

"Hey, I got the system, batteries and all," Parkay called out behind Tim. He was carrying a boom box and a stack of tapes. Seeing Tim, he said, "Hey, I thought this was gonna be a surprise."

"It was, numb-nuts," Cobra said, standing on top of a car stringing flags swiped from a used car lot from antenna to antenna.

"Alright, what's going on here?" Tim asked.

Mutt was stretching wires to make a grill to put over the fire but stopped to excitedly explain, "Well, we're…we're having a festival. We're going to have music and lots of food and dancing and singing. It's going to be great."

"I've got the booze!" Domino shouted, coming around a corner with two cases of Budweiser.

Tim bit his tongue. He didn't think that with all their existing troubles, they should add an alcohol problem, but he understood the desire to numb the pain that comes with being sad and lonely.

"Hey, Chief, ya want one?" Domino asked, tossing a can to him.

"No thanks." Tim tossed it back.

All the activity stopped. "You don't drink?"

"No."

"Why not?" Gatsby questioned, mystified.

Not wanting to sound preachy or give them a long lecture of the detriments of alcohol to his people, he answered, "I don't know. It's kind of for the same reasons you don't tell anyone your real name."

"Whadya mean?" Mutt asked.

"My mind, it's very important to me. It's all I have. If I were to get drunk, I wouldn't own it anymore; the alcohol would. I have to keep the one thing I have left."

No one said anything for a minute, and Tim thought he had brought down the whole party. Then Parkay pushed play, and the music started to cheers. Tim noticed, though, that more than a few boys deciding not to drink. They had, besides beer, lots of hot dogs and hamburgers with fresh buns and lots of condiments. Tim was amazed at all that had been saved or swiped for this party. He was touched that a story he had told had brought all this about.

They danced, first to hip-hop, some of the boys showing off their moves. For the first time in a long time, it wasn't for money. Then they put on some Reggae and Latin Mambo and started to dance so vigorously that soon they had removed their shirts and whooped them in the air.

Tim was the last to take his off, first of all because he was the last to start dancing and also because of the ugly scars that he didn't show anyone. Then he realized that everyone had scars, and they would understand that the scars did not define you. That's when he felt safe enough to dance the only way he knew how.

"Go Chief! Go Chief!" they began to chant as he started the precise steps of a Powwow dance that he must have perfected over the years until it was instinctual. He no longer heard the music that didn't fit the beat of his dancing, and he didn't hear the boys start to add their own beat. They picked up pieces of anything that they could drum with. Some had oil pans, some were pounding hoods with wiper blades and some were looking for a softer sound as they pounded on ripped-out car seats.

He danced for what felt like hours, and as he stopped and looked around, he smiled through the sweat. The boys, in between their drumming, had started painting each other with oil and mud to look like war paint, and some began to try to mimic his moves. He felt drunk for the first time in his life.

"What the hell is this shit?"

Everyone stopped what they were doing and jumped to fearful attention. A man who looked only a few years older than Tim walked into the circle, followed by six or seven other guys the same size and shape as him.

"What you bitches doin'? Havin' a little Tupperware party or sumpin?"

Tim studied the scene quickly and thoroughly. The man speaking was definitely the leader. As Tim glanced at the boys cowering behind him, he surmised he'd just been elected their leader.

"Who are you?" Tim demanded, stalling for time. He noticed a few of the newcomers were carrying weapons of the metal pipe variety. He did a mental check to make sure his knife was where it always was: in his back pocket.

The man laughed. "Hey, Mutt darlin', why don't you tell Cochise here who I am."

Mutt snarled. "Get outta here, Sisco. We told you, we ain't workin' for you no more."

Sisco laughed again. "Oh what a sweetheart boy you are. You think when all my hoes up and leave that I ain't gonna wanna know where they all up and got to?" He took a step forward and the others followed, as if choreographed. "I just came to pay a visit to the new pimp daddy in town."

Tim tried hard not to register on his face the horror and confusion he felt. He wanted to obliterate this vile thing standing in front of him, but he knew he must remain collected to guarantee the safety of not only himself, but of all the boys behind him. He was horrified to think of what it must have taken to bring them to the place where they would sell themselves but it also amazed him at how strong they must have been to stand up to this man and walk away.

"These boys aren't hoes, and I'm not their pimp," Tim spat out.

Sisco stopped smiling and started sizing up his new competition. Tim felt Sisco's eyes stop on his newest scars, especially the gash on his stomach. It was true that every one of the boys had their own scars, but Tim knew his gave away the fact that he was not new to fighting and probably was used to something more than sticks and pipes.

Tim put his hands behind his back, giving Sisco the false impression that he was exposing himself. What he was really doing with one hand was sliding his knife out of his back pocket while simultaneously signaling with his other hand for Gatsby to hand him the windshield wiper he was holding. Gatsby did.

Tim swung the longer, less threatening weapon and stopped it right at Sisco's throat. He kept the knife concealed. He'd really like not to have to use it. "You are not wanted here. I suggest you leave."

He watched, wondering fleetingly how this was going to end, as he saw the guys behind Sisco flex and prepare their weapons. Then he heard a strange sound behind him. It was the sound of at least a half dozen switchblades opening. Neither Sisco nor Tim flinched or looked away for a single second, but they both registered this unexpected turn of events.

Tim wondered why they all needed a bodyguard if they had the strength and equipment to defend themselves. Then he remembered where they were standing and figured it out. They needed his strength, his size and his belief in them to be able to stand up for themselves.

"Like I said," Tim repeated, "you are not wanted here, and I suggest that you leave."

Tim watched Sisco try to figure out how he could get out of there and still keep face. "This isn't over. I see any of you on my streets again, you're dead."

Tim applied pressure against Sisco's Adam's apple and made a threat of his own: "I ever see you again, and I don't care how many your girlfriends are with you, I'll have something much sharper than this pressing up against you."

Sisco put his hands up in a mock touché and slowly backed up, never taking his eyes off Tim. His guys followed his lead again like the good goons they were. Tim let out the breath he'd been holding, and while the boys whooped and hollered, he walked behind a car and lost his stomach and the last of his nerve. He wiped the cold sweat off his face, took two deep breathes, and joined the party that was celebrating something else now. Not only had they been given the gift of joy, they had also been presented with the gift of self-respect.

Tim let them have their party but couldn't get back into the celebration himself. He knew what they didn't. He knew he was all talk. *Well, I think that's what I am.* Truth was, he didn't know what he was capable of when cornered. He only knew that he didn't want to be trapped anywhere. *What am I doing here?*

He asked himself that all night and then the next day, he asked Mutt, "Why are you here?"

"Whatdya mean?"

"I mean, what were you running from and is that thing worse than what you're living now?"

"God, Chief, not you. Don't be that guy."

"What guy?"

"That guy that has to fix everything. I know I shoulda told ya about Sisco but I couldn't...I couldn't face it."

"Alright, it's alright. You don't have to tell me anything about your life. I just have to know one thing. Is what happened to you out there worse than it is in here?"

Mutt looked away and shook his head. "No...but there's no *there* left."

Tim didn't say anything, just picked up rocks from the ground and began tossing them, trying to get them into the busted out window of the car across the lot as he waited.

"I was in foster care since I was three years old. I'd been passed from crazy house to psychotic house my whole life, and after the last one, I said I'd never go back. I would stop being the punching bag of every drunken asshole in the Pacific Northwest. So this is all I got. I do what I have to do to survive."

"Don't you think there's something better than this? Somewhere else we could be?"

Instead of answering the question, he turned it back to Tim. "Why are *you* here?"

"Hmmm. That is a good question. Do you want the honest answer? Or do you want me to tell you something you'd believe more?"

"What the hell, let's try the truth."

"I don't know why I'm here. But I know I don't want to leave without you."

There was a long pause after this confession. "Why?" Mutt finally asked.

Tim shrugged. "Why not?"

"Okay, so where do we go if we're not here?"

"Anywhere. We could go anywhere." Mutt looked doubtful, so Tim continued, "First answer this, if you could go anywhere, where would you go?"

They had just finished reading Steinbeck, so Tim was not surprised when Mutt suggested, "California?"

"Alright, let's go to California," Tim said, standing up, like once the decision had been made, there was nothing left to do but go. "I'll be Lennie, and you can be George."

Mutt laughed, catching the fever of adventure. "Well, if I'm the brains behind this operation, we're in a lot of trouble."

Tim could do this. He could be Mutt's body guard and they could start over somewhere else. Tim could get lost in that life, in that dream.

The dream shattered though as the rest of the boys began emerging from their resting places in the cars around him and Mutt. How could he take Mutt away and leave the rest of them here with Sisco, who would now be looking for retribution and revenge and would take it out on the boys left behind? How could he travel to California, or anywhere else really, with a band of teenage boys? The logistics of it were inconceivable.

Mutt seemed to be thinking the same thing. "Chief, I'm going to go out and take care of some things, and we'll go tonight. If you wanna get some of the gang to come with us, that's fine with me. Only, I know it will be a lot harder to travel in a group, so maybe we should say our goodbyes when I get back."

"Where you goin'?" Tim asked, not liking the idea of Mutt leaving his side right now.

"I just gotta take care of some things."

"I should come. I am your body man after all," Tim said.

Mutt stood right in front of him and looked him sternly in the eye. "No. What I gotta do, I can do better on my own. I'll be done and back before you know it."

Tim watched him walk away. Saw the bulge of a knife in his back pocket, knew where he was going and what he was going to do when he got there, and Tim did nothing. He knew how it would end, could almost predict the last drop of blood, and yet he stood there. It was like he was watching a movie that he was in but had no control over the outcome.

He spent the next couple of hours trying to get excited about California, telling the guys that they were free to come if they wanted. He watched as they tried to work out what to do. Most of them were in this town, in this state, for a reason, and the thought of leaving it had never crossed their minds. It was a testament to how much he'd affected their lives that they even considered the move. He knew though, knew like he knew Mutt wouldn't come back, that they weren't going anywhere.

He had to go find Sisco. See for himself if Mutt had been successful. If not, if it was too late to save Mutt, Tim could save these kids who wouldn't leave but couldn't stay as long as there was a Sisco in their world. He stepped out of the lot and felt a fear that he couldn't explain but was familiar and belittling all at once. He heard a voice in his head: *To be human is to feel fear, and to be a man is to face that fear, to be a hero is to make that fear work for you. You are the destiny...*

He paused, looked both ways, and followed his instincts to where he'd find Sisco and, hopefully, Mutt. He walked only two blocks before he heard the footsteps behind him and knew if it wasn't Sisco, then it would be some of his boys. Of course, Sisco would station some of them outside the lot, waiting for Tim. He kept walking, quietly, and slowly pulled his knife out of his pocket. Along with the fear he'd felt before, there was another feeling even more familiar: a blinding rage that intensified as he counted the footsteps behind him. He guessed three, maybe more boys.

Just when they probably thought he'd start walking faster or even running, Tim slowed down. They practically bumped into him before he sprang around, backhanding the closest boy, sending him flying and then with the same hand, grabbed another's hair and slammed him into Tim's raised knee. The only kid left standing didn't seem to be as tough anymore as Tim pointed the knife at the boy's chest and began slowly dancing around him. The guy turned in a circle to keep the knife where he could see it.

"What did I tell you?" Tim snarled.

"Look, I'm sorry. I don't want this," the kid, who was probably no more than seventeen, said.

"Take your friends and get out of here. Don't let me see you around here messing with these kids again."

Turning his back, Tim walked away, no longer scared, but still, his heart pounded painfully in his chest. He did hear footsteps again, but they weren't the same guys, and they weren't walking. These footsteps were running. They belonged to other boys, his boys who were whooping and hollering. "Holy shit, did you see that?" Domino exclaimed.

Tim smiled despite himself as they went on and on about how cool he looked beating all those asses. They said they were coming with him no matter where he went.

"We have to find Mutt. I think he went and got himself in trouble," Tim said.

The boys led him to a place Tim had never been and hoped he'd never be again. He thought he'd witnessed all the dredges of society there were to see, but this was something else. If "The Ave" was where the hookers and pushers hung out, then this was where they lived. This was where the dark of their souls was unleashed and seeped into every brick of every burnt-out, boarded-up tenement and factory that lined the streets on both sides. Even the police had written this neighborhood off as beyond help.

So when they saw the sirens down the block, Tim knew that it was going to be bad. On a normal day, the blue and red lights painting their warning along the walls would have sent them all scurrying like rats, but this time, they had to see, had to know.

The police had barricaded the end of the street where all the action had taken place. Tim fought the crowd, getting as close as he could and saw a group of cops bringing out a person in handcuffs. Mutt. His arms and hands were covered in blood, and he smiled in a manic way Tim had never seen before. *Oh Mutt, what did you do?*

The answer came faster than he would have liked. After Mutt was put into the back of a police cruiser, the next group came out. Those were EMTs pushing a gurney covered by a white sheet. The blood was already coloring the fabric; starting in the groin and working up to the place where a heart should be. Two of the EMTs looked like they were close to being physically sick, and another one was holding a small, clear bag filled with what Tim could only assume was Sisco's manhood.

"Oh Jesus. Jesus," echoed the boys around Tim, who had slumped to his knees as the cruiser drove by, and Mutt looked at him with that unrecognizable smile for the last time.

The Way Compound
1988

I was happy. I know it seems hard to believe, but it's true. The Way was everything: It was my life, my family, and all I'd ever want. I didn't notice the changes occurring in the group; I was too consumed with the ones happening to me. I went from an angry, rebellious eleven-year-old to a soulful, happy twelve-year-old, and I barely recognized myself anymore.

My brother had transformed as well. His was more predictable, I guess, but still pretty amazing to watch. He went from shy, insecure outsider to proud, confident leader. He was Malachi's right-hand man, the son he'd never had. When Tim turned twenty, it was a week-long celebration. He was a man. He moved into a floor of his own right above Malachi's. There was surprisingly little opposition to all this preference. Tim wasn't just Malachi's favorite, he was everyone's. Even I wasn't jealous of the affections I now had to share with everyone else. After all, this was my family, all of them.

When I was twelve, I was given a lot more private time. Not that I wanted to be by myself, but there were things I didn't want to share, and my sisters and mother respected that. I had started to develop breasts, which I guess I knew would happen, but still didn't feel completely like they were really mine. I also didn't want to claim the changes happening down *there*. Besides a few accidental glances, I'd never seen the naked human body and was disgusted by the first appearance of dark brown hair.

A few months before my thirteenth birthday, I was down by the large stream, alone. In the hot summer months, I liked to bathe in the water. I looked around, making sure there was no one nearby, hung my towel on a low branch, took off my robe and shoes, and hurried into the water to submerge my nakedness. As I came up to the surface, I gasped at the cold. Maybe, I should have waited a month or so for the water to warm, but it had been so hot. I swam around, getting used to how the chill sent shivers up and down my body. Noticing for the first time how my nipples became hard pebbles in the cold water, I ran my finger around them, curious to what that would feel like. I didn't feel anything, but if it were possible, they became even tauter. I squeezed them, and the sensation shot through my body. I laughed loudly.

When I was alone in the woods, floating in the frigid water, I liked to pretend that I was a mountain girl. That I lived in the wild, ate only what the earth gave to me, wore only what I made, and even used the earth to cleanse myself. After I got used to the cold water, I swam downstream, found some large, durable leaves, and began rubbing them along my body. I liked the way it made my skin smell.

While cleaning myself, I once again felt an exciting sensation that made me laugh out loud when I reached between my legs. I clasped my legs together tight at the overwhelming throbbing in my center. Every slight movement of my hand sent another jolt of pleasure. This time when I cried out, it wasn't to laugh, but to moan as my finger slipped inside me for the first time. Even if I wanted to stop, I couldn't pull away. I began rubbing in slow, precise swipes, applying more pressure gradually, studying the new sensations each time. It might have been an accident that first time my finger slipped further into the cusp. I gasped as my head exploded with sounds and images. I twisted my pelvis, trying to release my finger, only to be bombarded with even more ecstasy as it rubbed against the nub of my clitoris. I felt light-headed as I found release. I closed my eyes and momentarily lost consciousness.

It felt like a hundred years later when I finally thought I was strong enough to stand up in the water. I looked at my hands to make sure they were still mine, and my heart stopped. On the hand, the exploration hand, a little blood tinged the finger, the archeological finger. *Holy Jesus, what had I done?*

I stumbled out of the water, not caring if anyone was watching, toweled off— speed replacing thoroughness— threw my robe and shoes on, and headed to the cabin for clothes, which I put on and ran to the bathroom. There it was: more blood, and with it, a pain in my abdomen. I panicked, shoving some tissue into my underwear and tried really hard to figure out what to do. As much as I loved and trusted everyone around me, this was not something I thought I'd have the nerve to tell anyone.

I decided that maybe, somehow, I had cut myself down there, and I would leave it alone. Maybe it would just go away all by itself. That night, it was still bleeding, so I put more tissue down there and went to bed, praying for peace to all nations, love to all people, and please, please, make this blood go away.

I knew it was no good when I woke up the next day. I changed my sheets, full of shame, and hoped my sisters wouldn't find out. Then I went to the bathroom to clean up before going to find my mom. I had to talk to someone. Maybe I wouldn't have to tell her about what I'd done, just tell her about the blood.

My mom spent most of her time at the rehab clinic, the same one she had been sent to cure her addictions. She said it was rewarding because helping people grow through their struggle and laying healing hands upon them was tranquil and helped her stay connected like nothing else could. She also believed it was good for the addicts to see that a new life is possible if they embraced The Way.

She saw me standing there in the entrance way, looking sheepish and ashamed and came to me. "Naomi, what is it? Has something happened?"

I shook my head, not able to get the words out. She studied me, feeling my forehead and gathering the hair hanging over my shoulders to the back of my head so she could look closer at my face. "You look different. You sure everything's okay?"

I mumbled, "I'm bleeding."

"What honey?" she asked, bending her ear to my mouth so I could whisper.

"I'm bleeding."

"You're bleeding?" she said, studying me again, this time looking for the evidence of my booboo. Then her face lit up. "You're bleeding in your *vagina*?"

I nodded, not able to look at her in the face.

She hugged me. "Oh darling, I'm...I'm so excited for you!"

I leaned back; that was the exact opposite of what I was expecting. "What does that mean?"

She cupped my face in her hand and gently forced me to look her in the eyes. "It means that you are a woman."

I was stunned. A woman? Me?

She brought me into the room I always called the Plant Room. It was floor-to-ceiling windows and full of green foliage. She explained what had happened, and I was shocked to discover that it didn't have anything to do with me touching myself, although I think in the back of my mind that I doubted that.

"It is the rite of passage from girlhood to womanhood. Your body tells you when you're ready. The whole world opens up to you from today forward. The privileges of womanhood are yours now." She beamed. "Oh, I'm so excited for you!"

I wasn't sure if I knew exactly what she was talking about, but it made me sit up straighter. I walked out of there, full of pride, ignoring the pain that was still there, or the constant, irritating drip, drip, drip.

That night and the next five after, we celebrated my entrance to the tribe of The Woman. We had feasts and danced, and I was honored and included. I moved into the cabin of teens and had my own room.

The day the bleeding stopped, my mom and the other women took me back to the water. In the meadow beside the stream, they gathered around me, holding hands, and began to chant.

My mother stepped out of the circle, her place being filled in by the others. "Today we welcome our sister, Naomi."

"Welcome, sister Naomi," they all chanted after her.

"Today, we introduce her to the Goddess Estsanatlehi, Changing Woman, who will bless Naomi with her gifts."

"Bless you, sister Naomi," they chanted.

She undid the one knot that was keeping my special gown on, and it fell to the earth. "We will take her to the water of our ancestors, and we will bathe away the childhood that has hurt and misused her.

We, her sisters, will lay hands on her, and we will prepare her for the gifts and joys of womanhood."

She took my hand and together, we all walked to the water. I stood before them, as they, one by one, undid their gowns as well, and, together, we walked into the water. They once again circled me, this time closer. My mom stood before me and raised my arms so that they were outstretched, parallel to the water. Each of the women put their hands on me and guided me to float on my back. They caressed my body lightly in circular motions as they chanted. I was so overcome with emotion that I was crying and smiling at the same time. This was a whole new level of love that my life up to this point had not prepared me for, not at all.

I thought the feelings I had in the stream that day were something I could forget about, but they weren't. Every month, right before I would menstruate, I would get these urges that took over everything. Suddenly, my body tingled and vibrated all over, and I was powerless to stop it.

And as I looked around my tribe, I had the feeling that it wasn't only me. Sex was everywhere. Women were having babies, men and women were kissing all the time, all over the compound. There was touching, so much touching. There always had been, but I hadn't realized what it might mean, until I felt the touching in a new way myself.

I had always thought of my brother as sexless. I never imagined him with a wife and children. Not even when he moved into the men's lodge did I think that.

Then I started noticing that, about one night a month, while sitting around the fire, Tim would excuse himself. About an hour later, Larry or one of the other men would approach one of the women, whisper something in her ear, and she would get up and go to the house. On those nights, there would be no meeting with Tim and Malachi for me to eavesdrop on, and I would go to bed without a good night. It was a different woman every time. They always seemed honored to be singled out, and the next day had a certain awed glow.

In the family cabin, I never really thought about what those nights might mean, but as I looked out the window that was all mine and no one else's, and watched as the girls entered the room, their silhouettes move, then the lights turn out, I wondered, *Did my brother have desires?* I'd never thought about it, but he must. As much as I'd built him up as a heroic God who was everything to me, he was still human. Did he love these women? And if he did, did he love them more than he loved me? It wasn't jealousy. That would be gross. Besides those feelings did not exist at The Way.

It was odd. As a girl, I mostly hung out with other girls. The moment I became a woman, I started hanging out with the boys. We hadn't had any new members in our tribe for a while, so I had practically grown up with them all. Usually, I still thought about them the same way, but like I mentioned before, about once a month, I started noticing who was the best hunter or fisherman, who ran fastest, who had the biggest muscles and the best body, who made me laugh and, most importantly, who noticed me.

It started to dawn on me as highly unfair that each man in the tribe had three or four "spiritual mates," but the women only had one. Not only that, but who decided who got whom? Did my mother choose Larry or did Larry choose her? Did they choose each other? How did they choose each other? And what if there was another man that she liked better down the road?

"Mom, can I talk to you about something?" I asked as we sat in the kitchen one day, shucking peas.

"Sure, darling."

"Well I was just wondering about stuff."

"Stuff?"

I sighed, figuring out how to best ask, "How did you know Larry was your man?"

She laughed, then saw my look of horror and stopped. "Sorry that just struck me as funny, *my man*."

"Well he is, isn't he?"

She shrugged. "Sorta but I don't think in the way you mean. I love Larry, that's true, but he doesn't belong to me."

"Do you belong to him?"

"No, no one *belongs* to anyone."

"Yeah I know that. I mean…I guess I want to know…well…how does it work? How do you decide?"

"You mean, what made me decide to settle down with Larry when there were so many losers out there that I could have, and did try, before him?"

I blushed, forgetting my mom's sordid past. "Yeah, that."

"Well, he was nice to me and saw in me all that I could be if someone believed in me. Let me tell you, that's a very attractive thing in a man. Then he introduced me to The Way and as you know, that changed my life."

"So how does it work? Why does he have three other mates and you don't?"

She smiled. "How do you know I don't have more than one mate?"

I was flabbergasted. "Do you?"

She shrugged. "No, not really."

"What do you mean, not really?"

She put down the pod she was working on and started to take this conversation seriously. "I didn't expect to have this talk so soon, but I guess it makes sense. You are having feelings right?"

I nodded.

She continued, "And you want to know what to do with them, what *I* do with them, right?"

I nodded again.

"Alright, so what we're really talking about is sex. That is a very important part of life, no matter what anyone says to the contrary. There are many people out there trying to tell us that we're wrong to have those urges. Bullshit. It's completely natural. Besides the fact that it feels incredible, it's absolutely necessary to repopulate the world."

"Sex feels good?" I asked, all my suspicions confirmed.

She laughed. "Oh God, yes. Sometimes it feels so good it's the only thing that gets me up in the morning. Or it used to be, and there was a time when I confused the way I felt about alcohol with the way I felt about sex. The feelings had been so mingled together for so long, but it turns out that sex sober is even better than being drunk.

"Someday you'll see, and know, you'll experience it as it should be, not how it was for me and for all those that came before me. Ending that cycle of alcoholism that's run in our family for too many generations is the greatest gift I could give to you and Tim and is what I thank God for every day. When you're ready, you'll have a great sex life, and you'll never confuse the high of lovemaking with the false intoxication of booze."

"So when does it happen?" I asked, not trying to sound too desperate.

"You in a hurry?"

I blushed. "No, I was just wondering. I mean, I don't want to have babies or anything, not now, but someday."

"It's alright to have the feelings, and believe me; they'll get stronger in time. When you're ready to experience it, don't you worry about it; Malachi will take care of it."

Now I was confused. "What does Malachi have to do with it?"

She smiled. "Well, it goes back to the idea of sex for reproductive purposes. In that, Malachi is very concerned. This family is very special to him, as it is to all of us, but he gets concerned about the future. If you've noticed, we haven't recruited from the outside in a long time. Malachi feels that we have all the elements to have the perfect family right here among us. He has special interest in your brother and you. So he's very concerned about who you choose."

"But it is my choice?" I asked.

She got up and went to the sink. "Of course," she answered in an unconvincing tone that I knew I should have questioned. But I had heard what I wanted to and the rest would take care of itself.

If my body awoke with a bang, I wasn't the only one. The minute I moved into the teen cabin, it was like we all simultaneously noticed each other at once. We hung out together all the time. We all helped out in groups, then every night and free moment, we were together.

It started the week after I moved in.

"Hey, Naomi, you want to play with us?" Damien asked.

I shrugged. I thought I had moved out of the family cabins so I wouldn't have to play anymore. He took my hand and led me out of my room into the hangout room where six kids sat in a circle with a bottle in the middle.

"What's this?" I asked. They explained the rules of *Spin the Bottle* as I sat down. Now this was *playing*.

The first couple times, the bottle got close to pointing at me, but it was the fourth time that Damien's spin ended right in front of me. He came to me slowly, on hands and knees. I held my breath, closed my eyes, and let the sensation of his lips touching mine wash over me. Then his tongue got mixed in as he licked my lips open, and I once again experienced the weakness of my limbs. Then it was done. I panted and felt as if my face was about 100 degrees.

Sunshine laughed next to me, putting her arm around my shoulders. "Your first time?" she asked.

I nodded, still unable to talk.

She caressed my back. "It only gets better. It's your turn."

I spun the bottle, and it pointed to her. This was the first time it had stopped at another girl, and I didn't know what to do.

She leaned into me and smiled. "Relax, I won't hurt you," she whispered, than she kissed me, softly at first, then working her tongue into my mouth and exploring me, licking my teeth, playing with my unmoving tongue. The tingles started in my crotch and worked their way to the rest of my body. She pulled away as I gasped. Everyone laughed this time.

Sunshine became my new best friend.

Two days later, we were walking home from the clinic where we'd been teaching a yoga class, when I asked, "Have you ever...you know...had sex?"

She laughed. "I'm only fifteen."

"What does that have to do with it?"

"Well, Malachi says that while the body is ready for childbirth at the moment of first menstruation, it's best if the body has reached the maturity of sixteen."

I had never heard Malachi's views on sex before, and I was intrigued. "Well, can't you have sex without having children?"

She laughed again. "You're a naughty girl, aren't you?"

I blushed.

"Having sex doesn't automatically make you pregnant, but we don't believe in anything that stops it from happening, so if you were to have sex before sixteen, there's a chance you could get pregnant. At sixteen, you become wedded to a man, you experience sexual intercourse, and hopefully you produce from that love a child that will make all of us proud and stronger in each other." She delivered this speech like a teacher before pupils, but then she laughed wickedly, saying, "Besides, there are other ways to enjoy yourself without intercourse."

For a long time, I was perfectly content with Spin the Bottle and other games that didn't go any further than kissing. Of course, sometimes it was just too much and I would need to relieve the tension myself. But usually kissing was enough.

Then one day, it wasn't.

I don't know if I started it or if Damien did, but one of us, while kissing, included our hands in the game, putting them places that they hadn't been before. We were out in the woods, looking for wild mushrooms and had stopped for a rest. He swatted a mosquito off my leg; I wiped a bit of sweat off his forehead. We kissed. He whispered in my ear that he loved me, and that's when I lost all control. That hot-breathed devotion in my ear put me right over the edge. I hugged him tightly, rubbing my nipples against his damp shirt. Next thing I knew, he had his hands on them, first over the shirt then I had my shirt off. He put his lips to my breast and I moaned.

I ran my fingers through his hair as he suckled my nipple. I laid in the soil and leaves and pulled him on top of me. I felt his erect manhood through our pants, and I suddenly wanted to touch it. I undid his button with shaking, impatient hands and gasped at the size as I took him firmly in my grasp. He moaned as I pulled at it, marveling on how the skin moved with my hand but under that skin was a rigid stiffness. I didn't realize I was wet until he put his hand down my pants. I gasped and shuddered. He put his finger in me, and I felt an instant release, but it didn't stop. He explored with that finger every crevice and crease I possessed while I was tugging up and down on him, faster and faster. He matched my rhythm with his own, in and out, in and out, breathing heavily in my ear, as I used my other arm to hug him to me, tighter and tighter. Until together, as if we were one, he released his essence onto my hand and I did the same. We lay there panting and gasping.

"That was incredible," I said when I could finally speak again.

He looked at me shyly. "You are so beautiful."

We kissed again before he rolled off me, buttoning up his pants.

"So are you..." I said, sitting up. "Have you ever done anything like that before?"

He shook his head. "Not that far. I'm only fourteen, like you. But I hope..."—he swallowed, looked away, then back—"I hope when I am wedded, it's to you."

I kissed him. "Me too."

When we walked back to the clearing, hand-in-hand, Malachi was waiting for us. The look he gave us filled me with conflicting emotions. He and the other elders had been telling us the urges we had were completely natural, as was the curiosity and exploration of the body. But I couldn't help thinking I had done something to displease him, like I had gotten blood on my hands again.

"Naomi, come with me please," he said without the slightest hint of displeasure. I figured, maybe I had misjudged his gaze.

I let go of Damien's hand and followed Malachi as he led me away from the compound to a meadow that I had never seen. "This is stunning."

"Yeah, it's my own little piece of heaven. I like to come here and meditate or when things get too much," he said. He sat down and I followed.

I'd never thought that things got too much for him. I guess I thought of him like I'd thought of Tim since we'd arrived: all-powerful, all-knowing, and at peace at all times. I looked at him for the first time like he was a real person. He had aged a bit in the past years, going greyer, becoming a bit pudgier, but his essence hadn't changed.

"So, what happened on your walk?" he asked.

"Nothing, we were just picking mushrooms. Olivia's making soup and..."

"Where are the mushrooms?" he asked at the same moment I realized I'd left my basket.

I blushed as he laughed. "Naomi, I think you've realized a few of our double standards and mixed messages. I'd like to clear things up for you."

Oh God, thank you, I thought but only smiled as he continued. "And you thought childhood was tough. I bet you had no idea how hard adolescence would be. With your body constantly shouting out to be paid attention to, your mind thirsty for knowledge, and people everywhere asking you to take on responsibilities you barely feel ready for.

"In society, parents tell children that what they are feeling is wrong. Some adults even make their children believe it is a sin to have those feelings, that they will go to hell if they engage in what their bodies are screaming for. We obviously don't agree with that stance. If we did, we'd separate you from the opposite sex; we'd have our eyes on you constantly. We'd make you unhappy and dress you horribly." He smiled, as if to reassure me that I could relax, unclench. I barked an anxious laugh and did feel slightly better. "So what we do is tell you we respect your bodies, we understand your desires, and there is nothing wrong with them. But then we ask you to have fun and be responsible. It's the responsible part that has you wondering, right? In society, they tell their teens they have to wait until they are married to have sex and then they say they may not get married until they are eighteen." I shuddered.

"It's true. Here we're saying we want you to have fun, but if you think being a teenager is hard, try being a mother. We don't want that for you when you should be having fun, right?"

I shook my head. Who wants to think about babies when all I wanted was a bit of affection? It all did make sense, but…

"Okay, so I know what you're thinking now. We've told you to go ahead and have fun and enjoy your bodies, and then we've told you to stop before there are repercussions. But I think you are at that point where it's gets hard to turn it off once you've started, and you might be scared about what to do when you can't stop."

I was becoming highly embarrassed by this entire conversation, but my need to know outweighed my desire to run away. I swallowed and nodded. "I don't want to do what I'm not supposed to, but sometimes, I feel like I have no control when it comes to…"

"Alright, I'm going to suggest something that might seem ludicrous, but there are ways to get around this."

"Like what?" I asked, trying to imagine.

He used the same harmonious tone that made everything seem logical and completely reasonable. "If it becomes too hard for you to deal with what your body wants from you, you go to Sunshine. If you have questions, concerns or need spiritual guidance, I hope you know by now, I am always here for you."

After a while, I learned to deal with those desires. I stopped thinking about the men around me constantly, wondering what they all looked like naked, wondering what it would feel like to have them inside me. Instead, I got into the spiritual side of my education; the God in my life took all precedent.

Most nights, I still went to find Tim in Malachi's office, and we still had our conversations. Now though, Malachi talked to both of us, not just Tim.

"I'm going to tell you something that I've never shared," he told us one night. "I dreamed you two into existence. Twenty-five years ago, while I was still experimenting with this idea of a better way to live, I had a dream. I wanted to create a family, like the one we have here, but I always wanted to have a different role in it. I know you see me as a father to you, and I cherish that, but I discovered about that time I could not have children of my own. It was then, in one of my darkest hours, that I dreamed of you two.

"I dreamed of what I would want my children to be like, and I pictured in my head everything: how they would look, what their background would be, who their mother would be, everything. That's why, when I saw your mother here, I knew it was an answer to my prayers. She had come to me, looking for a better life, and I had gone to her, looking for you two. You are the future of The Way; you are the destiny, my destiny."

The honor of that was immeasurable. It also made it harder to watch what was happening to him. He started to suddenly get weaker. It hadn't occurred to any of us that anything could happen to him; he aged years in just months. He didn't come out much, and many of his daily obligations were taken up by others. The spiritual learning and tribal training was overseen by Tim; my mother and Larry took over the running of the clinic and the everyday family obligations.

I did most of the caretaking for Malachi, and I felt blessed to do it. He liked when I lay beside him. He talked to me as he caressed my hair. I never felt as loved as I did in his arms, holding on to his life force. He talked to me, told me about his childhood, his upbringing, and what he hoped for us. Malachi was very concerned about the future of his family.

"Listen to me, Naomi. This is very important. I have a feeling Tim might have the same issues I have."

"What issues?" I asked.

"He's been with about every woman here, and he's yet to reproduce any children. It makes sense really. I went looking for my complete and total equal, and I found him. We only have one last hope. You are my last hope."

"Whatever you need," I said, not really understanding what he meant.

Two weeks before my sixteenth birthday, at 3:42 in the morning, while Tim, Mom and I watched over him, Malachi smiled at each of us, closed his eyes, and was no more.

Cascade Mountains
Spring 1993

Tim really had tried to see Mutt before leaving town, but without identification, they wouldn't let him. He had known he should feel worse about the way things turned out, but he really didn't. In his mind, this had been as close as it would get to a happy ending for Mutt. Prison might be horrendous, but so was the life he had before. At least in there, he would be sheltered, fed, and, hopefully, not required to prostitute himself for money and protection. Maybe he'd get a second chance.

As for the rest of the boys, Tim wasn't worried about them anymore. They had seemed to take Mutt's actions and consequences as a matter of course and nothing to concern them. Then Tim had remembered what Mutt had told him that first day: *"…If you go away tomorrow, I can say to myself, oh well, I didn't really even know him anyway. If you watch me get knifed to death, you can say, 'There went Mutt….' It don't mean as much; I don't mean as much."*

It's not like Mutt truly mattered to the other boys; they didn't even know his real name. They didn't know Tim's either, which he supposed was ironic since neither did he. He was Chief and that meant he didn't matter much either.

That was what he told himself one morning when, with twelve dollars in his pocket and a backpack with two changes of clothes, he walked away.

There was one place he needed to see. Living so close to an ocean all those months in Seattle and yet having the Puget Sound separating him from the expanse of never-ending water, he had wanted to see it, to experience the vastness of it, so he had hitched a ride north, and then let the sea air guide him the rest of the way.

He had to walk over a few cliffs and through sand and dried salted seaweed before he got to where the water touched the shore. The Pacific Ocean. He raised his hands into the air and prayed to the God of the Infinite Nothingness and felt His warmth for the first time in a long time.

He smiled and looked around to make absolute sure he was alone. "We are the same, you and I," he said to the ocean. "We have no past, we can't predict our futures, and God lives in us both."

He went to one of the cliffs and sat there all day, thinking about everything and nothing all. He had been heading west for so long, not sure why, but now he'd gone as far as he could. He didn't know if he had anymore answers than he did before, and what answers did he expect anyway? Where to now? *Maybe south,* he thought to himself, thinking of Mutt's desire to see California. But that had been Mutt's dream of some Steinbeckian utopia, not Tim's. Still, there was something pulling him south, something luring him like a whisper in his ear from another lifetime. *Remember Arizona...*

He had survived the winter in Seattle —where they don't call it winter; they call it The Rainy Season— by living in burnt-out, ripped-to-shreds abandoned cars. He didn't want to be enclosed in a smelly trap anymore. After inhaling the salt and algae of the ocean water, he yearned for a smell he recognized. He yearned for the smell of earth and pine needles. He had had enough of civilization, of buildings, streets, alleyways and danger. He had also grown weary of his constant search to find himself. He wanted to get lost again.

He still had his knife and he spent a few of his last dollars on the few supplies he needed and headed for the Cascades. One couldn't get more lost than that.

He walked east and then south; it was slow work, but he wasn't in any hurry. He fished, but he also hunted and gathered all the edible foliage he could find. He knew which plants were safe and which could kill you, or at least make your life incredibly uncomfortable.

He found a small hamlet deep in the mountains called Skykomish. It seemed like a ghost town that only came to life seasonally. The only retail store on the main street was a ski and wild-water rafting supply store.

He had a feeling while walking down the sidewalk that there were about a dozen people in this town, and they all had their eyes on him. He had tried to make himself presentable, but there's only so much you can do with mountain run-off and a sliver of a bar of soap. His clothes and hair were in desperate need of some attention.

He was only in the town proper for about five minutes before he was approached.

"Hey, Chief, you here about the job?" a man coming out of the train station asked.

Tim swung around. "What?" he asked, more aggressively than was necessary.

"Relax, brother. I just asked if you were here about the job, and if you are, you better hurry."

"Ummm. What job?"

Now it was the man's turn to be confused. He looked around him, finally noticing that Tim had come into the town, which was something like an oasis in a desert of trees, without any transportation. "How'd you get here?"

"I was hitchin' and this is where they dropped me. What was the job you were mentioning?"

"Lumberjack. The Cascade Lumber Company was here looking for help. They might still be at the office if you're interested."

It was as easy as that. Given directions to where to go, Tim entered the office of The Cascade Lumber Company, was looked over like a piece of meat, then hired. He was told to come back the next morning, and they would take him to the site where there were temporary shelters for the workers to live during the week. The job was only for two months, but he would be well-fed and paid $500 cash each week. He got weak-kneed just thinking about that part. He had no problem splurging his last few dollars on dinner.

The next morning, he and about six other big, beefy men were taken to the site. He knew instantly that he was going to hate this job. The site where the equipment stood was a crater in the depth of the wild. The devastation had been fresh; he could still smell the blood of the pine, spruce and cedar seeping into the ground. Wood chips lay everywhere like dismembered body parts. He closed his eyes and thought of the money. Enough money to start a life somewhere, someday.

"Hey, Chief," a big guy, older than the rest and clearly the boss, called out.

"Yeah, Boss," he answered.

"You ever done work like this before?"

This one he knew for sure. "No, sir, but I'm a fast learner."

"Good. We don't have time for Lumberjack 101, so you'll have to pick it up. What I need you to do today is go out with Ray here and start tyin.' We'll have you doing the heavy stuff tomorra."

"Thank you, sir."

The Boss studied him for a minute. "You messin' with me boy?"

"I'm sorry, sir. What did I do?"

"You're a throwback, aren't you?"

"Huh?" Tim felt like he was trying to interpret a foreign language.

"Sorry, never mind. I guess I just don't expect your kind to be so well-spoken."

Now, that was language that Tim recognized.

He walked away with Ray, who handed him a bag of long strips of orange fabric and instructed, "What you got to do is this, you take a piece and you find a tree. You want a healthy S.O.B., but not young. Too young and they are no good to us. Gov'ment meddlers tell us how many trees we're allowed to take, but hell, gov'ment not being paid by tree, are they?"

"We're being paid by tree?" Tim asked, mortified.

"Nah, not us. The company. But if the company falls behind in profits, what'd you think the first thing to go is? You and me pal, and that ain't no lie. Well, maybe me before you. I'm almost too old already. So what we do is we compromise. They says there needs to be 150 stems per acre, we do 'bout half that and it's still not what those dammed tree huggers like to call clear cuttin'."

While Ray talked, they tied the ribbons around the trees. Tim was reprimanded repeatedly for not being more liberal with the trees he chose. He was given instructions on what trees passed for acceptable and which didn't. Even when he meant to do it right, which wasn't very often, he was told he was incorrect. The rules seemed to change as the day wore on, until they arrived at the place where the cutting was actually taking place, and Tim realized they were putting ribbons on almost every other tree.

They arrived at the main site right at lunch time, so he was introduced to the rest of the group over sandwiches, chips, wilted fruit, and pop. He took a Pepsi, a half-dead apple, and a bologna sandwich. He was sitting on a stump when the only guy that looked his own age approached him.

"Hey, name's Blaine. Nice to meet you."

"Chief," Tim answered because that was the only thing that came to him.

"Really?"

"No, that's just what people call me."

"Oh, so you from a tribe round here?"

Tim shrugged. "Nopiinde," he said and was for a moment overwhelmed at the rightness of the name. He actually knew subconsciously it was right, something that was part of him.

"Oh yeah? Cool." Blaine answered, just like a man who doesn't want to admit that he doesn't understand something.

Tim knew that gave him the permission to make up the rest of the details as he went along; Blaine wouldn't know the difference.

Lunch was a lot shorter than Tim expected, and it was a long time after that until they stopped for dinner. He was unaccustomed to such long hours of work and was going to have to get used to it fast. They worked from sunup to sundown with very few breaks unless you were what Ray called "a lollygagger," which, Tim surmised, was one of the worst things you could be around this particular group of men.

That night, they started a fire with all the spare wood bits, and most of the men sat around it, eating their dinner and talking in small groups. There were about twelve of them and most were in their 30s and 40s and in different stages of decay, which told Tim that no one died of old age in this profession.

"So, Blaine, what brings you to this mountain?" Tim asked, as they finished their meal, and Blaine lit a cigarette.

"I'm a migrant. Travel from place to place, take seasonal work and don't settle down. How 'bout you?"

Tim shrugged. "Same thing, I guess. I'm looking for a place to settle, but until I do, I been traveling round, trying to find a home."

"Well, man, stick with me and I'll show you all the homes you could possibly want. Springs logging in the Cascades, summers fishin' in Alaska, winters workin' the fields in Texas or traffikin' in the border towns, falls pickin' peaches or oranges in California. Good money all year round and hot pussy in every town up and down." He chuckled wickedly. "Not that you need help, I'm sure, a big stud like you, but stick with me and I can get you laid every weekend of the year. Different chick every time if that's your thing."

Tim turned away to hide his discomfort. He hadn't heard sex spoken of so vulgarly since he could remember, not even the street boys talked that way. It somehow humiliated him. He changed the subject. "So, which of those jobs do you like the best?"

Blaine took the bait and pondered the question before answering, "I always like the one I'm 'bout to get to. Usually hate the one I'm at, and don't think much 'bout the ones I just did. So I guess, right now, my favorite is fishing. Jesus, you gotta come out with me. That is a real man's job. Half the cunt-rags at this gig wouldn't last a day on a boat."

The next day, Tim was allowed to abandon Ray and the orange ribbons and follow Blaine, who showed him how to use a chainsaw, a gin pull, and a one-man bucking saw and how to load a rubber-tired skidder. The work was hard and demanding with very little reward, until payday, then it was the best job in the world.

That Friday night, the boss paid them, and Tim almost wept as he held the five bills that represented freedom in his hand. They all loaded up in a flatbed truck that took them back to town. Once there, Blaine took him aside, and they got into his Honda Civic. Tim had expected Blaine to have a better car, or at least a larger car. If he traveled around in this thing and practically lived in it from time to time, how did it not feel like it was closing in on him?

Blaine drove for almost an hour to a larger town, a logging town. They stopped in the parking lot of a place called The Beggars Tavern, and Blaine checked his hair in the mirror, stuck another stick of gum in his mouth, offered one to Tim, and got out of the car, whistling. Tim didn't like this, didn't want to be here, and hoped he could leave early, but go where? He didn't want to blow any of his money on a hotel or on whatever they offered in the bar, but he didn't see any choice.

Tim walked into the bar and thought he had traveled back in time to the old west with cowboys on one side and Indians on the other.

"Dude, what're you drinking? I'll buy first round," Blaine said.

"Just a Pepsi, please."

Blaine stopped to look at him. "Whatdya mean?"

"I don't drink," Tim said, in what he thought was a non-negotiable tone.

Obviously not though, because Blaine kept questioning, "How do you mean? Ever?"

"No, never."

"Why?" he asked.

Tim shrugged, went to the bar, and ordered his own pop. Blaine might have wanted to keep up the inquiry, but he met some friends across the bar and left Tim to himself. That was completely fine with Tim; he could make a clean getaway.

"You new around here?" a soft voice from behind asked.

He turned around and saw a girl who didn't look old enough to be in there, looking scared shitless by her own bravado.

"Yeah. Just got the job last week. You live here?"

"Well, not here. I live just outside town."

"Oh," was Tim's only reaction. This girl was obviously too young mentally, if not chronologically. He turned back around.

She didn't go away. "So you're Indian."

"Yeah, but that wasn't a question, was it?"

She giggled uncomfortably. "No, I guess it's pretty obvious. But you're different."

"Because I don't drink?" he practically snapped. He couldn't understand his own anger.

"No, not that. I don't believe that stereotype; I know a lot of Indians who don't drink…no really, I do. You're different in a different way."

"Different in a different way?" Tim repeated.

She giggled again. "Don't you see it?"

"See what?" he asked, keeping his eye on the door.

"Your aura. It's the brightest I've ever seen."

Tim stopped watching the door and studied this enigma in front of him. "What do you mean, aura?"

"Aura, it's that…that light, or glow…the, well you know…"

Tim stared at her, and she withered in his gaze.

"Why don't we find somewhere to sit; you need to relax," he finally said, smiling reassuringly.

She sighed then smiled too. "Thanks."

He led her to a table away from the crowds, and Blaine's approving smirk. "So what were you saying?"

"I was telling you about your aura, but I was doing it very badly. What's your name?" she said.

He smiled. "You're all over the place, aren't you?"

She sighed, looking down at her hands, which she was ringing. "I have what you might call verbal diarrhea when I'm nervous. I have no control of it. I'm sorry."

"Why are you nervous?" Tim asked.

She shrugged, put her head down for a minute, then finally looked up at him again. "I guess it's because of what I was telling you about. I wanted to talk to you because…well because of…"

"Because of my aura?" he filled in.

She smiled. "Right, your aura. Because you're special, and special is special everywhere but it is damn near a miraculous occurrence around here. So I didn't want you to leave before I'd introduced myself, but I'm not used to this, well, this is a new thing for me."

"Talking to a stranger is a new thing? Well, you're doing it very well."

"Yeah right; nice of you to say, but I think you're messing with me."

Now he smiled. "Maybe just a little. So what's your name?"

"Rainbow. What's yours?"

"Rainbow? That's not your real name."

She blushed but didn't answer. "What's yours?"

"Call me Chief."

"So we're both using an alias?"

"Yeah, but you started it," he answered, starting to relax.

They talked the rest of the night. Tim was amazed at how easy it was. He knew within the hour that he could have her that very night if he wanted. He didn't know where the charm came from, but he knew he had it. Maybe that was the aura she had been babbling about.

They told their stories, sort of. She told him about her family, about growing up on the East Coast, coming to Seattle for school, now she was interning with Washington Game and Wildlife, testing water supplies in the Cascade mountain range.

He told her about his family in Oregon, how his father was a fisherman on the Columbia River, how his whole family had been fishers on the Columbia, his whole tribe, he told about the industry dying and him having to find a new job. He didn't know where this story came from, but he suspected he had read it somewhere. It was becoming easier and easier to tell stories as if they belonged to him.

He talked about his job and how he already hated it but that the money was too good to turn down; did that make him a horrible person?

"No. I know you're going to hear this a million times, but if you weren't cutting them down, someone else would. It sounds to me that you're the sort of person I want doing the job. Someone who understands how important it is that it be taken seriously, you know what I mean?"

He nodded, before standing up. "You want another?"

She shook her head, and he sat back down. "But you could…I mean…" she stumbled.

"No, I've hit my two Pepsi max. So, um, you want to get out of here?"

"Yeah, sure. Where should we go?" she asked.

"You're asking me? This is your town."

She blushed. "Well, I just meant, do you have a place?"

"Not yet, I just got into town, but I could get one."

"No, that's okay. You could stay with me…I mean if you want to…not that you have to…you know…" she stopped when she noticed he was laughing at her again. "I'll just shut up now."

"No, I like this verbal diarrhea issue of yours, very entertaining," he stood up and held his hand out. "I also like that I make you nervous."

She took his hand, and they walked out together, not looking back, not noticing all the eyes upon them. They walked to her car, a green Jeep Cherokee with a picture of George Washington on each door. They drove for about half an hour until they turned on a dirt road with No Trespassing-Government Property posted on all the trees.

"This is a good place to hide a body," Tim chuckled.

"Yeah, now you know why I use the alias," she answered.

"So, do you live up her alone?" he asked.

"Yeah, but only for three months. Then I go back to school and some other crazy person takes over this job."

"Don't you ever get scared or lonely?"

She laughed. "Yeah, sometimes, but then I go and pick up men, and I'm not lonely anymore."

"Yeah, but you're probably scared for a whole new reason."

"Uh, yeah," she said, looking at him out of the corner of her eye and trying not to laugh. "Now I am."

Tim was going to continue with this line of jokes but decided it probably wouldn't be funny too much longer.

The cabin was a small A-frame, all open on the main floor. Living room furnished with wooden furniture and mismatched pillows and throws, kitchen with limited and outdated appliances. There was a ladder that led to the loft bedroom.

Rainbow put on some twangy Hindu music, and they sat on the threadbare Persian rug across from each other, with their legs crossed, yoga-style. She was drinking red wine, and he had water.

They started talking; he couldn't remember talking this much to anyone, and he didn't know he had that many opinions. It started when she asked about his views on the plight of the indigenous people of the country.

He found himself starting to lecture, and she was mesmerized. There was a familiarity about it, this talking to girls with romantic ideas of the savage warrior, the mystic shaman that had very little idea of how they survived in modern times where the warrior had been replaced with the drunk and very little need of magic in their healing.

* * *

He took her hands and held them lightly, with their knees almost touching. His thumbs softly caressed her hands, their eyes locked, and they sat there like that for hours. He believed that if souls were to be intertwined, then the eyes would tell everything. If you felt a connection then, given enough time, all would be revealed through them. He hadn't known he believed this until he was talking to Rainbow, and the more he explained it, the more familiar it became.

When Tim's eyes started to droop, so did Rainbow's, and before he knew it, her head was in his lap, and she fell asleep while he played with her hair. After a while, he picked her up effortlessly and carried her to the couch, covering her with one of the blankets before getting himself comfortable with pillows and another blanket on the floor.

"Morning," she said the next day as she rubbed her eyes and slowly meandered into the kitchen, where Tim was frying bacon and eggs.

"Hey you," he answered, coming to where she was and kissing her lightly on the forehead. "Sleep well?"

"Amazingly well. I had the best dream."

"Yeah, what was it?"

She went to the other side of the room and began to make coffee. "I had a dream that I met this great guy in a bar and then brought him back here and had this great conversation and then…well, I couldn't begin to explain what happened after." She finally looked at him. "Oh my God, it was real…it wasn't a dream!"

"How is it that you can be cracking jokes at this time of the day?" he asked, taking two plates out of the cabinet, like he'd lived there his whole life, and arranging two eggs, two strips of bacon and orange slices on each plate before placing them to the table.

She shrugged and brought two glasses of milk and two empty cups for the coffee to him. "How could you have created this amazing breakfast this early in the morning? Thank you."

"It's the least I could do. Thank you for last night. It's been so long since I've had someone to talk to."

She smiled. "Me too."

He knew that he hadn't talked to a girl since he lost everything, but he somehow knew that he had been really good at this before. For the first time, he wondered if, out there somewhere, maybe he had a wife, a child.

He'd like to think that if he had been a husband, a father, then some of those flashes of memory would have revealed that. Also, he'd like to think, that if he belonged to someone in the fundamental way of being their father that he would just *know*. But he knew that wasn't how his brain worked anymore. He tried to push the idea out of his mind. There was nothing he could do about it at that moment and Rainbow was studying him with quiet concern.

She deserved his full attention, but still, the thoughts lingered. The feeling that there was somewhere he should be, someone else he should be with at that moment. And why it was now—when, for the first time he could remember, he was so very close to being almost happy—that this feeling overwhelmed him? That was the part he couldn't stop his mind visiting.

"Chief?" her voice finally broke through his revelry. He sensed that she'd called him several times before it registered.

"I'm sorry. What were you saying?"

"I was just wondering if you had to get back or if you could stay… for dinner tonight?"

He smiled. "I don't have to be back until Monday morning."

She beamed, then blushed, as if embarrassed by her own relief. "Is there anything you'd like to do?"

He thought for a moment, trying not to think of all the things she seemed to be asking. He wanted to be there in the moment with her, but he also needed to clear his mind.

"If you don't mind, I'd really like to take a quiet walk. I mean, I want to be here with you, but I haven't had a moment to myself since taking this job, you know? I mean, if that's okay—"

"That's fine," she rushed nervously. "I totally understand and I have to do a few things anyway. So, yeah. Take a walk. Don't get lost. Okay?"

He sighed into a smile. "Thank you. I won't be too long and I promise, I won't get lost."

* * *

When he came back, he was firmly in the present again, having talked himself into allowing this bit of happiness to override any lingering thoughts of his forgotten past. Rainbow was sitting on the porch shucking corn, trying not to look like she'd worried about him.

He bent down on one knee in front of her and took her hand before leaning in for a quick kiss. "Thank you."

"For what?" she asked, twining her fingers through his.

"Everything."

She didn't say anything, just leaned in for another quick kiss.

That night after dinner, Tim listened to her talk passionately about her schooling, forestry and environmental concerns and they continued their experiment. Again they sat across from each other, their knees touching, a fire kindling lazily in the hearth and them not talking or taking their eyes off of each other.

After about three hours, it happened. There came a time when everything was revealed, and all was known. They each gasped from the power of the other's experiences. Tim laughed for reasons he couldn't explain as he felt the joy and wonder of her life—until he saw her wailing and weeping at his experiences. He took her in his arms and apologized over and over. He felt the guilt of needing someone so much that he was willing to put her through that. In fact, she probably felt his sadness more acutely than he. The pain of forgetfulness and the fear of uncertainty had become comfortable and casual, so he didn't even register them. For her, they were new and heart breaking.

"Oh God, God, God…how can you live with this…this… sadness?" she asked through the tears.

He shrugged. "I could ask you the same thing. How can you live with this much joy?"

She took his face in her hands and looked into his eyes with her tear-stained ones. He dried her face. "You're amazing," she said.

He looked away. She gently turned his head, leaned in, and kissed him softly on the lips before pulling back to look into his eyes again. He didn't know what she was searching for now: He'd already showed her his soul. She smiled and then kissed him again.

Before he knew what he was doing, he had taken her hand and was leading her to the ladder up to the bedroom. Once there, he laid her down on the large bed and positioned himself over her, kissing her face and neck as she pulled her shirt over her head. She tasted clean and earthy. As she fumbled trying to get his shirt off, he worked on her pants. He was trying to take his time and revel in every single sensation, but he was overcome immediately with a hunger he needed satisfied.

The emotions that washed over him as he thrust himself into her were both brand new and comfortingly familiar. As he slowed down, she begged him to go on forever. He planned to do just that. He suddenly remembered others, many others with that same expression. He was shocked at the volume of faces that swam before him. As she screamed louder and louder the name of her God and every other god she'd ever heard of, he saw the face that stilled his heart as he exploded inside her.

It was the face of the girl he'd been seeing for months now, only this time she was older and she looked both more peaceful and yet sadder as well.

Now he and Rainbow shared opposite emotions in reverse. She laughed hysterically, choking on her joy and happiness, and he silently wept for a sadness he couldn't name.

She didn't seem to notice or assumed it was a post-coital reaction and wrapped herself around him. He lay beside her gasping, trying to sort all the rabid visions he was receiving. He felt her breath on his neck and realized that none of the flashes were of her.

"Oh my God!" she suddenly screamed out. "That was fucking amazing. There's just no other name for it. I've been trying to come up with a better word, a more precise, newly discovered expression to a…to communicate my…my…AWWWW!" she shouted, partly in joy and partly in frustration for her lack of vocabulary.

Shutting his eyes tightly against the images, which of course, didn't go away until he opened them again and looked at Rainbow, he smiled. He forced his mind to focus on her alone. He knew he'd have a lot of time in the next week to think of other things. "You are beautiful," he told her, kissing her on the lips and propping himself on his elbow to watch her.

She blushed and stared into his eyes and, after moments, they broke out into laughter, their souls clean.

They spent all of Sunday in bed, talking, loving, eating very little, and drinking even less.

Monday morning when she brought him to the pick-up site, all they could do was beam at each other. They made arrangements to meet the next weekend, and he watched her drive away as the rest of his coworkers stood, mildly curious. Blaine was the only one to interrogate him, and he continued it all the way to the site.

"Dude, give it up!"

Tim didn't say anything, only shrugged. He couldn't put into words what had transpired over the weekend, and he sure wasn't going to do it for Blaine. Instead, he just wandered away from Blaine and put his mind into the job and getting through another long week.

For the next two months, it was the weekends with Rainbow that helped him get through the week. He tried to convince himself that what she and Blaine had said was true: if it weren't him doing the job, it would be someone else. Probably it would be someone who didn't care at all, someone who would tie ribbons around anything as long as they got paid.

On Fridays, the day he got to see Rainbow and forget about the trees for a while, Tim would close his mind to everything but the intoxication of the physical labor as he worked through the morning. He spent hours in deep concentration as his shoulder blades pinched and released. His back muscles stretched, starting at the shoulders and smoothly worked further down with every swing. The sweet pain of his movements had begun to mirror the slow, deep inhale and exhale against his rib cage. He couldn't remember ever being this conscious of his life pumping in his veins.

Of course that was just one of the mountainous mass of things he couldn't remember. He was used to the fog his past was immersed in. It had been months since he'd given up the sliver of a dream that one day, it would just all come back and he would remember everything, would *feel* everything. He was finally becoming contented in the not knowing, in the everyday presenting itself asking to be lived.

"Hey, hello, anyone home?" Blaine asked.

Tim heard him, had heard him the past three times, but he raised his ax one more time. Just to hear that "hmpt" his throat made simultaneously with the sharp blade connecting with the downed evergreen.

Finally when he could put it off no longer, he had to look up. He observed the devastating carnage that he had been partly responsible for. The bodies lay everywhere. The short stumps sticking up from the earth were the only testament that there had ever been life here. He wondered why he was the only one who felt the suffering. Why didn't anyone else hear the wailing over the sound of the chainsaws, the pained sigh as the tall, living statue to God's grace fell to the ground?

"Hey, Chief, seriously, if we get to the lunch wagon and all they have left is bologna sandwiches and Diet friggin' Pepsi, I'm going to kill you," Blaine said, smiling to say he wasn't serious.

Tim sighed and swung his ax one-handed into the trunk of his latest butchering. They walked down the mountain together.

As they sat down with their bologna sandwiches and Diet Pepsi, after Blaine stopped cursing him, Tim asked again, "How does this not get to you?"

Blaine sighed. "It's a job. If we weren't doing it, someone else would, and it's good money."

"Blood money," Tim mumbled. "Don't you feel even a little bit like you're selling your soul?"

Blaine laughed. "What the hell are you talking about? *Selling your soul*. Really, that's your Comanche horseshit upbringing kicking you in the ass. The truth is they're friggin' trees man. What we take down today will be back this time next year. We're not clear-cutting, we're thinning, and that's good for everyone, even your weeping trees. So you and Pocahontas can live happily ever after."

Tim didn't think his being Indian had anything to do with his guilt. He didn't know what it meant to be Indian; the mirror was the only thing that told him he was. But he sometimes felt that he'd always been singled out for being odd; he just couldn't remember why.

That night, all the guys sat around the fire discussing their futures. Summer was coming soon, and the logging season would become the fire season. Die-hard Cascade men would soon become firefighters or lookouts. Tim and the other vagabonds would move on at the end of the month.

Blaine was trying to talk him into coming with the group to Alaska to work the boats. Tim was curious about being out at sea for three months with a boat full of men. He was even more curious about the place, Alaska. The way those hard-edged men, who pretended they couldn't hear the trees scream, would get mist in their eyes when talking about the wilds of Alaska made him wonder.

That night, he fell asleep by the fire with tales of Alaskan sunsets in his ears. After falling deeper asleep, the sounds became the laughter of the little girl in his memory. She was talking to him in his dreams more and more since his time with Rainbow. It was like Rainbow was the reminder his mind needed to rekindle his subconscious memories of that little girl. As usual, this dream started with flashes of images: walking down the highway, grasping her small hand, swimming in a lake together, holding her while she cried. There was no one else in these dreams, and they were almost always her as a child, no older than twelve. This night it was different.

She stood before him a beautiful woman. He didn't know how he knew it was her because she was so different, but it was her. She was crying and was extremely angry with him. She slapped him hard across the face and began screaming, "You promised! You told me we could leave! You said you would take me away from here if I didn't like it."

"Na-ho, this is our home, our family. They need me; we need them."

She slapped him again. "I was your family before they were. Honor your promise to me."

The scene changed, and he was standing in a room lit with many candles and the same girl was struggling, half naked, on the floor with a woman he knew was his mother. The woman was smacking the girl and shouting. "We tried to show you the way; we tried to fix the damage, tried to love the devil out of you. I thought we had gotten through, thought we had showed you that the family was everything. Malachi loved you like a daughter and this is the way you repay his faith in you? He depended on you to help your brother guide the family into the future and you... you dare..."

"I dare?" the girl screamed back. "I dare? You... you whore out your own daughter and then ask that? What is wrong with you? What is wrong with you all?"

The scene changed again. Tim was outside screaming at a pale man with a cowboy hat. They faced each other, stepping in a large circle around each other as everyone stood and watched, pleading.

"Were you in on this?" the man shouted.

"Leave her alone. She cannot be forced to do what she does not feel is right."

"It was already foreseen; it will come to be. Your mother will convince her of what is right. She will show her the way."

"No. My mother will kill her. It's been too long. I need to go make sure—"

"Your mother understands Naomi's role. She would never hurt her."

Tim lunged at him. "You have no idea what my mother will do. You've never met the real Virginia. Believe me."

The man pushed Tim away and pulled a knife from his pocket. Tim did the same.

"Do you understand what is happening?" Tim shouted as they continued to pace circles around each other. "It's over. It's all over!"

"That's not your decision to make, son."

"Son? You're my father now? Since when? If it's not my decision, than whose is it? Yours? My mother's? What would you have us be?"

The man swiped at Tim. "We are a family and we decide as a family."

Tim laughed. He couldn't help it. "Do you even hear yourself? Look at yourself, at your family. You're crazy."

The man screamed and came at him. Tim felt the skin separate and the wet release of hot blood. He lost all thought and lunged at the man. He knocked him down to the ground. Before the man knew what to do, Tim had his knee on the man's back and the twine from his back pocket around his neck. "This was not what Malachi wanted and it is not what I want. It's done."

He released the twine and stood up, gasping. The man did not move. Before Tim could fathom what he had done, he heard screaming. Looking up, he saw chaos illuminated by flames. The large house that held his sister and mother was on fire. The family he had tried to create was screaming and running away or running to him, but he had to get in there, had to save his sister.

They held him back with hands on every part of his body restraining him. He was close enough to feel the burn on his skin. When he watched through the tears as the house fell to the ground, he fell with it.

In the brief moment from dream to conscious mind, everything was revealed. He remembered everything, every name, every face and who they were and what they meant to him. Most importantly, he remembered who he was and what he'd done to the person he loved the most. He knew what he had to do.

After he stopped shaking with sobs, he rose noiselessly, went to the tent, threw his clothes in his pack, said a wordless goodbye to Blaine and the others, walked out of the camp site, and down the mountain.

The night was lit by the full moon guiding him. He walked past the carnage he had caused one last time, and all he could say was, "Sorry, sorry, sorry." He took it as his penance to apologize to each and every stump.

After a few miles and too many sorries, he came to the place where there was no sorry but instead big, tall trees swaying to the cool wind with orange ribbon around their trunks. He took out his knife and begun cutting off those death sentences and disposed of the evidence. Through the tears barked the laughter of a cleaner conscience.

He walked for two days, only stopping for food, water, and mandatory rest, before he found his way to Rainbow's house. He needed to see her, he felt the guilt of his life eating away at him, and he needed her to witness it, cleanse him if she would, give him a smile and goodbye if that's all she could.

He hadn't even stepped onto the property before she was in his arms, almost knocking him over with the power of her passion and fear.

"I was so worried. I went to the pick-up site last night, but you weren't there. Blaine said you just disappeared one night, and they hadn't seen you since. Oh God, you don't know how glad I am you're here." She said all this between planting kisses all over his face.

"I am so sorry. I forgot all about it being the weekend before I got here. I'm sorry you were worried," he said as he returned her kisses and walked to the house with her in his arms, her legs wrapped around his torso.

"So what happened?" she asked as they climbed the porch.

He put her down and tried to collect his thoughts by pacing the floor. Finally he just burst, using her again, this time as a confessional. He had to; he had to get it all out and sort through it. "It was me; I destroyed everything."

He stood above her, trying not to pace but to look her in the eye the whole time, and told her everything, everything that he could remember, everything that he had ever thought and all that he had done, right down to the moment when he watched them all burn. By the time he was done, he was on his knees in front of her. Both of them were in tears, and he couldn't figure out if she was crying for him or for herself.

She slid off her chair and fell into his arms. "Jesus, oh my God…I don't know what…I don't have anything to say…I'm so sorry…"

"I killed them; I killed them all."

"No, no. No! First of all, you don't know if all of this happened exactly the way you are remembering it…you don't…but you know what? Even if it happened exactly the way you remembered it, it was not completely your fault."

He looked away; he didn't agree, and he couldn't let her talk him out of his guilt. "They made you their leader and then they forced you to do things that you knew weren't right."

He was struck with more images, and he gasped again. "You don't understand. I was so desperate to be special, to be *important*. It did make sense to me. I did believe I was a God and that she was…she was…my destiny…oh God…I…I have to go…"

"Go where?" she asked.

"I've got to go...home, if there is a home. I have to know."

"I want to go with you. I want to be with you," she said through fresh tears.

He hugged her tighter to him. "I will come back for you. I need to do this alone. I do. But I don't want to say goodbye. You were the only one I trusted when I didn't even trust myself. I'm not taking that lightly. I don't. I just need to discover what I have done and what I can do to make it right."

The Way Compound
1992

It was my wedding night. I was nothing but nerves and emotions. I now understood why everything had been done the way it had been. Why I had been introduced to the joys of physical contact with the opposite sex but had been forbidden to partake in these rituals. It was all in preparation for that night. I would go to my husband, whoever that might be, with the longing and pent-up sexual urges of two years of experimentation and frustration.

My mother spent all day with me, pampering and preparing me. There was a ritual to this night that she observed delicately. She stood me up naked, perfumed me at all the pressure points with lavender and rose. She rubbed my skin with a fragrant, silky lotion and then presented me with an orange and red spaghetti-strapped, knee-length negligee.

There were no public marriage ceremonies, so I would not see my spiritual husband until that night, but I knew they had thought long and hard before deciding who he would be. They had to: Malachi had told me, and everyone else understood, that the future of the family lay in my hands.

As my mother walked me to the men's house, I began shaking, both with nerves and desire. She took me up the stairs and stopped before the door of the room that was once Malachi's and now would be mine: mine and my husband's. She smiled at me, kissed me on the forehead and on both cheeks, and through the tears of joy told me how much she loved me, and how proud she was.

I waited until she was downstairs before taking a deep breath and knocking on the door. I was so ready for this night where I would finally become a woman the family would be proud of.

Tim opened the door, and I was confused. What was this? One more step I'd have to take before facing my destiny?

"Tim, what are you doing here?"

"Come in and sit down, Na-ho," he answered, with a different voice than I've ever heard him use to me, but I'd heard it before with the others, more and more since Malachi's death and Tim's new leadership role in the family.

I sat down on a bench before the fire, my back facing what would shortly be my wedding bed and waited for his brotherly advice. "Na-ho," Tim sat beside me and taking my hands in his. "Do you remember what Malachi told us?"

I nodded my head. "He told us we were his dream realized."

"Yes, he told me in the days before his death that he needed us to do something very important for him."

"Yes?"

"We need to be mother and father of his tribe. We are its future."

"I know, he told me that, too. He said he depended on me to help him repopulate his dream. He worried that his histories might have been passed down to you, and, therefore, it was up to me."

He sighed.

"Tim, what is it? My husband should be here any minute."

He stood up and walked around for a minute then turned back, looking extremely sad. "No, he's not coming."

"What do you mean?"

He took a deep breath then knelt in front of me. "He's here. I'm him."

I didn't think I was a stupidly naïve person, but I started feeling all tied up inside. "Tim, stop it. I don't know what's going on, but stop it, now."

"You and I are to be the mother and father; we are to produce the next generation of leaders and..."

The knots got tighter until they were choking me; I couldn't breathe. In the spark of the second it took me to realize what he was trying to tell me, I thought I would lose consciousness. All I'd ever known was gone and replaced by people I didn't know, wanting from me things I could never give them.

Tim saw me starting to faint and stood up to catch me.

I screamed, "No, get away!"

He dropped me, terrified. I stood there looking at him, searching for the brother I knew in the man before me. If he was still my brother—the only person I always thought I'd know better than myself— then I'd be able to see him in there, behind all this. If he was my brother, he would have looked away in shame after what he'd just suggested. But he stood there, looking me directly in the eye, almost as if he was trying to hypnotize me.

I wiped the tears that had started falling so they wouldn't cloud my vision, but there was nothing there to see. My brother, my protector was gone, and I didn't know this man in front of me.

"Why are you doing this?" I asked.

"It has been foreseen" was his reply.

Without a thought, I reached over and smacked him. "Shut up. I don't understand how you could say that. *It was foreseen.* That makes no sense."

"Malachi told me he saw the answer in a vision. It was a vision of you and of me and—"

I slapped him again, hard across the face. "Did he envision that I would think you're all crazy? Or was I not included in that at all? Am I just some...some vessel for the seeds of everyone, anyone? Tim, you are my *brother.*"

He finally looked away and went to the other side of the room to sit on the bench in front of the fireplace. I wanted to run and never stop.

Sighing deeply, I walked over and sat next to him, covering myself up as much as possible with my flimsy robe. He retrieved a quilt from the bed and placed it around my shoulders.

I turned to stare at him, but he wouldn't look at me. "Tim, didn't you think of me just a little in all this? Didn't I matter?"

Now he turned, hurt. "Of course you matter. You matter more than anything."

"No, I don't mean my role in the family, or destiny...I mean me, your sister, the one who loved you when no one else did. Didn't you think of *me?*"

He looked into the fire for a minute then turned back to me. "I wanted to talk to you. I thought you might see it this way. The others though, they were convinced that you had gotten out of the demonic secular world before its ideals of right and wrong had taken root; that you would see it was destiny."

I did have an insurmountable amount of conflicting emotions, but I didn't think any of them were based on societal influences; they were gut feelings. "Tim, society didn't tell me it's wrong. You did."

"When?"

"My whole life. You always told me I was never to be with anyone I didn't have feelings for, no matter what. You told me I wasn't to listen to others when it came to love, that I would know when I found the one."

"Don't you love me, Na-ho?"

"Stop it. You are my brother. I love you more than anyone. I love you more than the man I was supposed to meet here tonight; that's what I mean." I reached into the pockets of the robe.

"Here." I handed him two bottles filled with blue wiper fluid and glittered with broken glass he had given to me hundreds of years before in the junk yard. I had been carrying them around forever. "I wanted to give this offering to my husband. My childhood, my whole life before this place is in those bottles, and I wanted him to take it, and, in so doing, make me a new person. But you, I can't give you that, you already have it. I can't give you this; I can't give you something you gave me. What's the word for that?"

"Indian giving," he said, handing them back to me and sounding like his heart was breaking more than mine.

We sat in silence for a long time, each watching the flames of the fire before us.

Finally I asked, "Tim, I have to know. Why did you think this was a good idea? We don't even know if you're capable of having children. You're willing to change our relationship forever on a desperate hope? If we did this," I gestured to the bed across the room, "we would never be brother and sister again, *ever*. Does our bond really mean so little that you can wish it away like that?"

"Na-ho—"

"Don't call me that! That was my brother's name for me."

"I *am* your brother. Don't say that. I will always be your brother. You asked me some questions. I'd like to answer them, if you'll listen."

I crossed my arms and glared at him. He stood up and began pacing in front of me.

"I admit, I did think it wasn't right. But the more Malachi talked..."

"Malachi told you this specifically?" I asked, the knots coming back. The man who was like a father to me was trying to get me to mate with my brother. Why hadn't I seen this coming? Was that what he had been telling me without using the actual words because of my age? Had I agreed to it?

"Yes, he's been preparing me for this from the beginning. He knew I was special from the start. You have to know how much that meant to me, coming from where we came from."

I did know that. In fact, it was Tim's lifelong struggle to belong and his finally being accepted and valued that was keeping me from completely loathing him right then.

"And it didn't matter to you that I'd been telling you that you're special your whole life?" I asked.

He moaned in exasperation. "Jesus, you're not going to make this easy are you? What happened to the little girl who listened to me and always trusted me?"

Before I knew it, I was on my feet and my hand was again across his cheek. "Easy for you? Are you kidding me?" I stood and glared at him for a long time, before I sat back down and wrapped myself tightly with the quilt. "I think it's obvious; I grew up. You used to be the only one I cared about who cared about me too. Of course I trusted you; how could I not? But this doesn't sound like the you I know."

"So, what I was saying," Tim continued, ignoring my outburst, "is that Malachi spent every day telling me about destiny. You know he believed in honoring God's signs for our lives, that he received these signs all the time?"

I nodded.

"You were a sign. I was a sign. He knew it didn't make sense; I knew it didn't make sense, but God doesn't always make sense." He was using his storytelling voice, the slow, hypnotic cadence that has a pause after each sentence, allowing time to ponder and visualize every image.

"So, not only my brother, who's my favorite person, and Malachi, the man who was like a father to me, but now God my Heavenly Father is telling me that this is my destiny. Why am I the only one who thinks it's wrong?"

Maybe I'm wrong.

I got up with weak knees and walked slowly to the other side of the room, giving myself some time and space to think. My head was buzzing with all sorts of opposite emotions. *How did I know it was wrong? If everyone thought it was destiny, why couldn't I see it?* I sat down on the bed and tried to picture it, my brother and me, here. I saw the time I'd spent with Damien, and even with Sunshine. *Could I feel those same desires for Tim?* I shivered. *How could my idea of my destiny be different from everyone else's? Did I even see my destiny?* Maybe that was my problem.

Tim came to stand in front of me, and I did want to jump into his arms. I wanted him to hold me and tell me that none of this was real, that everything would be okay, and he would take care of me. I wanted him to be my brother again.

"Nothing has to be decided tonight. You can sleep here on the bed. I'll go over there."

Taking his offered hand, I asked, "Tim, what happens if I can't do this?"

He looked sad and shrugged. "We'll figure it out."

"I really do love you."

"I love you too."

For two weeks, I stayed secluded in that room. I was terrified to go out among our people. Did everyone know what was to happen? Were they all okay with it? And if so, who were these people? What had Malachi done to them? To us all?

Tim spent every night talking to me, not always about our particular situation but about stories throughout time. He talked of the Greek god Zeus and his sister and wife Hera, of their parents, Gaia and Chronos, and of all the sacred lines that came from pure, incestuous blood. The children of Adam and Eve, he said, had to marry and reproduce. They had no choice, and they, miraculously, had produced the human race without the genetic defects of inbreeding. The Egyptian Pharaohs, descended from the brother and sister couple Isis and Osiris, kept their blood divine through such marriages.

"Brothers and sisters made that sacrifice in order to keep the blood of the gods in their veins. They did it for hundreds of years, until Cleopatra. Even she was married to her younger brother, Ptolemy," he said. He was sitting cross-legged on the floor, while I perched on the bed, listening.

"What happened to them?"

Tim looked away. "Cleopatra poisoned him while he was sleeping and seized his power for herself."

"Oh."

Tim was quiet again. I looked down to see the lines on his face. He looked older than his twenty-four years.

"You wouldn't do that to me, would you Na-ho?"

"Do what?"

"Poison me," he said. "Because of…this. Kill me and take our power for yourself?"

He sounded so sad. I wanted to run to him, to hold him, to cradle him in my arms the way that he used to cradle me when we slept in our mother's closet as children. Yet what he was suggesting was so arrogant.

"Oh Tim," I cried. "There is no power to take."

My brother looked taken aback, as if he were expecting me to protest that I would never hurt him. He said nothing, leaving a void where his words about sacred blood and holy incest had hung, and I leapt into that void, desperately filling it with my words.

"Don't you see? There is no power; there is no kingdom. There's just a group of scared people living together, afraid that they might be erased by the outside world."

Tim remained quiet, and I plunged back into the silence.

"Hera and Zeus and Osiris and Isis weren't real people; they were gods. And if the story about Adam and Eve is true, their children had no choice; there was no one else. And incest must have been normal to the Pharaohs. But we aren't Pharaohs, Tim. There is no sacred blood. There's just you and me."

It hurt me as I said it, because I had wanted to believe in everything, in Tim, in Malachi. Mostly, I wanted to believe that we truly were extraordinary. But I couldn't believe this was our destiny.

"I love you. I think you're special without a tribe to lead into the future. I thought you were special when we were kids. But I don't think you're the savior of this tribe. I don't think *anything* can save this tribe anymore."

I imagine any other man, when faced with an attack on the one hope on which he'd been pinning his entire existence, would have cracked then, rose from the floor and swung at me. Tim merely looked up at me, dry-eyed, and blinked. He knew, deep in his soul, that I was right. Or at least I hoped he knew.

His voice, at long last, reached into the void of silence, but it sounded husky, like a recording of itself.

"Malachi foresaw it," he said.

"Malachi was just a man," I replied, as gently as I could.

"So was the guy who first decided that the Pharaohs should all marry their sisters," said Tim. "That guy was just a man too."

"That's exactly right."

Tim looked up again, and I knew that he understood.

Now it was his turn to ask, "So what do we do now?"

I shrugged.

After another week of seclusion, my brother was called into a council meeting. I snuck down to hear what my fate would be.

"Has the marriage been consummated?" Larry asked.

Boy, they don't mess around, I thought.

"I understand that you have some interest in this, but please don't inquire into my business like that," Tim said with no apologies.

"Tim," my mother started, "we know that in a perfect world, this would be none of our concern, but you know what is happening; you've seen the panic that has set in since Malachi's passing. Our brothers and sisters are living with fear in their hearts. This has to work, or everything we have built here will be for nothing."

I wanted to ask what exactly they were trying to save, what was so fragile that Tim and I could destroy it, but I kept my mouth shut. Thankfully Tim was thinking along the same lines.

"First: if this family falls apart, it will not be because of me or Naomi. These people that leave us, they were never our family to begin with, and they have made that obvious. Second: we don't even know if this is going to work. It could be true that I am unable…"

As one, the entire council chanted, "It is foretold."

All, that is, except my mother, who, with a glare, snarled. "She has poisoned you, hasn't she?" Right then and there, she had turned on us.

And I finally figured her out: She was an addict. She had always been an addict; she had just changed drugs. She no longer needed to get her fix with booze and sex; now she tapped her vein with zealotism. Loving me was part of her obsession, what she needed to do to prove to her suppliers that she was worthy of their drug. But now? Now that I was threatening her mania, she let the façade fall away. I knew exactly where I stood with her. Exactly where I had always stood.

I-90 Heading East
Summer 1993

Tim watched the scenery disappear as the sun set behind his seat. He'd been on the Greyhound bus heading east for six hours, and although he'd been down these same roads about a year before, they looked different now. Then, he hadn't known anything about himself, and every road seemed foreign, frightening, and a bit exciting. Now, he knew exactly who he was and what he'd done and all roads led to home and guilt.

Many times in the hours since he'd said goodbye to Rainbow, he'd wondered what he was doing. Why was he going back to a place where he had destroyed everything? He had killed a man with his bare hands; he remembered that now. Larry was a good man, doing what he thought was right, and Tim had killed him.

He had been trying to save his sister, to set her free, but he couldn't even do that. He had stood there and watched her and the home they had created burn to the ground. He knew he hadn't started the fire, but he might as well have; it was entirely his fault she was dead.

So why was he going back? He had to know. Had to know what happened to this family that he was supposed to lead instead of destroy.

He just needed some salvation. Something to have survived. He didn't know what and he prepared himself for it not being there, but the not knowing seemed to him to be the biggest act of cowardice he had left.

Staring out the window as they made their way across Washington, he thought of his mother too, also dead. Like always, his feelings toward her were a jumble of devotion, fear, sadness and revulsion. He had loved her all his life, even when he didn't like her, even when he loathed her, but he'd *never* understood her. He had thought she had changed at The Way. He had truly believed in the healing power of Malachi and his teachings. Seeing the mother he'd thought they'd left behind at the reservation emerge in the last weeks of The Way had finally been the wake-up call he had needed to go along with Naomi's plan. It was clear to him then that only they could save the family, and if not, were the only ones who could save themselves.

It wasn't until after crossing Lookout Pass and entering Montana that more memories came back in an onslaught of good and bad, sad and joyful. He had remembered who he was back on that mountainside, but this was more than remembering; this was reliving.

He stood facing the water, mindlessly picking up and chucking pebbles across the surface, farther and farther each time. "Na-ho, this is never going to work."

She chuckled with the new scornful mirth that already started to fill him with guilt. What had they turned her into? "Of course it will work; I am fulfilling prophecy."

"Don't say that. You know that wasn't the way it was foretold."

She cut him off. "You know what? If I hear that word one more time, I'm going to cut someone's throat. Foretold. I loved Malachi as much as you did, and if he had ever, once, one time, told me that for his family to survive and prosper, I was going to have to sleep with my own brother, maybe we wouldn't be having this conversation. But he never told me that, and he told me everything. What I'm getting now instead of prophecy is skewed interpretations, mother's and yours. No offense, but I don't trust the translation and I certainly don't trust the motivations."

"My motivations?" he asked. "I only wished to honor Malachi's wishes."

"Over mine?"

"No, of course not. I've agreed with you, and I know that if Malachi were alive and you told him what you've told me, he would understand and we'd find a way. I truly don't believe that he would have forced you, and neither will I. I have told you as much."

Her tone and expression softened, but he knew there would be a long time before she truly believed him. "Thank you," she said and sat down on a fallen tree and watched him continue to throw rocks into the water. They hadn't been able to look each other in the eye for a long time.

"So, what is your plan?" he asked.

"If a baby is the miracle they need, then that's what they'll get. Who cares if biologically it's not yours? You will be the father, and I will be the mother and the family will accept it if you do. They will follow your lead."

"I don't know," he answered, wondering if he'd ever been as strong as everyone thought he was. "Mother suspects. The family seems to be splintered down two factions, those who remain true to me and you and those who can be persuaded anything by her and Larry."

She shrugged. "We can't save anyone who doesn't want to be saved, but I know Damien is on our side and can be trusted to go along with the plan."

"How do you know?"

"He loves me. He'll want to please me, and he'll listen to you."

"And if...?"

"And if that doesn't work, then we have to go."

He finally stopped throwing rocks and went to kneel before her. "Go where?"

She put her palm on his forehead and smiled like she had to calm him when they were children. He finally looked into her eyes and was relieved that the bitterness and scorn, if not completely gone, was extremely lessened. "We can go anywhere. Arizona. Remember Arizona? Remember when we first came here, you promised me that we could go if we didn't like this place?"

"How do we just go? How do we leave everything? Everyone who loves us, trusts us, and looks at us for leadership?" He got up and sat next to her on the fallen tree she was perched on so she couldn't see his weakness in his eyes.

"Relax. We don't have to even think about leaving now. I'm talking about if this doesn't work," she assured him. "Believe me, if this doesn't work, we won't be the only ones leaving."

The Way Compound
April 1992

After my weeks of seclusion during which the family was convinced that I had gone along with prophecy and was busy working on the future of us all, I finally left my "marital room" and walked among the people. It was time to present our plan to Damien and hope for his acquiescence. I walked out of the house and into the heat of the day. In my self-pity and disgust, I had forgotten the simple pleasures such as the sun on my back that warmed me from the outside in, and the love of a tribe who remembered who I was and loved me unconditionally, warming from the inside out.

The children who were about, playing games, ran to me, and before I had time to notice how few children there were, they had knocked me down to the ground with the force of their affections. I held them all to me and felt a connection to these children that I had never felt being my mother's daughter.

As they took their places on the ground around me waiting for a story, I put my hand to my lower abdomen and smiled. *I could do this.* I would make a wonderful mother. Summer Rain, my favorite toddler, plopped herself on my lap. I kissed her on the top of the head and, out of the corner of my eye, saw my mother watching me.

She looked approvingly as I laughed with the children hovering around me. And as an old, long-forgotten desire to rip her heart straight out of her chest and squeeze it 'til it popped came over me, I smiled back at her.

As I recited one of the children's favorite stories about how the coyote stole the moon, I thought to myself, amazed at my own calm and coldness, *Fine, if it is foretold, then I will make it so. If a child from my womb is what is needed for peace to be restored, then I will make this sacrifice. I will become what I was destined to become. I will be the mother of this tribe. And I will be the mother I always wished my mother would be.* Once more, I caught her glance before she walked away satisfied that I had conformed to her will.

I searched nonchalantly, strolling through the small village that we had created with our bare hands and pure hearts. I called out greetings to my neighbors that were closer than kin, as if everything was perfectly normal, and I had no purpose but sharing my light with them. All the time, anxiety rose in my throat as I calculated all the people missing from the family. I hadn't really thought too much about all those leaving. At first, before I'd started having my own ideas of leaving, I just assumed they'd all be back eventually. Where would they find a life that gave them all that this family did? Now though, well, I was desperate to find one person, frantically hoping he was not one of those who had abandoned us.

I audibly sighed and broke into a run when I saw him in the distance, coming from the Center. He had taken on more and more responsibilities in the rehab center—both his parents had been alcoholics and his father had died in a car accident when he was very young, his mother took years after to find The Way. Damien was determined to shield other children from the pain he had suffered. His compassion and desire to help others was one of the most remarkable things about him and why I knew we could trust him with this secret. "Naomi, how are you?" he asked, taking my hands in his, like he always did when we meet. I smiled and kissed him like always, but I noticed he was studying me, and I knew he, too, knew of the prophecy.

"Will you take a walk with me?" I asked.

I led him away from the group and to the only place I was pretty sure no one else would see us: Malachi's meadow. Many times I had met Malachi here as he told me secrets and taught me what he had wanted me to know when I was a child. Now I was going to defile that memory with lies.

I knew when I looked at Damien's eyes full of amazement, that he had no idea that this existed. "What is this place?" he asked, as I had asked Malachi all those years ago.

"This is Malachi's meadow, where he would bring me to tell me his secrets, and when he needed to tell me of the prophecy he hoped he would not have to tell the others."

Damien's eyes seemed to shimmer at the promise of secrets never told and prophecies never shared. When he saw that Tim was there waiting for us, he seemed puzzled for a moment, before his look of being singled out for greatness intensified.

"Brother," Tim said as way of greeting, holding his arms out for an embrace. It wasn't the first time I had been amazed at the power of my brother, of how similar he was to Malachi, but there, in that meadow, I knew that there was nothing he couldn't convince Damien needed done and making him feel special enough to go along.

"Damien, do you see what is happening to the family since Malachi has joined our heavenly Father?"

Damien looked down and mumbled, "Many have left." Then he looked up and his eyes had changed: they were ablaze. "They were not true to the family. They did not have faith enough in Malachi's teachings; they did not believe in the prophecies."

He spoke with such anger for those who doubted what was foreseen that I swallowed and momentarily questioned getting him, or anyone else in the family involved.

Then I thought something truly blasphemous that made me wonder if I had ever been anything but that angry, pessimistic, little girl that had arrived more than five years ago. I thought, *Hell, if Malachi could pull these prophecies out of his ass, so could I.*

I only remained shamed by the sentiment for a brief moment before that emotion gave way to something much more potent: the giddy arousal of power. "You have heard what was foretold by Malachi, but now I must tell you of what was told to us, something we'd have to do if the prophecy doesn't come as quickly as the family needed to believe."

"Can we trust you?" Tim asked.

Damien swallowed hard and nodded.

Tim cleared his throat and looked at me quickly, needing reassurance that we were doing the right thing. I nodded and he started, "Malachi, in his infinite wisdom and communion with God, did see a time of struggle for his children, but he also saw a few, true believers who were strong enough and wise enough to make the sacrifice needed to save the family.

"You know of what is needed of Naomi and I. Now I must tell you of what the family needs from you."

Damien swallowed again, and I was suddenly reminded of how young we both were. I felt ancient, and I was getting older every moment, but he should have been left to stay young and innocent forever. What were we doing to him?

We were doing the same thing that had been done to me, to Tim—we were using him.

"Me?" he asked.

I gently touched his forehead with my own, willing him to understand and comply. "I hope you won't find what we need from you too disagreeable, but the hardest part of what you have to do is to keep a secret. You have to contribute to the well-being of this family, but no one must know."

Kootenai Salish Reservation
July 1993

Tim had no problem finding a ride up north. He'd never had a problem finding a ride, he thought as he threw his bag and himself into the back seat. He used to think it was because he was a good person, and people could sense that, but now his self-loathing tainted every thought he possessed.

He had to pass the reservation he had grown up in to get to The Way, so he decided to check in on his grandfather. He hadn't seen him, or thought too much about him since the day he had driven away all those years ago with his sister, mother, and Larry. The chance that his grandfather was no longer alive was pretty good. To Tim, he had seemed barely alive his whole life anyway. It wasn't like his daughter and grandchildren had taken care of him, but they had been there, they had made sure he had a roof over his head and food in his fridge. There were occasions too that Tim had carried him home when he passed out in some ditch between the bar and the house.

Tim was thinking of this when his ride pulled to a stop right in front of the place where he had spent his first eighteen years of life. He recognized nothing. He was shocked by all that was different. *Yes,* he reasoned, *it has been eight years since I'd been here, and even longer since I cared about tribal business.* But in his whole life, they hadn't even so much as changed the message on the board that had always read: "Welcom to India C untry."

Now, not only was the sign gone, so was everything else, including his house. His whole neighborhood, which admittedly had been the slums, was now replaced with a large building with a larger parking lot. "What is this?" he asked.

"It's the casino," the girl in the passenger's side answered. "Aren't you from here?"

"I used to be" was Tim's answer. *Now what?* he thought. The only thing he wanted to do was check on his grandfather, to check if he was alive and well—or as well as a man like him could be.

He thanked his ride and decided there was only one place he could go to find answers about his grandfather. He just hoped that had not changed. He never thought he'd say *that* about The Broken Arrow.

He walked into the bar for the first and last time in his life. He'd been to other bars to pick up his mother when she'd lost her keys or had pissed off her rides, but The Broken Arrow was close enough to their house that he'd never had to rescue her from there.

"What can I get you, son?" the bartender, the only person to notice his entrance, asked.

After Tim's eyes grew accustomed to the weak light of the bar, he scanned it for signs of his grandfather. Even if they took his house, there is no way they'd take him from this place; he'd die there. Or so Tim thought.

"Yeah, I'm looking for a man who used to live where the casino is."

The bartender snorted. "Lots of people used to live there. You got a name for this fella of yours?"

"Amos, sir. Amos West."

At that, everyone looked up from their drinks and their silent dislike for strangers. That was what Tim was to them. Even if they had known him as a child, none recognized him now. Tim wanted to keep it that way.

"How you know Amos?" the bartender asked.

"Friend of the family."

The bartender snorted again. "Sure you are. Well I hate to tell you this, but your *friend* Amos West doesn't live here anymore."

Tim was so prepared to hear that his grandfather was dead that he was momentarily confused to silence. Everyone watched for his reaction. "What do you mean?"

"Amos took the settlement he received from selling his house and moved to Arizona."

Tim still didn't understand; this was not the grandfather he knew. "Amos West moved to Arizona?"

"Yeah."

"When?

"Jeez, it's been about, well little less than a year I guess."

"Why Arizona?"

The bartender shrugged then turned to a man at the far end of the bar. "Hey Hank, you know why Amos moved?"

Hank mumbled something that sounded vaguely like, "Family."

"Family?" Tim asked, now knowing they were talking about the wrong guy. "What family?"

He read on the bartender's face that, as a stranger, he had asked one too many questions. "Listen, son, how the hell should I know? If you really knew Amos West, then you'd know he wasn't much into talking and sharing his plans. One day, he was here and the next he wasn't and the rest is none of your business."

Tim thanked them, apologized, and left the stale warmth of the bar for the bright sunshine of the outside world. He contemplated what he'd been told as he walked north with his thumb extended over the road. It didn't make any sense. He knew for a fact that his grandfather had no family other than his daughter and his two grandchildren, and since Tim was the only one left, they were both orphans of sorts.

Tim chuckled to himself as he tried to picture his grandfather marrying a woman and starting a new family in Arizona. It was too ridiculous to imagine.

He walked along Highway 93 for about two hours before he got a ride. He didn't really mind; he was in no hurry to get where he was heading. Besides, he didn't want to accidentally catch a ride with anyone who knew him from the old days when he had been the tribe's punching bag. He was past Ronan when he was finally picked up. The boat attached to the shining Dodge Ram told him that they were tourists and weren't anyone he might know.

Thankfully the tourists asked a lot of questions about the scenery and history of the land, and Tim could distract himself with the answers. But as they got closer to his destination, Tim grew more and more terrified of what he'd find. By the time they had dropped him in Whitefish, Tim had to tell himself to breathe as he imagined charred bodies and blood everywhere. His breathing would become so stilted he had to remind himself that a lot of time had passed to begin breathing properly again.

He still had a long walk to get to The Way, but he decided to make the rest of the journey on foot. He didn't want any witnesses to this reunion.

He walked through the night and arrived at the drive leading to his disastrous past at the cool breeze of dawn. The driveway to the clinic looked just the same as it always did: paved and enclosed in forest to suggest immersion in nature and peaceful surrender from the outside world of addiction and destruction.

He walked around the perimeter of the clinic, which looked, surprisingly, just like he remembered, maybe even better. He noticed a new totem with an eagle on top, underneath that a bear below an owl. He watched the eagle, and he saw Malachi looking down at him.

The sign had been changed. The wooden banner had been replaced with a wire and ribbon Dream Catcher and circled around that, the words: "The Way Heritage Rejuvenation and Wellness Center."

He was both confused and heartened by what lay before him. Confused because he couldn't imagine that The Way was still functioning if what he remembered happening had actually taken place. Heartened because this all seemed to suggest somehow the family had survived! He was tempted to run to the door, fall to the ground and weep. First though, he had to see what remained.

The clinic might have been almost the same, but its surroundings were completely different. The road that led to the commune used to be hidden, but now it was nonexistent. The fence was no longer electrified; in fact, it was barely standing, which was good, because the undergrowth was so high, he was practically tripping on the fence before he realized it was there.

The gate that used to open on a slider was lying on its side. He prepared himself as he followed the weed-infested pathway that had once been a road. The place where he had once built his life was gone.

The only building standing was one that he had built the year after he turned twenty-one. He, along with a few of the other men, built a sweat lodge, where tribal traditions of spiritual rites and vision quests—real vision quests—would be honored.

The rest of the compound had been bulldozed, cleared, re-soiled, and now saplings grew in its place, so that when they became full-grown trees, the sweat lodge would be invisible behind them.

Walking carefully through the new life, he laid hands occasionally on the fledglings, as he made his way to the building. He was still yards away when he began to hear voices raised in chant. They seemed to be reverberating from the stained glass windows and filling the air with their healing essence.

"way hey ya, way hey ya way hey ya, away
way hey ya, way hey ya, way hey ya way"

Caught up in the music and the warmth echoing around him, Tim didn't see the monument that had been erected outside the lodge at first. It was a wooden statue of himself and Malachi that was eerie in its likeness. He approached it without a thought and placed his hand on the face of the man who had been more than a father to him. "In memory of those in our tribe who sacrificed themselves to show us The Way. We honor them in all we do," he read as he ran his fingers along the inscription then to his own face.

He wondered where the carving of his sister who had sacrificed the most was when the door to the lodge opened. Frozen, hand still on the statue and eyes darting, Tim was trapped.

Three men walked out talking and stopped when they spotted him. Tim didn't recognize the first two, but the third one had Tim in an embrace before he could place him.

"Damien? Is that you?" Tim asked through his shock, both of being recognized and of being welcomed.

Damien didn't answer right away; he was too overcome with tears that silenced him. "We...we thought...we thought you were..." he couldn't continue.

Tim *sh, sh, sh'd* him in his arms like he would his own child. Damien wept and tried to get the words out, and as much as Tim wanted to hear what he had to say, he thought it was more important to calm him first.

Finally Damien remembered the other men there and disentangled himself. "Michael, Robert, this is Tim. He has returned. He is saved. She said you would, but we lost faith. Then she left, and we were thrown into despair."

Tim tried to think of who Damien was talking about. The only person he could think who would have that much faith in his strength was dead; he had seen the house with her in it fall to the ground. So he had to ask, "Who's she?"

They both shared the same confused look before Damien said, "Naomi. She told us you'd be back."

Tim's vision blurred and knees buckled under him so that Damien had to reach for him to keep him standing. "When? How…"

"Before she left. She told us you'd be back; you'd come for her."

"Left…?" Tim stuttered, not able to form the words in his frazzled mind. "She's not…not dead…?"

Damien seemed to realize finally what Tim had been thinking all this time. He wrapped his arms around him in a bear hug. "Naomi is alive, Tim. She survived."

The Way Compound
June 1992

It had finally happened. After years of yearning, longing, hoping, and fearing for my future, I had at last entered adulthood as Damien entered me over and over. After the years of waiting and my body screaming for it, the actual occurrence was, sadly, a bit of a disappointment.

I convinced myself it was all the anticipation, topped with all the lying and the stress of the future of an entire group of people that had dampened the joyful experience. That and having to come up with a feeble excuse to explain away the blood as we had told Damien that Tim and I had tried and failed to conceive.

I reasoned it would get better, and with each passing day, it did. I knew my cycle like I knew the moon's, and every night when the moon first waxed and then waned we met in the meadow, in the farthest corners of the forest, or anywhere else we wouldn't be seen. At first, I was so consumed with my objective and the thoughts of sacrifice that I felt we were finished the moment he found his release inside of me.

As the nights flowed one into another, his enthusiasm overcame my thoughts of obligation, and I began to put everything else out of my mind, focusing on my own pleasure as well. That's when my moans and screeches became as loud and vigorous as his.

I suddenly returned to my adolescence when I wanted physical contact constantly. I needed him to need me, to be so excited to be with me; he was aroused just looking at me across the compound. The power of that was so great that I desired him always, and it didn't matter anymore why.

So one night, into our second month, after being with each other everywhere from on the soft grass to against trees and even in the river, I made plans for me and him to be alone at the compound. This fortunately coincided with the annual tribal weekend retreat.

Tim suggested that Damien stay to keep his eye on the clinic. I should also remain because it could be that I was with child, a miracle child, and precautions must be taken.

As far as anyone knew, I was Tim's perfect wife and was active in promoting all aspects of my tribe. I spent my mornings in the clinic with the other wives, afternoons were spent educating children; I taught pottery and yoga. After class, I would spend a few hours in either independent study or enrichment classes. The evenings were filled with family dinners and sitting around the fire, pretending that the family wasn't dwindling and immersed in fear, waiting for prophecy to show them that they had been right to put all their faith Malachi and the family.

This was the only time I didn't have to make believe. I wasn't frightened about my future. Tim and I had taken our destinies into our own hands, and I just knew that no matter what, we'd be fine.

I stood at the beginning of the trail and waved goodbye to all my family. Then I went to prepare the room that I would bring Damien to. It was the room Tim and I had been sharing all these months we had been pretending to be united. I lit candles all along my marital bed in the direction and color of the medicine wheel and prayed to the Great Spirit for help and guidance.

"O' Great Spirit,
Whose voice I hear in the winds,
And whose breath gives life to all the world,
hear me! I am small and weak, I need your strength and wisdom.

I lit the red candle at the foot of the bed.

"O' Great Spirit of the South,
I light this candle in your honor,
Let the passion of our love here tonight,

Enflame my womb with the greatest gift you
Can bestow on your children."

I lit the yellow candle at the East side of the bed.

"O' Great Spirit of the East,
I light this candle in your honor,
Grant a new day to your faithful children,
Empower me to fly above my fear and do what is needed,
For the future of my family."

I went around to the other side of the bed and lit the blue candle.

"O' Great Spirit of the West,
I light this candle in your honor,
Allow the love that flows within me to protect those I love
Quell the anger I feel and let it be swept away,
So that I may be whole again."

Finally I lit the green candle at the head of the bed.

"O' Great Spirit of the North,
I light this candle in your honor,
Endow me with your wisdom, so that I may know your will,
And let the Earth around me,
Heal me."

Turning off the lamp light, I took off my robe and stood in the middle of the room. I was wearing the special gown my mother had given me the day I was to meet my husband. Closing my eyes, I extended my arms to embrace the spirits and feel them wash away the resentment of choices being decided for me. I heard the timid knock on the door. Taking one last cleansing breath, I went to him.

Damien took a long, solemn look at his surroundings before he even noticed me standing beside him. He swallowed before he spoke, "It's beautiful; you're beautiful."

I turned to face him and took his hands in mine. "So will our child be."

A pained expression flashed in his eyes, and I realized how heartless that was to say to him. We both knew that wouldn't be "our" child. I kissed him as way of apology.

When the kiss ended, Damien still looked sort of wounded. "You know, I always wanted to have children, to be a father. I always thought it was the perfect way to heal my own childhood, you know? The one I had before I came here."

"You will be an excellent father. Whether this child is to be yours or Tim's doesn't matter, not here, not in the family. We are all responsible for each other and in the nurturing of the young. You already are a great father, a great brother. We're lucky to have you." Times like these, I truly did believe in family. Just not the one my mother and her followers were willing to manipulate into being.

"I thank God every day that I have found The Way and especially you," he whispered in my ear as he hugged me tight.

"I do too."

I felt every possible emotion simultaneously as I wrapped my legs around Damien's torso, looking into his glazed-over eyes and felt him release inside me at the same time that I orgasmed. But then a wail from across the room stopped my heart.

"No! No! What are you devil children doing?" my mother's screeches finally forming words.

"You slut! Whore!" she continued screaming as she approached. Before I could think to get away, she yanked me by my hair, dragged me off of Damien and across the room. When she finally let go, I lay on the ground too stunned to move. She straddled me and began wailing on my head, face, and shoulders, going from slapping to punching as Damien tried to pull her off.

I was fighting against the darkness that was trying to pull me into numbness when I heard my brother's voice. I opened my eyes and saw in the haze, him lift her off of me.

"Stop it!" he shouted as he wrapped his arms around her and tugged her up.

Others stood at the door and looked from me to Damien then to Tim and mother. Confusion the only thing all faces shared.

"What has she done?" my mother kept chanting over and over. "She has ruined everything. Everything."

I stood up and wrapped a blanket around myself. My mind raced with the list of options I had contemplated in the last months. There were so many Tim and I had discussed and debated, and one we had not.

"Let me talk to her," I ordered.

She stopped flailing in his arms but he held her tighter.

"I don't think that's a good idea," both Tim and Damien said. The others still looked too confused to weigh in. Plus, besides the outburst they had just witnessed and couldn't make sense of, Virginia West had never been anything but peace and love.

"Please, let me explain," I said, trying to sound as calm as collected as I could. I knew it wasn't helping that my lip was bleeding and one of my eyes was swelling.

"This I got to hear," Larry said, stepping forward. He turned to Tim, "Let her go."

Tim and Larry looked at each other for a moment. The struggle for power made public, finally.

"Please," I said again.

Tim looked at me, trying to plead with his eyes; I just nodded.

"Fine, but I want to stay in the room," he finally said.

"So do I," Larry said.

"No," I said pointedly to Larry before turning back to Tim. "You've been our middle ground for long enough. I need to talk to her alone. See where I stand on my own with her and not just because of her devotion to you. Please understand and never forget… Arizona."

He looked hurt but it was the confused expression that worried me the most. As he turned and ushered Damien, Larry and the rest out of the room, I called after him. "Tim, remember Arizona!"

"What does that mean?" my mother asked, her voice filled with scorn.

I didn't answer her and instead went to the bathroom to get dressed and see if the physical damage my mother had done finally match the mental scars she inflicted all those years ago.

I knew the first plan was no longer going to work. I was going to have to put our escape into action. I didn't want to leave the only place that had been home and the people that had been my family, but it was clear to me now that I already had. Things would never be the way I had believed they were. All I could do now was try and save us from our mother, once and for all.

As my mother raged on the other side of the door, pounding her fists, shouting for me to come out and face her, I tried to calm my nerves. Looking in the mirror, I watched as my face seemed to swell. Blood trickled from my forehead, around my ears, and from my split lip. I took a towel and warmed it under water before applying it to my face. I felt my whole head throb under the pressure.

To take my mind off my injuries, I thought of something else equally as painful: My mother. I would never understand her, never. What had I ever done to deserve the treatment she had given me? Had she ever really meant those things that she had been telling me since we had gotten here? I thought I knew the answer to those, but the most troubling question was, why did I care so much?

I stayed in the bathroom until my mother had stopped her shouting. Then willing to be as ruthless as her, I took a deep breath and walked out of the room.

"Why?" she asked before I'd even closed the bathroom door.

Relieved that my waiting had paid off and her rage was less manic, I walked over to a dresser, opened a drawer and pulled out the bottle of Jack Daniels. I had always prayed our plan would work—that I would get pregnant, have a child that would resemble Tim, or at least me, and no one would be the wiser. If that didn't work, I planned to get us the hell out of there, anyway I could. I was prepared for anything.

"What's that?" she asked, sounding scared for the first time.

"Oh you know what this is. It's your favorite, isn't it? You think I'm a whore, right? Show me how you do it right. Let's get drunk together, just you and me; no one will know." I opened the bottle and tilted it into my mouth. "Hmmm. Kinda burns; is it supposed to burn?" I asked, holding it out to her.

It took her longer than I thought it would for her to reach for the bottle, but she did finally take it and lift it to her lips. She took a long drink and moaned with guilty pleasure.

She held it in her mouth for a long time before gulping and shoving the bottle back to me. "Why are you doing this?"

"You know why. I couldn't do what you wanted me to. This was the only way I could make it right." I put my thumb over the top of the bottle and once again put it to my lips. I handed it back to her. It again took her longer than I thought it would to take it, but she did and again she took a long swig. This time she didn't give the bottle back.

"Would it have been so hard for you to do what was required? Was it too much to ask for the family that embraced you when it should have seen you for what you were and locked you out of their hearts and minds?"

Instead of answering, I watched her take another drink.

I took the bottle back from her. "It's coming back isn't it? How good it tastes, how it will make you feel. Tell me, how will it make us feel?"

She took it back and guzzled deep again. "We will be laughing in about five minutes. In ten, we'll forget that we hate each other." She took another drink before handing it back to me.

I held the bottle up to toast—"Well, here's to ten minutes then"—and took another fake swig. "Why do you hate me? Why have you always hated me?" I asked as she took the bottle back. I just needed to hear her say it, hear her put it to language once and for all.

She rolled her eyes before mockingly giving me a sad expression. "Oh baby, I never hated you. Hate is a strong word, and I never felt that strongly for you. I simply never liked you. I know that seems harsh and makes me a horrible mother but," she shrugged, "what're you going to do? You can't control who you love, and you can't be forced to like someone who is everything you despise."

If it were possible for words to stab, then I felt them slash at my heart. I almost staggered from the pain of it, and I felt drained, as if I were actually bleeding. I gave myself only a moment to grieve, however, before I took a deep breath and pretended that she wasn't even talking about me. I forced a laugh, took the half empty bottle of Jack and faked another swig.

"You know, my life probably would have been a lot easier if you would have told me this earlier."

She smiled again, and I wanted so badly to reach out and smack her, but instead I handed the bottle back to her and waited for it to do the work for me. "Well, whoever said life would be easy? Besides, how dumb are you? I told you that every day in every way. I tried to like you. I came here, found people that were willing to like me for me, and then they made me bring you here. I tried, but you make it so hard."

I had to keep laughing or I'd have cried and I would *not* give her that. "You despised me because I am an Indian, just like you, but I refuse to hate myself like you hate yourself. You also hate that Tim loved the Indian in me. But I never deserved the way you treated me, and you don't deserve to have Tim love you, and now he won't."

"Is that what that 'Remember Arizona' thing meant?" she asked with a laugh. I recognized that laugh even though it had been a long time since I'd heard it. She was right; it had only taken five minutes. "You think he's going to give up all of this? For you? We have made him a god, what have you given him?"

She laughed manically, but I was panicking. The bottle was almost empty, and she was still conscious. I knew she used to be able to hold her liquor, but I figured since it had been years since she'd drank anything, it wouldn't take nearly as much now.

Then she stood up and tried to walk. Watching her stumble around as if her legs couldn't contemplate how to work properly relieved me greatly. Still she laughed.

"Tim, they're being mean to me! Tim, save me!" she shrieked mockingly. "You're pathetic."

"I'm pathetic? Look at yourself!"

She stopped prancing on her drunken legs and looked at me as if trying to see through a haze. She seemed to finally put it together what was happening. "What have you done?"

Now it was my turn to laugh. I held up the almost empty bottle. "I have shown you what you really are, what you will always be, a worthless, dru—"

She lunged at me, but she was drunk and I was not. I shot to my feet and slapped her hard across the face. She crumbled to the floor and didn't move. I stood over her, my hands in fists, waiting for her to wake up. She didn't.

"You're pathetic," I repeated, putting the bottle to my lips and taking my first real drink of the nasty fire whiskey. I spat it onto her hair-covered face, dropped the bottle beside her, and walked away.

I bent down and pulled out the box I'd kept under every bed I'd ever slept in. I opened it and took out the jars of sparkling liquid Tim had given me all those years ago, remembering what he had told me when he gave them, *"But if anything happens and they break, you have to throw them away. It's beautiful but dangerous and highly flammable: glass and windshield wiper fluid. I know you're a smart girl and will now what to do with them."* I slammed them on the hardwood floor by my mother's body and was shocked when she flinched as they shattered around her. She still didn't wake up though.

The rest of the items, the letters from Tim I'd saved from the foster care years, the picture of my father, the gum wrappers I'd saved from my grandfather's daily gift just got sprinkled out over her. Next, I went to the side of the bed, took the candle of the West, brought it to her and dropped it onto the flammable liquid, amazed by my own calm as the fire licked the liquid and danced around my mother.

"This is my childhood, the pains I've endured, the things that kept me down. I will not be destroyed, and I will not suffer from your wrath. You are going to the only place you've ever belonged, but I, I am Soaring Fire and I will rise from these ashes. I will be washed clean by the flames of my anger and my love."

The Way Heritage Rejuvenation and Wellness Center
Summer 1993

The world stopped along with Tim's heart as he heard the words reverberate through his whole body until that sentence was all that existed. "She's alive...She survived."

He tried to swallow the buzzing, but he felt his throat tighten and his tongue swell, as if he had been stung by his own swarming emotions.

"Come sit down with me," Damien said, almost carrying Tim away as the other men excused themselves.

Damien brought him to a place by the river that Tim knew well. Tim remembered the time, days before the tragedy when he and Naomi had met there and planned their future.

"I'm not sure about this," Tim said, handing Naomi the bottle of Jack Daniels he had taken from the Center. It had always amazed him the things alcoholics thought they could sneak into their recovery.

"It's just a test. I need to know that if I'm doing all of this, if we're all going through all of this that she really has changed. If you're right and she has, then I won't need this. If not...if I'm right...and it's not just that she's scared..."

Tim was just trying so hard to make everything work. If things could just be like they were when Malachi was alive and everyone believed.

Now his mind reeled. "How is it possible? I saw the house burn to the ground."

"We all saw the house burn to the ground, but what we didn't see until the smoke had cleared was that Naomi had somehow gotten out and ran for the safety of this river."

"And Virginia?" he couldn't call her *mother,* not anymore.

Damien bowed his head. "They found her at the fire's origin. She was passed out drunk and a burned candle was pooled around her." Damien mistook Tim's silence for shock and not the dawning realization that when Naomi had told him about a test that she had prepared for their mother, this was the test. She had failed miserably.

Damien continued, "Such a tragedy, such a waste. I know that she was livid, that she didn't understand, but I thought Naomi would be able to reason with her, to show her the way. I had no idea that she'd resort to her old ways."

Tim shrugged. "So where is Naomi now?"

"Phoenix. She left with the deprogrammers—"

"Deprogrammers?" Tim asked.

"Yeah. After the investigators came and couldn't get any of us to talk to them, they labeled us a cult. We were swarmed with agencies wanting to split us up, study us, try to figure out how we were brainwashed, and help us back into society." Damien seemed scornful, and Tim understood why. None of that sounded like what they wanted The Way to be, but that was what they had become.

"So, anyway, we were down to a handful of us living here and trying to rebuild our lives. The government wanted to take it, the building, the people, all the land around here, but they couldn't. Malachi might have suffered from—what did they call it?—Charismatic Messiah Complex, but he wasn't stupid. He did everything right, everything legal, and, in his will, he left everything to you and your sister so they couldn't touch anything."

Tim was shocked and overwhelmed by this discovery, but he kept his tongue, needing Damien to continue.

"Since Naomi was under age, she had us call her grandfather to do the paper work. She was going to stay here and fix everything, but then folks from The Phoenix Center came and talked her into going with them. She kept saying she needed to get to Arizona."

Suddenly it all clicked in Tim's mind:

"Arizona, Remember Arizona."

"Amos West is gone, he moved to Arizona to be with family."

He stood up. "I have to go."

"Now?" Damien asked, disappointed.

"I need to see her. Have to…to…" he couldn't continue.

"Can I come with you?" Damien asked, if he noticed Tim's struggle he didn't mention it. He continued, "Saying goodbye to Naomi was the hardest thing I'd ever done. Then you wondered back here, like a miracle."

Tim was torn; he did want Damien with him, not only for the company but Damien could fill him in on what happened after Tim had fled that night, but Tim reasoned there was just a bit more he needed to do on his own.

As he looked around though, he saw the perfect excuse. "Damien, it looks like you're needed here. We'll come back."

"Promise?"

"I can't speak for Naomi, I can't even imagine what she's been going through, but I will come back." *Eventually,* he finished to himself.

Damien nodded solemnly. "I understand."

"Tell me about the place she went, the Phoenix Center? Who are they?"

Damien snorted. "They're this born again group that wanted to turn us around and get us on the right path; yeah, like they're not brainwashed themselves. But Naomi went with them. I think she just wanted to get away for a while and sort things out."

Yeah, Tim thought, *she needed to find her way to Arizona. After all this, she still believed that we would find each other, and maybe, somehow, find our happily ever after, our lost tribe.*

The Phoenix Center For Deprogramming
Phoenix, Arizona
July 1993

So, I got myself out of the house. I ran to the river and just floated there, unable to do anything, go anywhere. I wanted to just float away and never come back, but I had to know. By the time I came back to the compound, my mother's body had been discovered along with Larry's, the police were everywhere, and Tim was gone. I looked for him, sent people out to all the hospitals and truck stops, we even went back to the reservation—the last place he'd go. I had to believe that he had understood my last words to him and had gone to Arizona. Then you showed up, and I suddenly had my own way to get there. I was so naïve, thought it would be so easy to find our way back together.

Now you know everything.

I've been here for, Jesus, eleven months? You know, I've been through a lot since I've been here. You knew before I came I'd been through a lot; now you know just what. I know that you think that I haven't gotten better, that I'm still haunted by the demons that have held me down, but I'm not.

The reason I don't talk now is different than the reason I didn't talk when I first came here or when I started writing this tale. Then, I was angry, and I used my silence to keep what little I had left: my story. Now that I've given that away, I don't know what I have anymore, who I am. I want to talk; I want to tell you that I'm going to be okay, that I'm ready to get on with my life, but I can't. Can't talk, can't get on with my life. What is there? No, I don't mean there's nothing to live for; you know I have my reasons for living. I just have no idea of the where and how anymore.

I guess I'm still waiting for him. I know he must be dead; I mean he has to be. It's been a year; if he was going to find me, he'd have found me already, right? Maybe it's time to give up that dream, but how? It's been a part of me for so long; what am I without it? What am I without him?

The Phoenix Center for Cult Recovery
July 1993

Tim drove the SUV that Damien had given him for almost twenty-four hours straight, only stopping for gas and caffeine. In the end, he didn't need anyone there to talk to; his impatience kept him company.

He thought about his last year, what he'd been through to figure himself out, and he wondered how Naomi survived it. Then he wondered who she would be when he did get to see her again. Would she be the angry woman she had become since she had been turned into human breeding stock, or would she be the trusting sister who had shared all his hopes, dreams and nightmares? Would she even want to see him? What would he do if she didn't?

He reasoned that he would do whatever it took. The one thing he had learned that last year was they didn't need a tribe to be complete. She was his family, and that's all he needed.

He started sweating as he crossed the border into Arizona, and by the time he got to the Phoenix Center, he was shaking so badly he had to pull over and force himself to breathe.

He was surprised by the look of the Phoenix Center. He had expected a prison environment, not the green, lush oasis he drove up to. Palm trees lined the path on each side, and the circular driveway opened up to poppies and orchids. He sighed, feeling better about Naomi being here all this time. Maybe they really could undo all the damage he and The Way had done.

The woman who welcomed him through a large plexi-glass window stared, dazed when he told him who he was and inquired about his sister. After a long moment, she opened the door beside the window and stood before him. "Oh my sweet Lord, wait right here," she whispered excitedly.

She rushed down the marbled hallway and disappeared around a corner. He tried to stay calm and not give into the urge to run down the halls screaming his sister's name.

Before he knew it, he was surrounded by smiling, overly enthusiastic people in brightly colored shirts and khakis.

"Tim? Are you really Tim West?" one of them asked.

Tim was overwhelmed by the crowd's anxious study of him and could only nod.

"You don't know how happy we are to finally meet you. Oh, you couldn't come at a better time. This is so exciting! Why don't you follow me?" The short woman, who looked like everyone's favorite grandma, bustled and took his arm.

Tim studied her. She was about sixty, had a long, grey braid down her back, and was wearing a formless sky blue dress and Birkenstock sandals. She wasn't Indian but wasn't exactly white either; she probably came from a Latin background, but Tim decided that it didn't matter.

She led him to an office with an unbelievable amount of plants and motioned him to sit down on one of the red and orange Southwestern-style couches.

"Naomi's therapist, Rose, will be right with you," she said as she left.

It was only a moment later when another woman entered. This woman looked a bit more professional and a bit younger, but still looked kind and caring. She was definitely Indian, probably Navajo, Tim guessed.

"Hi, my name is Rose, and I know you're dying to see your sister. We just need to talk first. You know why Naomi's here, right?" she asked.

Tim knew the answer, but how do you tell a perfect stranger it was because of him. She was here because of him. "What has she told you?"

"There's not much she hasn't told me. I worry about her. I worry about you. I need to know where you've been and where your head is before I can allow you to see your sister."

Silence. He knew those were perfectly valid questions, but he was now terrified of the woman before him. Suddenly it was as if she had razor sharp teeth, claws for fingers, and fire coming out of her eyes. But more than that, everything he said would have an effect on whether or not he got to see his sister.

Naomi obviously trusted her, so taking a deep breath, he told her everything. Everything that he'd been doing this whole last year; how he didn't know who he was until just recently, how he'd thought Naomi was dead, and it was entirely his fault.

She listened, didn't interrupt, then put her claws and her killer teeth away, and her eyes smoldered and died out.

She smiled at him. "I'm sorry if I came across rough. I just wanted to get all the unpleasantness out of the way. We have worked too hard to get her where she is to let anyone come in and disrupt her wellbeing."

"That's never going to happen," he interrupted. "Obviously she's told you about what The Way wanted from her, and she must have told you about my part in it, but I know now, and I think I even knew then that it was wrong. I think part of me agreed to it all along because I knew she would refuse. I guess I always expected her to be the conscience for both of us. Does that make sense?"

She nodded. "But, you know, the community you lived in, something was wrong even before. You know that, right?"

Looking away, he shrugged. It was the first place that had accepted him fully and made him feel the love he'd been starved for, so he never questioned too much the things that seemed strange or too good to be true. He had gone along with everything. "I thought they were just like me. Proud to be Indian but saddened by what our tribes had turned into."

"It might have seemed that way, but, didn't it seem odd that it was run by primarily Caucasian men, and that they mostly recruited from a place where they were in charge of broken, abused Native Americans?" she asked.

"They wanted to help people and show them the true way to live better lives," Tim answered, reciting the old mantra. He had believed that up until Malachi had died.

"Maybe, but what was in it for them?"

He paused, never thinking about it that way before. It had seemed obvious then, but now? He didn't know. He shrugged again.

"Could it be they wanted something from you? The one thing you could give them that they didn't have. They wanted your heritage. The Indian in you.

"They discovered that people who were already damaged, already searching for someone to tell them how to live, would accept almost anything from their leaders without question. I'm not saying it's all bad. I know family meant a lot to you and Naomi; she still reveres Malachi as the father she never had through all of this.

"The people who come here don't know what to believe anymore; they don't know who to listen to, and they've stopped trusting their own voice and believing in their own judgment. When Naomi got here, she felt guilty for many things, but none more than that she couldn't do the one thing her 'family' asked of her. She didn't trust herself that she had refused her 'destiny' for the right reasons. She's come a long way in the past months, but I don't think she'll truly be healed until she can forgive herself for what happened."

Standing up impatiently, he said, "I have to see her. I have to tell her she has nothing to forgive herself for. Whatever she did was self-defense. Whatever was done was because she was pushed. Please can I see her? I promise I won't ever hurt her."

There was a look in her eye, like she wanted to tell him one last thing, but then she sighed and stood up. "Of course. However, I am going to need to supervise the meeting."

He bowed his head. "Of course."

She led him down one hall after the other until they were at the other end of the building and then out the door into the bright, late afternoon sun. There, sitting under a tall, swaying palm tree was his sister. Although her back was to him, he knew it was her and that she wasn't going to be the angry woman who had been turning into her own mother. Her head was tilted as if studying something in her lap, and she looked peaceful.

He ignored the woman beside him and walked slowly to Naomi. He was right behind her, before she felt his presence and turned her head. For a traumatic minute, his heart raced as she just studied him. Then her eyes welled up with tears. But still she didn't stand up to greet him, didn't say anything, and so he asked timidly, "Na-ho? Do you hate me?"

She shook her head and slowly turned the rest of her body as Tim fell to his knees. The last thing he ever expected was to see his sister, his little baby sister, cradling a little bundle of hair and limbs in a blue blanket on her lap. He stared at the squirming figure for so long, he almost forgot who was holding it. He looked at her apprehensively, and when he saw her sweet smile, he returned it gratefully and leaned in closer.

She still didn't say anything, but she pulled back the blanket and gave Tim the first look at his baby nephew.

He had to swallow to speak. "He's beautiful."

Naomi put her hand on Tim's forehead, and he broke down in sobs that shook his entire body. He wanted to take her in his arms and hold her until he stopped. But he just continued to sit there with her hand on his forehead and him trying to stop crying so that he could see his nephew more clearly. The baby looked just like Naomi, but there was someone else in his eyes, something that reminded him of his mother when she wasn't being hateful.

"What's his name?" Tim asked.

Naomi just looked at Tim.

"What's the matter Na-ho? Why won't you talk to me?"

She held out the baby to Tim, who took him. She stood up, put her hand out for him to stay, and then backed away. He watched her puzzled, as she went and brought over Rose who had stopped a few yards away.

Rose sat down where Naomi had been earlier, and Naomi sat next to her, not looking at Tim or her son. "Timothy, Naomi really wants to talk to you; she does. She also is extremely glad that you are here. She was about to give up on the dream of your return, but now she is happier than she's been. Unfortunately though, Naomi hasn't spoken since the day she arrived, since the day she discovered she was pregnant."

Naomi finally looked at him, the tears still streaming down her face. He nodded that he understood and said to both of them, "That's okay. She doesn't need to talk for me to understand. I just want her to know that nothing that happened was her fault."

She shook her head violently, and he continued, "It wasn't. It was my fault. I wasn't strong enough to stop them. I was never as strong as you thought I was, as everyone thought I was. I tried to be. I wanted to be, but I was only strong when you were by my side. You made me strong; your strength was mine."

They were both crying now as she still shook her head. "It's true." Tim continued, "I've been spending this last year trying to remember who I was, and the only thing that kept me going was the belief that somewhere out there was someone that needed me. I knew it was you even when I didn't know who you were. I knew you even when I didn't know myself.

He started chanting:

"Na-ho-a-ah-me-i-ah
Na-ho-a-ah-eh-me-a-eh
Na-ho-a-ah-me-i-ah
Na-ho-a-ah-eh-me-a-eh
Na-ho-a-ah-me-i-ah"

When he finished, he said, "And I will spend the rest of my days showing you that you were the good person in all of this."

She continued to cry, and the baby started wailing as well. She reached her hands out to Tim, who gave her back the baby. "What's his name?" Tim asked Rose.

"His name is Renna. She says it means—"

"Cleansed in Fire."

She nodded.

Naomi stood up and walked away with the baby, still crying, in her arms.

"She's going to nurse him. She'll be right back."

Tim took his eyes off his sister's receding presence and focused again on the lady in front of him. "She's okay though right, deep down?"

Rose patted his arm. "She'll be fine. We just have to let her heal herself. She has to know for herself that she's worth the love people feel for her. It will happen. It will just take time. You both are welcome to stay here as long as you'd like."

Tim looked into her eyes. She really was a beautiful soul but he didn't see how staying here listening to others telling them how to live or think would be any better than what they had escaped. Just when he was starting to wonder where they should go, he saw a figure emerge from behind one of the trees along the perimeter of the field.

He rose to meet him. "Grandfather," he said, taking him into his arms. They held onto each other wordlessly for a long time. He never loved his grandfather as much as he did right at that moment for being there for Naomi. He never considered that his grandfather really thought about them at all and was touched to discover they did matter, to the extent that he would uproot himself and move down here, just to be close to her.

"Thank you," Tim said into his ear. The other man issued a breathy sob, and Tim wasn't surprised that it was the only answer he got. Some things would never change.

They were about to walk back to the building and look for Naomi when she came out, still holding Renna. She gave the baby to Amos and took Tim in her arms, holding him tight as they both shook with sobs. When they finally pulled apart, she handed him a piece of paper. "LETS GO HOME" was all it said.

"Where's home?" he asked.

She took the paper back and wrote "WHEREVER YOU ARE."

"Wherever *we* are," he corrected. He folded the piece of paper and said, "Okay, let's go."

Epilogue

Pacific Coast Highway
September, 1993

Dear Rose,

I know you would have liked us to stay with you for a little bit longer, but I hope you understand that eventually we would have to leave to find the path for ourselves. I do truly appreciate everything you and the others have done for me, especially your tremendous patience and kindness, even when I really didn't think I deserved any of it.

We are still looking for a place that feels right. I think we both have given up the idea of the Nopiinde. Maybe they were an illusion. I think what scares us most is what if we find them and discover they are no better for us than The Way was. I guess we've found out the hard way that the only tribe we can believe in is ourselves. Tim does talk about a girl named Rainbow and how he wants me to meet her, and there's someone I want Renna to meet. Soon.

For the days we have spent endlessly searching, I truly feel for my brother. I can't imagine what it must be like for him to be in a car with two grown adults who won't talk and a tiny baby who switches without warning from laughter to tears. Tim probably never thought there would come a time when he was the most talkative person in this family.

I know one day I will be able to use my voice. Until then, I store up all the things I want to say and the questions I want to ask. When I finally do open my mouth to talk, I fear that I'll never shut up. So until then, I exercise my throat with humming the chants that have been the only thing putting my precious baby to sleep.

I'd like to tell you that we left your home and rode off into the sunset, but that's the cowboy's version of "Happily Ever After" that usually meant the Indians were all slaughtered or enslaved. I don't think we Indians have a "Happily Ever After." I don't think our stories ever end.

Much Love and Appreciation,

Naomi, Tim, Amos and Renna West

About the Author

Tamela's truck driving father taught her the value of stories, travel and adventure. Her housewife mother taught her the value of daydreaming, family and escapism. Though she was raised in Spokane Washington, it wasn't until she moved to Missoula Montana that she felt she was "home." She currently lives in Virginia, but still dreams of the Big Sky. You can visit her online at http://www.tamelajritter.com.